Praise for the Drama High Series

"The teen drama is center-court Compton, with enough plots and sub-plots to fill a few episodes of any reality show."
—*Ebony* magazine on *Drama High: Courtin' Jayd*

"You'll definitely feel for Jayd Jackson, the bold sixteen-year-old Compton, California, junior at the center of keep-it-real Drama High stories."
—*Essence* magazine on *Drama High: Jayd's Legacy*

"Edged with comedy and a provoking street-savvy plot line, Compton native and Drama High author L. Divine writes a fascinating story capturing the voice of young black America."
—*The Cincinnati Herald* on the *Drama High Series*

"Filled with all the elements that make for a good book—young love, non-stop drama and a taste of the supernatural, it is sure to please."
—THE RAWSISTAZ Reviewers on *Drama High: The Fight*

". . . A captivating look at teen life."
—Harriet Klausner on *Drama High: The Fight*

"If you grew up on a steady diet of saccharine *Sweet Valley* novels and think there aren't enough books specifically for African American teens, you're in luck."
—*Prince George's Sentinel* on *Drama High: The Fight*

"Through a healthy mix of book smarts, life experiences, and down-to-earth flavor, L. Divine has crafted a well-nuanced coming-of-age tale for African-American youth."
—*The Atlanta Voice* on *Drama High: The Fight*

"*Drama High* has it all . . . fun, fast, addictive."
—Cara Lockwood, bestselling author of *Moby Clique*

Also by L. Divine

THE FIGHT

SECOND CHANCE

JAYD'S LEGACY

FRENEMIES

LADY J

COURTIN' JAYD

HUSTLIN'

KEEP IT MOVIN'

Published by Kensington Publishing Corporation

Drama High, Vol. 9
Super Edition

HOLIDAZE

L. Divine

KENSINGTON PUBLISHING CORP.
www.kensingtonbooks.com

DAFINA BOOKS are published by

Kensington Publishing Corp.
119 West 40th Street
New York, NY 10018

All Kensington titles, imprints, and distributed lines are available at special quantity discounts for bulk purchases for sales promotion, premiums, fund-raising, educational, or institutional use.

Special book excerpts or customized printings can also be created to fit specific needs. For details, write or phone the office of the Kensington Special Sales Manager: Kensington Publishing Corp., 119 West 40th Street, New York, NY 10018. Attn. Special Sales Department. Phone: 1-800-221-2647.

ISBN-13: 978-0-7582-3109-3
ISBN-10: 0-7582-3109-1

First Kensington Trade Paperback Printing: October 2009

10 9 8 7 6 5 4 3 2 1

Printed in the United States of America

One of my aunties said to me over the holidays that she doesn't get the lingo of *Drama High* and she couldn't stand the language. I wasn't hurt by her truthful words because I honestly didn't write them for her generation. I am well aware that there are people out there who don't get my flow and never will. That's the beauty of having multiple writers for multiple audiences. And that's why I write this series: for the readers who get how we live, write, and speak. Our culture is real and prevalent. What can I say? Fiction mimics reality and vice versa. I'm tired of writing about drive-bys, car jackings, and other violent crimes. But they are the reality of daily life for many of us. And hopefully the day will soon come when I can write about these and other negative deeds in the past tense only.

When I heard that another family member was a victim of violence, I was in an immediate daze. This volume is dedicated to my cousin on both sides of my lineage, Khary Kidd, who was murdered during this novel's creation. I will miss you always and treasure your bright smile and deep voice eternally. I love you and will keep a candle lit for you on my shrine.

i live in fiction

it's all in my head.
i live in a world
between here and there,
every and nowhere.
i live in a place where I have the same face
i had as a child.
where ancestors come back in their prime
and spend time refining our
perfection.
i exist in a place where
word count is my sun
and page count my moon.
i come to and wash dishes, do laundry, cook dinner, and
  supervise the
real lives of two other real
people.
and then, back to my
characters.
back to the weaving of this reality I crave to
be in.
i live for this fictitious place.
i breathe in this make-believe space.
my body is a vessel for its stories.
and I live to tell them.

l. divine
2009

Acknowledgments

I'd like to go back and say thank you to the many educators who have influenced my life's work. This list is in no way complete, but it's a great start.

Dr. Walter Allen, Dr. Valerie Smith, Dr. Richard Yarborough, Dr. Maureen Silos, Dr. Jenny Sharpe, Dr. Sid Lemelle, Dr. Robert Hill, Dr. T.J. Desch-Obi, Thomas Ennison, Nathan McCall, Baba Medahochi Kofi Zannu, Dr. Kwame Kalimara, SongoEniola Oladeji Kalimara, Elbert Shitamoto. And a special thank you to Khisna Griffin for being the best college counselor ever and to my first West African dance teacher, Nzingha Camara, whose course changed my life.

And a very special thank you to my agent, Brendan Deneen, and my publisher, Dafina/Kensington, for keeping the series going. Thank you for your faith in *Drama High*. Our novels nourish my children, my audience, and myself. For that I am forever grateful. I feel like I'm living in a dream sometimes because life as a working writer is a divine blessing. Thank you for the sweet reality.

The Crew

Jayd

A sassy sixteen-year-old from Compton, California, who comes from a long line of Louisiana conjure women. She is the only one in her lineage born with brown eyes and a caul. Her grandmother appropriately named her "Jayd," which is also the name her grandmother took on in her days as a voodoo queen in New Orleans. She lives with her grandparents, four uncles, and her cousin Jay. Jayd is in all AP classes and visits her mother on the weekend. She has a tense relationship with her father, whom she sees occasionally, and has never-ending drama in her life, whether at school or home.

Mama/Lynn Mae

When Jayd gets in over her head, her grandmother, Mama, is always there to help her. A full-time conjure woman with magical green eyes and a long list of both clients and haters, Mama also serves as Jayd's teacher, confidante, and protector.

Mom/Lynn Marie

At thirty-something years old, Lynn Marie would never be mistaken for a mother of a teenager. Jayd's mom is definitely all that and with her green eyes, she keeps the men guessing. Able to talk to Jayd telepathically, Lynn Marie is always there when Jayd needs her.

Esmeralda

Mama's nemesis and Jayd's nightmare, this next-door neighbor is anything but friendly. She relocated to Compton from Louisiana around the same time Mama did and has been a thorn in Mama's side ever since. She continuously causes trouble for Mama and Jayd. Esmeralda's cold blue eyes have powers of their own, although not nearly as powerful as Mama's.

Rah

Rah is Jayd's first love from junior high school who has come back into her life when a mutual friend, Nigel, transfers from Rah's high school (Westingle) to South Bay. He knows everything about her and is her spiritual confidant. Rah lives in Los Angeles but grew up with his grandparents in Compton like Jayd. He loves Jayd fiercely but has a girlfriend who refuses to go away (Trish) and a baby-mama (Sandy). Rah is a hustler by necessity and a music producer by talent. He takes care of his younger brother Kamal and holds the house down while his dad is locked up and his mother strips at a local club.

Misty

The word "frenemies" was coined for this former best friend of Jayd's. Misty has made it her mission to sabotage Jayd any way she can. Living around the corner from Jayd, she has the unique advantage of being an original hater from the neighborhood and at school.

KJ

He's the most popular basketball player on campus, Jayd's ex-boyfriend, and Misty's current boyfriend. Ever since he and Jayd broke up, he's made it his personal mission to persecute her.

Nellie

One of Jayd's best friends, Nellie is the prissy princess of the crew. She is also dating Chance, even though it's Nigel she's really feeling. Nellie made history at South Bay by becoming the first Black Homecoming princess and has let the crown go to her head.

Mickey

The gangster girl of Jayd's small crew. She and Nellie are best friends but often at odds with each other, mostly because Nellie secretly wishes she could be more like Mickey. A true hood girl, she loves being from Compton, and her man with no name is a true gangster. Mickey and Nigel have quickly become South Bay High's newest couple, even if Mickey's not sure who's the father of her unborn child.

Jeremy

A first for Jayd, Jeremy is her white ex-boyfriend who also happens to be the most popular cat at South Bay. Rich, tall and extremely handsome, Jeremy's witty personality and good conversation keep Jayd on her toes and give Rah a run for his money—literally.

Mickey's Man

Never using his name, Mickey's original boyfriend is a troublemaker and always hot on Mickey's trail. Always in and out of jail, Mickey's man is notorious in her hood for being a cold-hearted gangster, and loves to be in control. He also has a thing for Jayd, but Jayd can't stand to be anywhere near him.

Nigel

The new quarterback on the block, Nigel is a friend of Jayd's from junior high and also Rah's best friend, making Jayd's world even smaller at South Bay High. Nigel is the star football player and dumped his ex-girlfriend at Westingle (Tasha) to be with his new baby-mama-to-be, Mickey. Jayd is caught up in the mix as a friend to them both, but her loyalty lies with Nigel because she's known him longer and he's always had her back.

Chance

The rich, white hip-hop kid of the crew, Chance is Jayd's drama homie and Nellie's boyfriend, if you let him tell it. He used to have a crush on Jayd and now has turned his attention to Nellie.

Bryan

The youngest of Mama's children and Jayd's favorite uncle, Bryan is a dj by night and works at the local grocery store during the day. He's also an acquaintance of both Rah and KJ from playing ball around the hood. Bryan often gives Jayd helpful advice about her problems with boys and hating girls alike. Out of all of Jayd's uncles, Bryan gives her grandparents the least amount of trouble.

Jay

Jay is more like an older brother to Jayd than her cousin. Like Jayd, he lives with Mama but his mother (Mama's youngest daughter) left him when he was a baby and never returned. He doesn't know his father and attends Compton High. He and Jayd often cook together and help Mama around the house.

Prologue

"Jayd, can you hear me?" *Mama says, but I can't see where her voice is coming from. I know I'm dreaming, but it feels too real to be a dream.* "Jayd, snap out of it before you get hurt!" *Why is she yelling at me? All I'm doing is walking around the living room, and I could walk around this entire house with my eyes closed and not trip over a thing. But wait, this isn't our living room. It looks like it, but I can tell from the furniture I'm back in my great-grandmother's time again and this must be her house.*

"Jon Paul, no! Give her back to me," Maman screams at her husband, who's holding their daughter tight. The baby screams loudly as Maman's cries become even more powerful. She begins to shriek like an opera singer and my great-grandfather can't take anymore. He slaps Maman hard with the back of his hand and she falls to the floor, hitting the Christmas tree on the way down.

"Lynn Mae," Maman cries, holding her bloody face with one hand and reaching her free hand up toward her daughter, who is still in her father's arms.

"Jayd, wake up, now!" *Mama shouts, but this time she's not in my dream with me. Where is her voice coming from?*

"What is she doing here?" Jon Paul asks my great-

grandmother, looking dead at me. Oh hell, no. I don't want to be in this dream. Maybe I should wake up, but I can't. I wish I had more control over when I wake up from or fall into my dreams.

"You do, Jayd, and now is the time to exercise that power. Wake your ass up!" *Mama's talking to me in my head, but not like my mom does. It's as if I'm dreaming, but in reality I'm awake. What the hell? Before I can get a grip on what's really going on, Jon Paul charges at me with his daughter in tow like he's going to slap me, too.*

"Jon Paul, Sarah has nothing to do with this. Leave her alone," Maman says, now on her feet, her green eyes glowing like I've never seen before. Unlike in my last dream with Maman, this time her eyes look like emerald fireballs. He's in for it now. And who the hell is Sarah?

"She's always here. You know all about her whoreish ways, don't you, young lady?" How did he hear my thought? I back away from my great-grandfather, frightened of his temper. As I stumble over a chair, I land in it and catch my reflection in a clean pot on the kitchen stove. The face staring back at me belongs to a girl about my age, but she's not me. I'm bugging for real. This is too much for me to handle.

"Jon Paul, haven't you heard of picking on someone your own size?" Maman's voice begins to get higher in pitch and her eyes even brighter as she focuses all of her attention on him. His head begins to pulsate, just like it did in the vision that Mama and I shared on Christmas Eve, and he can't take it anymore. He begins to charge toward the kitchen door, but Maman's not letting him go anywhere with her daughter.

"Aren't you forgetting something?" Maman says, putting her arms out for her daughter, whose eyes are also glowing. "Sarah, come here. And bring Lynn Mae with you. He can't

hurt you now." I stay put because I don't realize that she's talking to me. But when she focuses her glowing gaze in my direction, I jump up from the table, walk toward my now mentally paralyzed great-grandfather, and take my grandmother out of his hands. When I reach my great-grandmother, she pushes us behind her and focuses all of her energy on crippling her husband. Maman's powers are completely off the chain. And I thought Mama was gangster with her shit.

"Jayd, drink this," Mama says, still talking to me from outside of my dream. *I look down at the baby in my arms and she smiles back at me, making me think of what my ex's daughter Rahima must be doing now, wherever she is. But this is Mama, not Rahima, and I'm about to freak out completely if I don't wake up soon.*

"Why is Jayd standing in the middle of the living room floor so late at night?" *I can hear my uncle Bryan ask, but I can't see him either. What's really going on?*

"She's sleepwalking. Help me keep her safe, but don't touch her," *Mama says. Sleepwalking? Damn it. I haven't done this in years and it's never good when I do.* "Jayd, focus on my voice, not on whatever's going on in your dream, and snap out of it, please." *The urgency in Mama's voice scares me, but I still can't find my way out.*

"Okay girls, it's time to make our move," Maman says, not letting go of her visual hold on Jon Paul for a second. "As you can see, he kicked in the front door, so we're going to have to make our way out the back. Stay behind me. And Sarah, whatever you do, don't let go of Lynn Mae." We follow my great-grandmother back into the kitchen and walk around her husband, who is now crippled on the floor and holding his head, which looks like it's going to burst. "Walk right by him. Don't look at him. Just keep moving and everything will be okay."

"Jayd, stop walking," *Mama says, but I can't. I have to follow Maman and get baby Mama out of harm's way, no matter what my grandmother says.*

"Jayd, it's not real. Stop walking, now. Bryan, follow us." *I follow Maman out of the back door, hand her baby to her, and she looks me in the eye, releasing me from my dream state.*

Upon waking, I fall back into Bryan's arms, completely lifeless. He holds me upright as Mama brings me to.

"Here, Jayd. Swallow this," Mama says, forcing some thick concoction down my throat. I resist at first because the smell is putrid. Whatever's in this cup reminds me of when Mama used to make me drink orange juice mixed with castor oil when I would get constipated as a child. I still don't drink orange juice to this day because of that experience.

"Y'all are too much for a nigga sometimes, you know that?" Bryan says, holding on to me tightly as Mama continues force-feeding me. I hate it when this happens.

"Watch your mouth," Mama says to Bryan. I look up at the both of them and realize we are standing on the back porch. It's dark and cold outside. Mama's dog looks at us from her post on the bottom step and seemingly shakes her head at the sight. All Lexi does is sleep and scratch herself, so I'm not really worried about disturbing her.

"Jayd, are you okay, baby?" Mama asks. Sometimes it's too much for me, too. If I could just leave my powers at the curb right now, I'd do it in a heartbeat. I'm getting sick of this shit.

"I'm fine," I say, coughing up some of the thickness she's made me swallow. I'm shivering in my thin nightgown and sweat pants and my feet are bare, causing the cold to run straight through my body. "Can I go back to bed now?" If Bryan's just getting in from his radio show, it must be close to two in the morning and it's a school day for me, no matter what kind of dream I just had.

"Not until you tell me what that was all about, Jayd. Whenever you sleepwalk, it's serious, girl, and you know it."

"Mama, I start a new semester tomorrow and I have to drive my mom's stick shift all the way to Redondo Beach for the first time. I need sleep. Please, can we talk tomorrow?" Mama looks into my eyes and feels my pain.

"Fine, but don't forget any of it. I need details." I'm sure she's already got the summary in her mind. I wish I could forget, but this dream was too freaky. I've never dreamt of being someone else before. I hope that was the last time it happens. I have enough to deal with as it is. I just want to get through this day with as little trouble as possible. With new classes, Mickey and Nellie tripping, and Nigel still out because of his wounded shoulder, there's going to be enough drama to deal with this morning as it is.

~ 1 ~
Walk on By

"That's all that I have left so let me hide/
The tears and the sadness you gave me when you said goodbye."

—DIONNE WARWICK

After this morning's sleepwalking episode, I could barely get myself out of the bed, let alone dressed and ready to go. Luckily, I don't have to get up as early as I did before my mom let me take her car, but six is still early in my book.

Speaking of books, I forgot my backpack as I was rushing out the door this morning, which means my day's not going to be easy at all, especially since we're being issued new books and have to take them home to cover.

I'm not excited about my new class schedule because not much has really changed. That's one of the major problems with being on the Advanced Placement track: the monotony is grueling and there's also the added curse of having to deal with Mrs. Bennett's evil ass. With any luck, I won't run into her or Misty today. That would make the day tolerable.

"Damn it," I say aloud while attempting to shift the car into first gear on the steep hill near campus. There aren't many hills between Compton and Inglewood, so I never got to practice balancing the clutch in various situations. Where's Rah when I need him? He hasn't talked to me since his ex Sandy took off in his grandfather's car with Rahima. I know he's pissed, but it really wasn't my fault. How was I supposed to know she would make a copy of his car keys and jack Rah the first chance she got?

"Because the bitch is crazy," my mom says, feeling my frustration.

"Mom, you can't call her a bitch. She's young enough to be your daughter," I think in response while still trying to work my way up the hill without rolling back too far. The cars behind me are honking at my slow progression, but I don't care. I'd rather they be mad at me than hit anyone. All I need is to have an accident. My mom would never let me live that down. More than likely I would also find myself back on the bus, and I'm not having that.

"You worry too much, Jayd. And no, Sandy isn't old enough to be a child of mine. That girl's eighteen and a mother, therefore she's fair game—and a bitch is a bitch, as I'm sure you already know." My mom's got a valid point. If there's an official bitch club, Sandy's got to be the president.

"Can you help me drive this thing or what?" I say aloud. If the traffic weren't so slow trying to get into the parking lot, I wouldn't have this problem. I've experienced more stop-and-go traffic in the ten minutes I've been waiting in line here than my mother does on the 405 freeway during rush hour.

"You have to learn how to navigate the road ahead in all situations, Jayd. Besides, it's good for you to know how to drive a stick. It's an irreplaceable skill to have. The first thing you need to do is calm down, little one, and put the car in neutral." I follow my mom's instructions and the car starts to slide backwards. *"Put your foot on the brake, Jayd. Damn, girl, you always have to use your common sense."*

"Mom, I had a very rough night. Please cut me some slack," I say, near tears. I notice the new girl, Shawn, walking past me and looking at me like I'm crazy. I guess she heard that, and probably thinks I'm talking to myself. I don't care what she thinks of me. As long as she keeps walking without saying shit, it's all good.

"Okay, I'm sorry. Now, ease off of the brake and apply an equal amount of pressure on the clutch before shifting into first gear. Then press slightly on the gas. If you do it right, the car should go up the hill smoothly." At first the car lurches forward, but then I ease up on the clutch and simultaneously press on the gas pedal. It works smoothly, just like my mother said it would.

"Thank you, Mom," I think back.

"That's what I'm here for. Now, what about this rough night you had?" I pull up in line and feel like an old pro at driving a stick the way I'm handling the hill. I'm almost in a good mood for the first time in days and don't want to mess it up thinking about my dream.

"Mom, I really don't want to go into that right now." I'm next in line to get through the gate and really want to get on with my day. It's bad enough Rah still hasn't returned any of my calls or text messages since he picked up his Acura from my mother's house yesterday. I want to know if he's heard from Sandy. I know he feels like he's the only one missing his daughter, but she left me too and I need to know if he's heard from her crazy-ass mama.

"Okay, fine. But I will remind you this weekend when I see you. Have a good day, baby, and let me know how your day went later on."

"Alright, Mom. You too," I think back. I have to watch it, talking aloud to her when I'm in public. I already have a reputation as a voodoo girl, which is the truth. The last thing I need is the school thinking I'm a schizoid, too.

"Hey, Jayd, new wheels again?" Jeremy asks from his car to mine, catching me off guard. Somehow he's made his way beside me, putting his car in the perfect position to ease his way behind mine and be next in line to get through the gate.

I guess being the most popular guy on campus has its advantages even before the school day officially begins.

"Yeah, my mom had sympathy on me and let me roll her car until I get some more wheels of my own." I haven't heard from my daddy since I left the dilapidated vehicle he bought me for Christmas in his driveway Saturday night, and don't expect to hear from him anytime soon. I know he's pissed and his ego's shattered. It'll take awhile for him to come around and call me this time.

"Sweet. So when are you taking me out, for a change?" I'm still irritated with Jeremy for the way he didn't react when I told him about Nigel and Tre getting shot last week, but what can I expect? His reality is surfing all day and living the life of luxury, while mine is making potions with my grandmother and dodging the occasional bullet. We exist in two different worlds.

"One day," I say as I pull into the lot to find a spot. Jeremy's right behind me, ready to get on with this school day as well. I don't know how I'm going to stay focused. But as Mama says, the day will pass whether I participate in it or not. So, we'll just have to wait and see how it goes, because right now I feel like time is passing me right on by and that's not good.

My first two classes haven't changed, and they went by without incident. But there was one mistake with my schedule. They registered me in a non-AP speech and debate elective when I should've been registered in the AP journalism class. They usually do this when there's a class cancellation, but I'd rather make my own adjustments than have them made for me. I requested a meeting time to talk to my counselor, Mr. Adelizi, about the change, but as busy as it was in the main office this morning, I doubt I'll get to see him today.

While I was in the main office this morning, I ran into Ms. Toni, the ASB teacher, and gave her a quick hug before she had to run off to a meeting. She's been so busy lately we haven't had time to catch up on all that's happened. I know she's still a little pissed at me for participating in Mickey's downfall, and consequently losing my part as Lady Macbeth, but there's still love there for me and I can feel it. She also mentioned she wanted to talk to me about Nigel's shooting.

I'm sure Ms. Toni still has questions regarding Laura's accusation about me choking her up with my special spray, and how I got my part back on opening night of the play. It is true: I did make a potion to get my crown back, but Laura can never prove it. Telling Ms. Toni about my powers isn't an option, but letting her in on my lineage may be okay. Mama wouldn't be happy to know that someone in the administration knows all about our work, but who we are is no secret. I have to tell Ms. Toni something when she asks, even if it isn't the whole truth.

"Can I walk the lady to class?" Rather than look for someone new to hang with at break, I've decided to chill in the library until further notice. I guess Jeremy figured this out and came looking for me, which is nice, but still not enough to make me forget about his non-reaction to my friends' drama.

"Okay, since we're both going to the same place anyway," I say. He takes my books from my hands and tucks them under his right arm. We walk in silence away from the media center where the library is housed and toward our government class. Jeremy looks down at me, waiting for me to say something, but if I speak first the words won't be so nice.

"What's up with you this morning? Did I do something wrong?" I look up at Jeremy and realize just how clueless he really is. Who knew boys could be so naïve?

"It's not so much what you did as what you didn't say."

Jeremy shakes his thick brown curls and gives an exasperated sigh. I know I'm a bit much for him sometimes, but no one said friendship was easy.

"Okay, what was it this time?" The bell rings and students start to leisurely rise from their seats and join us in our trek to class. Third period is my least favorite, and will remain that way until Mrs. Peterson is gone permanently. I thought she was retiring at the end of last semester, but it seems the old crow's going to wait out the rest of the school year. Lucky us.

"Look, the last thing I want to do is argue with you, Jeremy. We're just different people and I accept that. There's no need to go into it any further." I look around at a few students staring at us as we walk on by. They're probably wondering if we're back together. That's how rumors start.

"What the hell are you talking about? What could I have possibly done between now and the last time we talked two days ago?" He stops in front of our classroom, looks down at me, and puts my books behind his back as if he's going to hold them hostage until I give him the information he wants. Of all the days to forget my book bag. Well, at least I only have to carry them to the car and not from one bus stop to another. That would suck. Papa Legba, my father Orisha, does have some mercy on me.

"Can we get into this some other time? We have to get inside before the tardy bell rings. You know Mrs. Peterson would love to mark us both for being late while we're standing right in front of her door." I think she heard me because she looks up from her newspaper and scowls at me before taking a sip of her coffee. I wonder if her drink is as bitter as she is.

"Jayd, I hate it when you do this. How can you give me the cold shoulder without telling me what I did to deserve it? That's not fair."

"Fair? Who said anything about life being fair? One of my best friends was shot a few days ago while another one died, not to mention that I've lost both of my homegirls over some bull. And another one of my friends got his daughter and car jacked at the same time by his crazy-ass baby mama, who he was trying to help. Fair my ass," I say, walking past Jeremy and into the classroom, leaving him standing in the doorway under the ringing bell. I know that was a lot of information to drop in his lap and he didn't deserve all that, but he kept pressing me and I haven't had much sleep lately. I was liable to snap any minute and Jeremy just happened to be the one there at the time to vent on.

I feel slightly relieved letting it out, but not completely satisfied. Now I feel bad, especially with the look on Jeremy's face from where he's still standing with his mouth open. He can keep the damned books for all I care. I'm not feeling this day anyway and we still have three more classes to get through after this one. Hopefully, second-semester business will take up the majority of the day and I can skate through the remainder without having to pay it too much attention. I take my seat and start flipping through the new textbook.

"Miss Jackson, did you hear me?" Mrs. Peterson asks as I turn around to face her. All eyes are on me as our teacher waits for my response.

"Yes, Mrs. Peterson. I'm sorry," I lie, because I didn't hear a damned thing she said before she snapped me out of my thoughts a second ago. Jeremy looks at me and I can see the worry in his eyes. I guess now he's coming to understand how serious it is when a friend gets shot. I didn't even tell him it was Rah's baby-mama drama that I was speaking of before because he wouldn't understand that either.

"Well then, why aren't you moving? Come get your pass and go on to the counselor's office." Damn, I didn't hear any of that, but I'm glad to get out of here for the rest of the period. All we've been doing is looking through our new textbook and class syllabus. Talk about monotonous. My counselor must have time now to help me get the class I want.

"Jayd, I'm sorry for not saying I'm sorry about what's going on with your friends earlier." Jeremy's blue eyes look mournful as he gently caresses my hand with his fingers. I know he's sorry, but I don't know if that's enough. I need someone to feel me right about now and I just don't think he can.

"I appreciate that," I say, gathering my books and papers before getting up from my desk. "I'll holla later." My phone vibrates in my purse and I look down at it, hoping and praying that it's Rah, but it isn't. It's my calendar, reminding me to call and schedule a doctor's appointment. Mama must've had Bryan program it after I went back to sleep this morning, because I know she didn't do it. She's not funny. What do I need to go to the doctor for?

"I don't know, but it must be serious if Mama's telling you to go. You know if she can't figure out what's wrong with you she'll find someone who can. You'd better listen to her, Jayd," my mom says, committing a mental drive-by of her own before I can comment back. As if I need another thing to think about this morning.

When I reach the main office, there's a long line in front of most of the counselors' offices, including Mr. Adelizi's. Rather than join the procession of anxious students who either forgot to request changes in their schedule before the deadline or students—like me—who did, but still got screwed up in one way or another, I look at the available class list posted outside of his open door.

"Miss Jackson, come on in and have a seat. The rest of the students don't have a pass," Mr. Adelizi says. The pensive student seated across from him looks up from his schedule to give me a once-over and then back down like he's about to cry. He reminds me of a disgruntled postal worker, so I'd better make this visit quick just in case he decides to go off. I sit in the other chair across from Mr. Adelizi's desk in the cramped office, and explain my situation.

"Mr. Adelizi, I don't know what happened, but somehow my fourth period journalism class got bumped for speech and debate, and it's not even on the Advanced Placement track. There must be some mistake."

"Well, good morning to you, too," he says, trying to make me smile, but I'm not in the mood this morning. "So serious so early?"

"This is serious business. I can't afford to get off track." Mr. Adelizi looks at me over his thin-framed glasses and sees I'm in no mood for small talk.

"Miss Jackson, your schedule won't work if you choose to take the journalism class, which was moved to fifth period." He's right. I'd have to give up drama and that's never going to happen.

"Well, can't I have a study period or something instead?" I really don't like the idea of being in a speech class open to all tracks. It leaves the door open for too many unknown variables, like having Misty and KJ as classmates, and that just won't work.

"Sorry, Jayd, but study periods are for seniors only. The only classes available that will fit into your Advanced Placement schedule are speech and debate, or home economics: it's your choice."

"Fine, speech and debate it is," I say, signing my schedule before getting up to leave.

"Debate class starts tomorrow, so you'll have a free fourth period for today." A free period means we have to check in at the library and spend our time studying, which is just fine with me. Normally, I wouldn't mind being in a debate class, but being outside of the AP track is always tricky, because the environment is less controlled than it would normally be. But I have to enroll in another elective, and home economics ain't it. I get enough of that subject living with Mama.

"You know, Jayd, you can talk to me about other things. I'm not just an academic counselor," Mr. Adelizi says. I look down at the schedule printout and notice there's no teacher listed for the debate class. Damn, another unknown variable. I can't stand it when that happens. "We heard about the shooting and I know all about your friend Mickey being transferred to the continuation school. You must be having a tough time adjusting to all of this change."

"The only constant in the world is change," I say, borrowing lyrics from India.Arie, leaving Mr. Adelizi to ponder how a little black girl could be so insightful when I know the thought is far from original. If I know anything to be true, it's that statement and, like all the members of our tribe, we keep moving through the change, no matter how painful the move may be.

Driving back to Compton from my high school in Redondo Beach is a pretty straight shot. You never know how many unnecessary stops there are on a bus route until you take an alternate path. I'm also looking for the roads less travelled when it comes to me learning this clutch. Mazda never lied when they made *zoom-zoom* their motto: this little Protégé's got spunk. The last thing I want to do is accidently hit someone while trying to balance the gas and the clutch like I did this morning before my mom intervened.

There are several ways to get from school to home without taking the freeway, and all of them involve getting caught up in mall traffic. There are two major malls between here and Compton and some people are still taking advantage of the after-Christmas sales. If I had some money, I'd be right in there with them. I haven't braided any heads since the shooting, and don't anticipate hustling this weekend either. Mama says I can't touch anyone else's head until I get mine straight. I'm pretty sure her and Netta will hook a sistah up tomorrow, whether I'm ready or not.

When I get home, I know the first thing Mama's going to ask me is if I made the appointment with our family physician, Dr. Whitmore, yet. I have insurance through my mom's job with Kaiser, but Mama doesn't trust them with shit like my sleepwalking. I don't blame her, because the last time something like this happened to me and my mom took me to my pediatrician, they tried to give me antipsychotic drugs, as well as send me to a shrink. When Mama found out she wanted to crucify my mom, and I was right there with Mama.

Walking up the driveway and up the porch, I look over my shoulder to make sure the alarm lights come on, indicating my mom's ride is somewhat safe parked in front of the house. I doubt anyone will jack it because we protect our own on our block, even if Gunlock Avenue is notorious for being the spot to take jacked cars to get money for the parts. So a sistah still has to be cautious.

As soon as I walk through the front door, Mama walks into the living room from the kitchen. She looks ready to harass me about my sleepwalking incident this morning.

"Hi, baby. You didn't forget any of the details from your dream last night, did you?" she asks, wiping her wet hands with a kitchen towel before giving me a hug.

"No, ma'am," I say, returning the hug. It feels good, embracing my grandmother, whose vanilla scent is comforting.

"Good. And did you call Dr. Whitmore to make an appointment? I had Bryan put a reminder in that fancy phone of yours."

"Mama, I just got home," I say, putting my pile of schoolbooks down on the dining room table before taking off my shoes. It's been a long day and I'm in no mood to get drilled.

"Don't you sass me, young lady. Tomorrow afternoon we're at Netta's, but you tell him that Wednesday works for me. And now that you're driving your mama's car, it should be good for you, too. Now, get on that little pink phone of yours and make the call." Damn, Mama can be harsh sometimes. You'd think she was the one sleepwalking instead of me.

"Yes, ma'am," I say, near tears. Mama looks up from her spirit book, also on the dining room table, and sees the emotion written all over my face. She pats my hand with hers, letting me know she's here for me.

"Look, Jayd, I know it's hard right now, but it won't always be this way. We need to immediately get to the bottom of why you're sleepwalking, and Dr. Whitmore will be able to help me see what I can't right now. And more importantly, he'll be able to help you get some solid sleep. The sooner we take care of this, the better." I couldn't agree more with her final statement. The last thing I want to do is have another episode like the one I had this morning.

"I know, Mama. I know." I take my phone out of my purse and put it on top of my stack of books. I look around the living room and notice my backpack isn't where I left it by the dining room table. Mama follows my eyes as I search the room.

"Your backpack's in my room, Jayd," she says, reading my mind. "You have to be careful, girl. You know these fools around here will snatch it and anything else up without a second thought." Mama's right. I have to be more careful and pay attention to what I'm doing. Maybe a visit with her doctor is just what I need to get myself together after all. Between his work and Netta's head cleansing tomorrow, I should be straight by the weekend.

* * *

After Monday's eventful day, I opted to hide out all day yesterday, and with it being a usual short Tuesday because of the weekly staff meetings, it went by pretty quickly. Mama, Netta, and I also had a quiet afternoon at the shop. But even with Netta's *rogacion de cabeza* and Mama there to assist with the head cleansing, I still didn't sleep well last night. It seems like as soon as I close my eyes, it's time to get up. There's no dreaming, no hard sleep, nothing. Just lying down and getting up. That's what usually leads to more sleepwalking episodes and no one wants to tune in for that show, least of all me.

There was still no teacher for the debate class scheduled to start yesterday, so I had another free period in the library. According to Mr. Adelizi, today we will definitely start speech and debate.

I haven't seen Mr. Adewale this week and I miss his presence. I've become accustomed to seeing our AP substitute teacher on a regular basis. I hope they find some work for him to do soon.

Walking down the main hall gives me the same familiar feeling I had when I walked down these same halls during the weeks before Christmas break. It's only the third day of the new semester and ASB has already moved on to the next holiday. Valentine's Day is over a month away and they've already got fliers up advertising the annual dance and secret valentine telegrams. Who knew a holiday supposedly about love could provide so many different fundraising ideas?

As with all holidays, the true meaning is hidden behind the commercial bull. The original Valentine's Day is based off of bloodshed, just like Thanksgiving. It seems that no matter the celebration, there has to be a sacrifice of some sort, and usually the person with her ass on the line has no idea she's about to be butchered.

"Ah, look who it is, baby. The bitch who death follows," Misty says. I don't know why, but her words give me the chills, and not like when a cold breeze blows across my face. I feel like she just invited someone—or something—into our space, and whatever it is doesn't feel good.

"What's that supposed to mean?"

Misty's eyes look cold and empty as she thinks of a response to my question. I never thought I'd see the day Misty reminds me of Esmeralda, but today she does. Our evil next-door neighbor has been incognito ever since Misty and her mom became Esmeralda's godchildren in the religion. Mama says that some twisted voodoo priests use their godchildren like vampires, and this newfound family they've concocted is a prime example of that type of sick relationship.

"It means that wherever you go, someone gets hurt. If I didn't know better, I'd say someone cursed you." Misty, KJ, and his crew laugh at her joke, but it's anything but funny to me. Those sound like fighting words, but I'm too tired to front her physically, so my words will have to serve as fists today.

"So, KJ, I see you have a thing for voodoo girls." He looks at me like he wants to eat me up, but he knows better than to try to get with me again. That'll never happen.

"Not anymore," he says, playing off his obvious attraction to me while adding to their morning comedy routine.

"Oh, Misty did tell you she's in the same religion as I am, didn't she? Or did you forget to mention that little fact?" I say, wiping the smiles right off all their faces. The last thing KJ or his hella Christian parents want is to be associated with any hoodoo mess, as they call it. But all priests know that hoodoo is simply the work. Voodoo, Santeria, Ifa, or whatever branch of the religion we choose to refer to ourselves as, is a whole other world KJ and his folks want no part of.

"Don't pay her any mind, KJ. She's a very troubled girl," Misty says, rolling her neck and hips at me. Misty's eyes aren't the only thing that's different about her. She's also lost a lot of weight over the break. When I saw her at Tre's house after the shooting, I could tell she was shedding the pounds, but now she looks like she's been starving herself.

"Whatever, Misty. You and I know the truth, and whenever you're ready to come with it, bring it on," I say to Misty's back as they exit the main hall, heading in the same direction I'm going. KJ looks back at me and I nod my head to confirm my words. If Misty's going to call me out on my shit—which I'm not ashamed of—then I'm calling her on hers. One of the rules of our religion is to not out other practitioners, but Misty's far from being a true devotee of the Orisha, our West African Gods. And because she's a fake, I think it's my duty to out her wannabe ass for the trick she really is, in as many ways as I possibly can.

I take my class schedule out of my purse to check the room number for my new fourth-period class. It's in the language arts hall at the opposite end of the building from my English class. At least it's not far from my third period government class. Jeremy conveniently ditched third period today, starting out his second semester the right way, as far as he's concerned. Lucky for him the absences start over again at the beginning of each semester, which means he's working with a clean slate now.

"Lost?" I hear a familiar voice ask. As if my prayers were answered, Mr. Adewale comes walking down the main hall looking as fine as ever. Damn, why does he have to be my teacher and too old for me to date?

"Hey, Mr. A. Fancy meeting you here." Mr. Adewale looks down and smiles at me, falling into step with my quick stride. As we walk down the long corridor, we notice the crowd of students waiting at the other end of the hall. Among the masses are KJ, Misty, and their crew. Please tell me they're not in class with me.

"Not really. Seems they had another opening for this semester and I'll still be subbing for Mrs. Peterson when she needs me, as well as the other teachers, just like I did last semester."

"So what do you do when you're not teaching here?" I ask, all up in his business this morning. We never have a lot of time to talk so I have to get in the important questions whenever I get the chance.

"I study. I still have to pass my exams at the University of West Los Angeles in the spring, before they award me my master's degree in conjunction with my bachelor's."

"Wow, that must take a lot of time out of your day." I feel him though. "Between my schoolwork and my work at home, I always have my head in a book."

"Is there a better place for your head to be?" Yeah, resting on a pillow in a deep sleep that keeps me still, but he doesn't need to know all that. Ending our brief conversation, Mr. Adewale stops in front of my fourth-period classroom and unlocks the door. Yes! He's my teacher after all. There is a God.

"Oh hell, no, she's not in our class," Misty says, following Mr. A and me into the cold, dark classroom. If I recall correctly, this room wasn't used last semester. It smells stale in here and has a strange feeling, like it's vacant, but not really. If I didn't know any better I'd say there were ghosts up in here, but I think that's my sleep deprivation talking.

"Now, this should be interesting," Jeremy says, talking over KJ and Misty's heads while looking down at me from behind. I look up at Mr. Adewale, who shakes his head before turning on the lights.

"Please take your seats," Mr. A says over the loud crowd.

Most of the students from my government class are in here, as well as other displaced AP students. But there are a few new faces as well. One dude in particular catches my eye because he seems to be staring at me. I quickly swoop up the seat closest to Mr. Adewale's dusty desk, and Jeremy's right next to me, as usual. Misty, KJ, and the rest of their crew, including Shae and Tony—her mute man, who never speaks unless spoken to—take the seats in the back, and everyone else files in and gets comfortable in our new space.

"Excuse me, I'm supposed to have you sign this," the cute Latino dude who was checking me out says to Mr. A. He glances at me and gives me a shy smile, making me blush from the inside out. Damn, he's fine. I wonder if he's met Maggie and the rest of El Barrio, the Latino clique. If not, I think introductions are in order and I'll be glad to make the connection.

"Sure," Mr. A says, taking the yellow enrollment slip from our new classmate and signing it. "Okay, class, today we're going to get our seat assignments in order and pass out the textbooks. Tomorrow I will hand out the syllabi for the semester and I expect everyone to familiarize themselves with the various sections of the textbook by tomorrow."

"Damn, dude, chill. It's the first day," Del says, causing KJ and followers to chuckle. Now they should know better than to mess with the same brotha that served as the referee for the game between them and my boys. Jeremy shakes his head, crosses his arms over his desk and puts his head down for a quick nap. He has no tolerance for drama of any kind.

"It's not the first day, it's the third and I'm not your dude nor do I chill." Mr. Adewale slams his teacher's edition onto his desk, causing a cloud of dust to rise up and silencing the chattering class. Jeremy doesn't budge. "No disrespect of any kind will be tolerated." Mr. A walks over to Jeremy and taps him on the shoulder, waking him up.

"Sorry, man, my bad," Jeremy says, sitting up straight in his chair. I wish I could fall out that easily.

"Jeremy, would you please pass out the textbooks that are in the back corner of the room. KJ, you can help." Wow, Mr. A is serious about his shit this morning. "Rule number one of debate and speech is to respect your opponent, just like in any other sport. You may not like them or agree with what they're saying, but they still deserve to be heard. Rule number two is to remember rule number one."

Feeling someone's eyes on me, I turn around and look behind me, scanning the other faces in the room. I catch Misty staring at me. She's been going back and forth with Shae the whole time we've been in here. Just then, Nellie and Laura walk into the room, completing my nightmare of a class situation. I feel like I've died and gone straight to hell, and I don't even believe in the place. Mama says life, like hell, is what you make of it, and this is as close as I could get to it on Earth.

"Like I said, this should be interesting," Jeremy says, placing a book on my desk before continuing with the rest of the row. He's no prophet, but Jeremy hit this one on the head. Mama's definitely got to tell me how to deal with this situation, because keeping a cool head this semester will be next to impossible.

~ 2 ~
An Unholy Day

*"This reminiscing with my past/
Has got me caught up in a daydream."*

—LISA "LEFT EYE" LOPES

Mama's still not comfortable with me having a license to drive. She refuses to get in the car if I'm behind the wheel, saying she values the rest of her living years too much to let a teenager drive her around. Rather than me pick her up from the house and we both ride together to Dr. Whitmore's office, which is next door to our neighborhood liquor store, Miracle Market, she'd rather meet me there. With all of the walking Mama does on a daily basis, it's no wonder why she's in such good shape. No one would ever guess she's a mother of eight children and in her mid-fifties. Her salt-and-pepper, shoulder-length hair only adds to her youthful look, because her skin is seamless, not a crack to be found.

"Hey, Mama," I say, walking into the small office. There's a waiting room with Zen qualities, and two patient rooms on either side of us. It feels more like an Eastern medical clinic than a general practitioner's office, like the sign on the door reads.

Dr. Whitmore delivered all of Mama's children and has taken care of them ever since. My mom never liked Dr. Whitmore, just like she felt about Netta, and delivered me at a hospital in Bellflower. Mama's never forgiven my mother for that, and blames her for my caul not receiving the proper burial it deserved. But Mama's been taking me to Dr. Whitmore on her own since then, and he's cool with me.

"Hey, baby," Mama says, moving her right cheek slightly up to meet my kiss. "How was your day?"

I take my purse off of my shoulder and sit down next to Mama on the futon to wait for the doctor.

"It was cool until Misty said something that freaked me out." Mama looks at me and her green eyes begin to glow as she probes my thoughts; looking for what, I'm not sure. But, by the way her eyes widen, I'd say she found what she was searching for.

"What exactly did she say?" Mama asks in a low voice that gives me the shivers. What the hell? The next time she asks me about my day I'm giving her a simple one-word answer. Dr. Whitmore's office door opens and we can hear him wrapping up a phone conversation. "Word for word, Jayd. This is important."

"She said that I'm 'the bitch who death follows.' " Mama turns grey as soon as the words leave my lips. Before she can say anything, Dr. Whitmore walks into the waiting room to greet us.

"My two favorite ladies in the whole world," he says, opening his long arms to hug us both. Daddy's always been jealous of Mama's relationship with Dr. Whitmore, but he really can't talk, as many church women as he's laid his healing hands on from the pulpit and beyond. "So, your grandmother tells me you're having some problems sleeping, Jayd. What's going on?"

"She's been hexed," Mama says matter-of-factly. When did she come to that conclusion and why didn't she share it with me? "By Esmeralda and one of her latest followers."

"When did this happen and where was I?" I ask as the conversation goes over my head. This always happens when Mama and Dr. Whitmore get together.

"While you were sleeping, I assume," Mama says. Now she's scaring me.

"That old bat. She still doesn't get it, does she?" Whenever Mama's around Dr. Whitmore, their body language becomes relaxed, but I know not to ask her too many questions regarding their relationship. Mama taught me at a young age to be quiet unless spoken to when I was out with her. I broke that rule once and can still feel the sting in my ass from that spanking.

"No, and she never will. We need to get to work on Jayd right away. Her powers are growing swiftly and Esmeralda knows it. She's got one of Jayd's school friends doing her dirty work now."

"Misty's not my friend," I say. They both look at me like I've lost my mind for speaking out of turn. Mama's eyebrows tighten into a frown, the usual scolding for intruding in what she calls "grown folks' business." I'm sorry for being rude, but that had to be said for the record. Misty's no friend of mine. And with all of the adjectives there are in the English language, I know we can come up with something better than that to describe her relationship to me.

"No, she's not," Dr. Whitmore says, taking my chin into his cold hand and forcing me to stick my tongue out. "Mmhmm," he says, looking closely into my mouth. I never get used to this part. I always think my breath stinks, especially after the Funyuns I ate for lunch today. "Go ahead and make yourself comfortable in room number one. I need to get my tools and I'll be in momentarily." Mama walks me into the first patient room and closes the curtain, which serves as a door for the intimate space.

"Mama, what's he looking at when he's eyeing my tongue?" I ask, making myself comfortable on the table in the center of the room. This is a sanctuary compared to the other doctors' offices I have to visit from time to time. There are several bamboo trees lining the walls and soothing Chinese music playing in the background. Mama sits down on the loveseat opposite where I'm seated. I notice hanging on the wall above her head are copies of Dr. Whitmore's acupuncture and medical licenses, as well as the certified oath he took as a traditional healer, just like the one hanging up in Mama's spirit room.

"He's checking your vital signs."

"Doesn't he need a stethoscope and a thermometer for that?" Mama rolls her eyes at my line of questioning, knowing I'm doing it mostly to antagonize her and less out of curiosity. I don't want to be here and I'm tired. The last thing I want is someone poking at me today.

"No, he does not." Mama's stern voice let's me know that her patience with me is wearing thin. "You act like you haven't been coming here all of your life, Jayd. What's gotten into you today?"

"I'm just saying, what's my tongue got to do with my temperature?"

"You can tell a lot about what's going on in a person's body by looking at the color of their tongue. Part of being a natural practitioner is taking the path of least intrusiveness, and that starts with you being quiet and sticking out your tongue." Mama throws her soft pink cashmere shawl across her shoulders and covers the slight cleavage she's letting pop today. She looks like she's going out on a date or something.

"Chilly?"

Mama smiles at me and I can't help but smile back. Mama's a grown, attractive woman and she's not dead. If anyone deserves some innocent flirting and positive attention from a man it's my grandmother. Dr. Whitmore walks through the curtain and sets my chart and a small tray of instruments down on the table next to my feet. He looks at my grandmother and takes in her presence fully before turning his attention back to me.

"As you already know, your visit alludes to a larger spiritual problem and I know your grandmother's already on top of that." Dr. Whitmore winks at Mama and she blushes like a schoolgirl. If they keep it up they're going to make me sick instead of heal me, which is the reason I'm here. Taking the miniature flashlight off the tray, he looks into my eyes, ears, and nose. Dr. Whitmore returns the light to the tray and takes out seven thin acupuncture needles. Mama rises from her seat and walks over to the sink on the other side of the room where his shelves and cabinets are housed, and washes her hands.

"Lynn Mae, do you remember the first time we performed acupuncture together?"

"Of course I do. You let me in the room knowing I'd never poked anyone with a needle before."

"Yes, but even then your acupressure was exceptional." Dr. Whitmore watches as Mama reaches for two of the small tincture vials lining the wall above the sink. She takes two cotton balls from their jar next to the sink and joins Dr. Whitmore for my session. "Lie down, child. This won't take long."

"Jayd, I want you to breathe deep and try to relax," Mama says, patting my thigh with her right hand as she pushes the cotton ball down on one of the tincture jars with her other hand. She then applies the effervescent ball onto the center of my forehead, my temples, the top of both shoulders, and on the side of both big toes. These are the points where Dr. Whitmore will place the needles. As I inhale the lavender and patchouli oil intermingling in the air, Dr. Whitmore follows Mama's trail, and I'm directed to be still and let the needles do their job.

I know it sounds crazy, but these little needles really do

get some things moving in my body. I don't have acupuncture very often, but every time I do I feel better afterward. It's just the poking and prodding that bugs me. After they are done placing the needles, Mama cleans up and returns to her seat while I drift off, enjoying the surge of ashe, or spiritual power, flowing through me.

After what seems like only a few minutes, I can feel Mama rise from her seat and begin to remove the needles. I open my eyes and glance at the clock on the wall. I've been lying here for close to an hour. Mama smiles down at me and Dr. Whitmore smiles down at her. They both look like they enjoyed my nap more than I did.

"How do you feel?" he asks, again forcing my tongue out while he searches for signs of life. He gives a nod of satisfaction and Mama does the same thing.

"I feel okay. I slept."

"Yes, but did you dream?" Mama asks. In any other household parents would be happy to know their children were sleeping, but not in mine. Mama's got to have the dreams too, and damn the REM sleep.

"No, I didn't, or if I did I can't remember. I didn't even realize I'd been out for this long." Mama breathes a sigh of concern and looks up at Dr. Whitmore for suggestions. Dr. Whitmore walks over to his medicine cabinet, pulls out a jar of huge brown capsules, and hands them to me. "Whatever or whoever's stressing you out, let him go. That goes for you too, Lynn Mae." Mama and I both look at him and reluctantly smile. We've both got our share of boy problems and, unfortunately, that always leads to hating females like Esmeralda and Misty.

"Thank you, Dr. Whitmore."

"Don't mention it, young lady. You just take care of yourself and watch your back. Esmeralda means you harm and that's real. But we won't let her get the best of you, little

Jayd." Mama takes out her wallet to pay, but Dr. Whitmore puts his hand over hers and directs her to keep her money. "Let me know if you need anything else."

"Thank you again," I say, following Mama to the door.

"Yes, thank you, and we'll talk to you soon." Mama looks back at him as he walks us to the entrance. They look at each other like they want to say more but can't because I'm here. I step outside in front of Mama and let them have a moment alone. I walk to my mom's car and open the passenger door, tossing my purse into the backseat. I look at the bottle the doctor gave me and study the Chinese characters.

"What are these?" I ask Mama as she exits the building. She walks over to me and looks around to check out our environment. Mama's always on red alert, and rightfully so. We've got plenty of haters out here.

"They are vitamins to help strengthen your ashe. You're going to need all of the help you can get to fight off whatever this girl's put on you. And even more than that, you're going to need to learn how to control your dreams before they end up hurting you, or worse." I've never heard Mama this scared before. *Worse?*

"The only thing that could be worse is death, and I know that's not what you're talking about, is it?" I search her eyes for a hint, but she's not giving in.

"Jayd, you ask too many questions," Mama says, answering my question with a straight poker face. "Just focus on getting some sleep and leave the rest up to me." No problem. I have enough on my plate as it is.

"Can I drive you home?" Mama looks at me like I'm really crazy this time, but I have to ask. Without responding, Mama drapes her shawl over her shoulders and begins her trek toward Gunlock Avenue. "Okay; see you at home," I say to Mama as she turns the corner, walking toward our block. As fast as she steps, she'll probably beat me there. I didn't have a chance to ask her about how to handle my new classmates, but that can wait until tomorrow. I don't want anything else on my mind for my date with some much-needed sleep. The drama will definitely still be there come morning.

With Tre's service on Friday and Rah still not talking to me, the last thing I need is something else to worry about. Mickey's still pissed at me for telling her off about Nigel getting shot, and I can't get any information from Nigel himself because his parents have confiscated his cell. It seems like life as I know it has changed permanently, and there's nothing that I can do about it. After I finish my homework I'm going to take my meds, and if they work like they're supposed to, I should get some good sleep tonight.

"Lynn Marie, please stop. You don't know what you're doing!" Mama shouts as I empty the contents of one of my three large Hefty trash bags that house my clothes, underwear, and other possessions. Bryan's bottom bunk bed is covered with all of my things—except they're not really mine and I'm not me. I'm my mother at my age. Oh hell, no, not again.

"You don't own me, Mama. I can do what I want, when I want." I continue to empty the bags onto the bed and sift through my mother's things. Damn, she has a lot of shit.

"No, you cannot, little girl, and as long as you live under my roof you will do as I say." Mama grabs my arm and turns me toward her. When I look into her eyes I see it's not Mama but rather Maman, and she's looking at me so intently it's making my head hurt.

"Problem solved," I (as my mom) say, without moving my lips. I'm talking to Maman from my mind into hers. This must be before my mom lost the use of her powers on other people. It's like I can hear the words as they form in

Maman's head before she speaks them aloud. I can even hear her changing her mind. What a trip.

"What are you talking about? You can't leave home. You're only seventeen." I keep sifting and throwing things I'm taking with me into one bag while piling everything else onto the floor to discard later.

"Mama, Jayd's doing it again." *I hear Bryan yelling outside of my dream, but I can't stop it. I can also hear Daddy and my other uncles grumbling about losing sleep, but they're not the only ones. Do they think I want to be walking around the house this time of night and completely out of control?*

"Bryan, go get a glass of water. Jay, help me follow your cousin." *Mama's voice sounds weak and terrified. Whatever's going on is scaring Mama and that alone is enough to terrify me.*

"I'll be eighteen in three months and then I'm getting married, so I can just move in with Carter now." I've never heard my mother call my father by his first name before. I almost forgot he had one.

"If you move in with Carter, Lynn Marie, it'll be the death of you." Maman's words are so strong they resonate through my mother's head like bells in a chapel: loud and clear.

"I'm sick of you and this house and your curses. It's over," I shout, stuffing as much shit as I can into two new garbage bags and passing Maman by in the hallway. I notice my uncles in the living room watching the scene. I see a young Bryan sitting next to the lit Christmas tree, crying at the sight of his mother and favorite sister arguing for what I'm sure is the hundredth time. Damn, another holiday gone bad. Why do we even celebrate them when we know there's bound to be some drama?

"Omi tutu, ona tutu, ile tutu, tutu Laroye," *I hear Mama*

chanting as she sprinkles cold water on my head. Even though I can hear her and feel her, I still can't snap out of it. I follow the path of my mother through the living room, ready to head out of the front door to God only knows where.

"Man, it's too early in the morning for this. Why can't she have a breakdown during the day when we're all awake?" *Jay asks.*

"Jay, shut up your whining and stand behind your cousin just in case she falls back. Bryan, you walk in front of her and don't let her hurt herself." *Mama continues praying in Yoruba and I unwillingly continue my sleepwalking through the past.*

"Lynn Marie, I'm warning you. Turn back around before you get hurt." Maman's shrill voices shocks me and my mom both, but my mom continues to move toward the front door. "If you walk out that door I can't help you, Lynn Marie. My hands are tied." I look back at Maman, my uncles, and the house before opening the front door with my bags in tow.

"I'll take my chances," I say. Before I exit onto the front porch, I catch a glimpse of my reflection in the glass door and see my mother's green eyes staring back at me. They're glowing like Mama's and Maman's do in my visions. I guess with the powers comes the glow, because although my mother's eyes are pretty, they don't shine like this anymore. I smile at the reflection and can feel my mother's long hair sweep across my back. I walk outside and begin to descend the front porch, but not before Esmeralda has a chance to rear her ugly head. She looks younger, but with the same cold, blue eyes, which catch my mother completely off guard.

"Lynn Marie!" Maman yells, but it's too late. My head starts to throb as Esmeralda locks onto my eyes with hers.

The pounding in my head is getting louder and louder, drowning out whatever Maman's saying in the background. I can feel hands pulling me back into the house but I can't tell if they're Maman's or Mama's. This feels too real for me.

"You evil bitch," my mom says telepathically to Esmeralda, who hears her loud and clear.

"You haven't seen evil yet," Esmeralda says, not letting go of her visual hold over my mother for a second. They continue their mental tug-of-war for what seems like an eternity before my mother finally starts to lose the infamous battle I've heard about all of my life.

"Mama, help," my mother whines. Maman looks down at me, her green eyes glowing, not from her powers but from the tears she's shedding.

"I can't, baby, I can't. You've been cursed, and when you disobeyed me, you locked it in. I'm so sorry, my daughter," she says. I can feel her staring into my eyes, searching for some recognition of my mother's powers, I assume. But like Esmeralda, they're gone.

"Mama, what happened? I can't see anything!" I scream. It's like someone turned out the lights and everywhere I look there's only darkness.

"Oh, baby girl, why didn't you listen to me? She took your sight," Mama cries, holding my head in her lap. Esmeralda overpowered my mom to the point that I'm lying on the front porch and didn't even realize it. "I can't hear you in my mind anymore. Why aren't you talking to me?"

"Oh girl, it's over. She took your powers right out of your eyes. Your sight will come back eventually, but your powers are gone forever."

So that's how my mom lost her powers. Wicked.

"Jayd, snap out of it." *I can hear Mama but it's Maman's voice that I'm following.* "Jayd, now!"

* * *

And with that final command, Mama pours the entire glass of cold water over my head, forcing me to wake up. We're seated on the front porch, just like we were in my vision. I try to look around but everything's dark.

"I can't see," I say, wiping the water out of my eyes. But it's no use. Everything's still black, and I know I'm not dreaming anymore. Oh shit, this can't be good.

"Damn, that's rough," Jay says, expressing my sentiments exactly, but without any sympathy.

"I'm glad I'm not a Williams woman," Bryan says. I wish I could see the smirk on his face so I could slap it off. Whenever Mama and I celebrate the women in our lineage, all the men in the household hate on us. Even if they would never wish anything serious on us, seeing me and Mama suffer must be the best dessert for them all.

"Shut up, both of you. Bryan, help me get Jayd back in the house. Jay, go get her a towel to dry off." Mama grabs my right arm and Bryan my left. They lead me back into the house and to my bed. The early morning cold has once again gone straight through my thin gown and straight into my bones, but I could care less about that. I want to know how long I'm going to play the part of Ray Charles in my mother's life story.

"Mama, what happened? Why can't I see anything?"

"Well, you stayed in your mother's past for too long and brought some of it back with you. That's why you have to learn to control your dreams, baby. Otherwise, they will get the best of you. You can't keep sleepwalking like this, child." Who's she telling? This shit is wearing a sister down, and I can't afford to lose any more sleep. It's killing my energy, and that's draining my wallet and my social time.

"What time is it, anyway? I've got to get up soon to get to school. You think this will wear off by then?" Not that I'm in any rush to get to South Bay High, but the day's going to start whether I can see it or not.

"Obviously you can't go to school like this. You'll have to stay home until it wears off. Here, take your medicine and go back to sleep."

"I don't want to go back to sleep, Mama. Every time I do I either wake up walking around as someone else or I feel like I haven't slept at all, which is worse." Ignoring my protest, Mama hands me a cup of water to accompany the pills she places in my other hand. I smell the nasty things and curl up my nose. "I thought these were supposed to make me better? What kind of help is it if I go blind in the process?"

"You have to have more faith and patience in your process than that, Jayd. It's not magic, I keep trying to tell you, girl. Now, drink up and get some sleep." I don't see how, with Tre's memorial service tomorrow afternoon. But at least I'll miss school, which is always a plus.

~ 3 ~
Pour Out a Little Liquor

"Pour out a lil liquor young queen."

—TUPAC

After yesterday morning's sleepwalking incident and sleeping most of the day away, I feel like a zombie this morning. Today is Tre's memorial service and I'm going no matter how cloudy my vision may be. My eyes are still blurry, but at least I can see what's in front of me, unlike yesterday.

When I didn't show up to class yesterday, Jeremy called to make sure I was okay. I told him I was fine, just feeling a little out of it and that I'd be back by Monday. I already requested today off because I knew Tre's funeral would start in the early afternoon and I didn't want to miss a single moment of it. Speaking of which, if I can't drive myself to the church I don't know who's going to take me. I'm not talking to anyone who'll be there, and I know Bryan's not going. There's too much gang activity on that side of the train tracks for him, and he's grown out of that stupid shit, for real. Hopefully between now and the four hours before the service begins my eyes will be good enough to drive.

Because my sight is almost at a hundred percent, Mama took the opportunity of having me home during a school day to give me an assignment. She made me read two chapters in the spirit book: one on the living dead and another one on the power of dreaming in our lineage. I learned that when I master my powers, in my dream state I should be able to see through my ancestors' eyes, literally *as them* with their gifts, Mama's included. Now that's some powerful shit right there.

"So, Queen Califia's power of sight was her ability to see treasure buried deep in the earth, no matter where it was. No wonder she was so wealthy." Califia was one of our ancestors—whom the golden State of California happens to be named after. Lexi looks up at me, yawns, and lays her head back down, ready for some more history.

"And it says here that Maman could influence the body's blood supply through her sight. No wonder she was a revered healer. Our powers are generational, sharpening with time and changing with every rebirth. That makes sense. I want to know more about Mama's gift of sight." I flip through the numerous pages of the heavy book to my mom's notes on Mama, which aren't as plentiful as the ones she and our ancestors kept. It's usually the job of each generation to keep notes on the one before it, but my mom gave that up along with her lessons. I guess that's my job now.

"According to my mom's notes, Mama can borrow anyone's powers, even people outside of the lineage. Baller," I say. Damn, this is getting good. I knew Mama was fierce, but I had no idea her game was this tight. "No offense, Lexi, but I wish Rah were here to talk to. I need some feedback, you feel me?" My phone vibrates and I look down to see the one name I've been waiting on to call all week long: Rah. Well, it's about time he got one of my messages. If all I had to do was send it through psychic mail, he should've called days ago.

"I thought you were dead," I say, even if it's not funny. Rah basically dropped off the face of the Earth, or at least it seems that way to me. This is the longest we've gone without talking since we started talking again, and it doesn't feel good.

"Nah, I'm here. I wish someone weren't, though."

"Don't even play like that, Rah."

"You started it." I guess I did. We both pause, unsure of what to say next. "Are you going to the memorial service this afternoon?" he asks, making the first move. I'm so glad to hear his voice I don't even hear Mama come into the spirit room, and Lexi's no help. She never gives away Mama's position.

"I was planning on it but I need a ride now." Mama looks at me, quickly inspecting my eyes with her glowing ones before stepping back outside. I close the spirit book and slide it to the corner of the table. I readjust myself on the stool, because it looks like Mama's coming right back.

"I thought you were driving your mom's car. Did it break down, too?"

"No, it's nothing like that." I'm glad he's concerned about a sistah's transportation issues. I still feel bad that I let Sandy drive his Acura when he had offered it to me first. If I'd never let her borrow the car she would've never got her hands on Rah's keys and made copies of them. But, like my vision, Sandy's going to come back eventually, and when she does, her ass is mine. "Let's just say my eyes aren't working like they used to."

"Okay. I won't even ask if this has something to do with you and Mama," he says, already knowing the real deal. "You don't sound like you're at school; are you?" I look at the clock hanging on the yellow wall above the stove and can barely make out the numbers through the blur. I realize Rah's calling me during a nutrition break. I like that our schools are on the same bell schedule.

"No, I had to stay home today."

"Oh, well if you need a ride, I can pick you up. Why didn't you call me if you needed me, girl?" He acts like we've been talking since Sandy stole his grandfather's car and ran off with their daughter last weekend. Talk about selective amnesia.

"I have been calling, or didn't you get my messages?"

"Jayd, I didn't get a call about you being sick. I just needed time to cool off from the other shit, you know that." Rah takes a deep breath and lets it out, forgiving me in the process. I already forgave him before he called.

"Well, I need a ride. I'm in Compton. The service is going to be at my grandfather's church." Mama walks back into the cottage-like environment and rolls her eyes at the mention of Daddy. Why are they still married if they can't stand each other? I hope I never have to deal with that type of drama.

"Alright, bet. See you at two."

"Thank you, Rah. And it's good to hear your voice." I can hear his smile through the phone, but Mama's glare tells me not to share that piece of information right now. Her body language reveals her impatience and I know it's time for me to get off the phone and give her my undivided attention.

"Jayd, tell Rah I said hi and bye. We have a lot of work to do to get you ready for Tre's service," Mama says, pulling back the white fabric and revealing the altar in the east corner of the room dedicated to the ancestors. Mama has several miniature shrines back here, instead of one joint shrine with shelves, like the one in her bedroom.

"I've got to go," I say into my cell. I begin to separate the fresh herbs Mama picked from the garden and placed on the table. She's got thyme, basil, chamomile, rosemary, and more lavender. Whatever we're about to make is going to smell good. She passes me an orange and a grater to make fresh peel to soak in the grapeseed oil she puts down in front of me. I could have gone to school if I knew I was going to have to do so much work today.

"I know. Tell Mama I said hi," Rah says.

I hang up my pink phone and set it down on the table, away from Mama's fresh ingredients, and start grating. I notice a tall bottle of gin on the counter next to the sink, which means we are feeding the ancestors this morning along with the rest of our duties. Mama always says a priestess's work is never done, and I see what she means. From morning to night Mama's doing something for someone. I don't know how she keeps up with it all, but she does it like a pro.

"So, what did you learn from your studies this morning? Have any new ideas on how to control your dreaming?" She takes the small pieces of orange peel and stuffs them into the oil vial. She then crushes a small amount of the lavender and places it in the same container before putting a cork in it. I follow suit with the remainder of the grated peel and share my thoughts.

"I learned about the powers in our lineage and why they evolve like they do. I also learned that we need to keep better records around here because your stories and Maman's stories are incomplete." Mama smiles as she sits down on the other stool across from me. She carefully inspects the herbs and then passes them to me to wash in the sink. I rise from my seat and begin to rinse them off. "But really, I'm very interested in the different ways we've used and misused our gift of sight."

Mama takes what I've washed so far and puts it in a large marble mortar with a pestle to crush it. "Yes, go on," she says.

"I also read up on zombies. That was some strange and cruel stuff my great-grandfather's folks were into."

"That's why we don't call on Jon Paul's ancestors. It hurts me that my father was such an evil man, but truth is truth." Mama shakes the excess water off the remaining herbs and dries her hands on her apron.

"Why did you have me read that?"

Mama looks into my eyes, searching for the right words to

say what she doesn't want to. The fear in her eyes is all the validation I need: Misty's trying to make me a zombie. Oh hell, no, this can't be happening to me. I've got AP exams in a few months, not to mention all the money I'm missing out on by not working. I don't have time to be someone's personal pushpin doll.

"Jayd, I don't want to scare you, but you should know the truth. Esmeralda is trying to make you a zombie of sorts. She really just wants to control your dream state, therefore controlling your powers and stealing another one of my girls' sight. And we're not having that." I hear Mama on that one. Williams women don't go out like that—ever.

Cortez tried to take Califia's power, but her lineage still lives on through us. Maman lives on in my dreams and she's like Wonder Woman with her shit. Mama's, well, Mama. And my mom reclaimed her powers through mine. Now it's up to me to keep my ancestors' legacy alive and in our hands; not Esmeralda's, or Misty's either, for that matter. That trick has yet again picked the wrong clique to join.

"No, we're not. What do we need to do?" I ask. Mama cracks a slight smile at my enthusiasm to jump back in the ring after I was just down for the count. The sooner I get Misty off my back the better.

"Well, it seems that Maman is the ancestor fighting for you this time around. In both of your sleepwalking incidents she was trying to get you out of harm's way, and exiting through a door was the way you both got into and out of trouble. Transition has to be dealt with, and we need to go to the ancestors for that. They'll tell us what to do next."

"Well, that explains a lot." Maman is my joto, or sponsoring ancestor, in my lineage. Every baby born has an elder who made transition before his or her birth, and that ancestor is like a guardian angel for the baby's lifetime. "Why do I need to keep taking these horse pills?" I ask as she hands me a tall glass of water to back them. "They don't seem to be working at all. I'm still not dreaming like I usually do."

"On the contrary, Jayd," Mama says, taking possession of the spirit book and the tall bottle of gin before rising from her seat to kneel before the small ancestor shrine. Lighting the white candles, she directs me to kneel beside her at the altar. "Your powers are growing stronger by the day. To fight off Iku, your powers will have to be as strong as they can become before your formal initiation."

"Iku. Did you say what I think you just said?" Mama looks at me and then up at the luminescent white altar. There are pictures of all the women in our family who've made the transition to the ancestor world with the inevitable help of Iku, or death, in Yoruba. He's not someone you want walking with you until it's definitely your time to leave this world as we know it.

"Don't worry about that now, baby," Mama says, patting my hand like she would when as a child I'd go to the doctor to get a shot. She'd tell me not to worry about the pain when I'd ask her if it was going to hurt. "Just focus on channeling Maman's strength and gift of sight through your dreams. That is, after all, the pinnacle of your powers once you reach them."

"But, did you just say that basically Esmeralda is trying to kill me and literally make me her zombie?" Mama looks at me and smiles at my simplification of a very serious process. From what I read, people usually get caught up in zombie world by crossing over a threshold where there's a poisonous powder laid down for the victim to unknowingly step on. This powder works quickly once it comes into contact with the skin, causing the victim's heart to stop and their body to be taken over.

"Yes, but only in your sleep. Don't worry, we'll fix her." Mama sounds very sure—but me, not so much. I was just blind for twenty-four hours and that was a little too close for my comfort.

"Mama, I don't want to die in any way, shape, or form. Besides, if I die in my sleep doesn't that mean I'm dead in real life, too?" I remember Mama telling me when I was a little girl to wake up, every time I had this one recurring dream of falling off of a tall building. Mama would wake me up right before my head hit the pavement, warning me that if I didn't, I would never see daylight again. From then on when I'd have that dream, I'd wake up at a certain point with Mama's help.

"There are different types of deaths, Jayd. Not all of them are tragic and not all are fair. But they all have one thing in common: they signify the end of one thing and the beginning of another. Sometimes it's new and sometimes it's old. I hope you don't have to repeat the mistakes of our collective past. But if you do, it just means that it's meant for you to learn your lesson in that way. In a lineage, you could have karmaic debts owed in past lives or the lives of your ancestors. It's interesting to me how a lot of the mistakes Maman made, I also made, and still may be destined to make. And you and your mama may be, too."

"This isn't making me feel any better." Mama opens the bottle of gin and takes a glass of water off of the shrine.

"What do you want me to say, Jayd? Yes, in most instances when you die in your dreams you die in this life, too. That's why it's vital that you learn how to control your dreams. Embrace your power, Jayd, and let your ancestors help you use them. Learn from their mistakes, as a witness rather than as a participant; and, more importantly, master the art of waking up."

We pour the libation to the ancestors, first giving them cold water and then gin while calling all the names in our lineage. We are going to need the collective power of our ashe to beat Esmeralda's evil ass, and we've got the strength and wisdom to get the job done right. After our worship, we talk about Tre's service and my taboos in dealing with Iku. Mama warns me to be careful of being around too much wailing and gossiping, because that could be a form of Iku and I need to stay as far away from death as possible while Esmeralda's curse is in effect. She also advises me to honor the ancestors at the ceremony, especially those in our lineage.

"Jayd, when your grandfather asks if anyone else would like to say a prayer on Tre's behalf, I need for you to speak for the ancestors. Pour the libation for Tre, just like we do to our ancestors, no matter what anyone says." Damn, why do I always have to be the one to stick out?

"Yes, ma'am. I need to get dressed now if we're finished," I say, following Mama's eyes to the clock on the wall. We've been in here for over two hours and a sistah's got to eat before I get going. I also need to pack to go to my mom's this weekend.

"Yes, go ahead. And remember to wear mostly white, Jayd. Tell Rah I said thank you for taking care of you, too." I'm glad at least one of my homies is hanging with me again. I know the entire neighborhood and my former crew will be out today, Misty included. It's been nice not seeing the haters at school for the past two days, but hopefully they won't make up for lost time this afternoon. All I can hope for is a peaceful going home for Tre, and for Misty to stay as far away from me as possible.

When Rah and I arrive, the church is packed with friends, family, and others, here to say their good-byes. I was a little nervous about Rah being singled out for shooting back at Mickey's man, whose bullet ended Tre's life and got caught in Nigel's shoulder. But since he wasn't the one who killed Tre, no one's really tripping off of Rah right now. Tre's body is still being autopsied to help with the case against Mickey's man, and then will be cremated, per his sisters' wishes. I feel bad for Brandy and her unborn baby, who'll never get to know its uncle. She and Tre were so close, unlike their older sister, who looks like she's ready to go.

"Where do you want to sit?" Rah asks, eyeing the pews in the quaint church. Most of the crowd is hanging outside, waiting for the service to begin.

"This is fine." We make our way into one of the pews closest to the front. My grandfather winks at me from the pulpit, where he and the other ministers are seated, waiting for the choir to begin. I love watching my grandfather preach because he's so enthusiastic when he talks about his faith. It's the fanning hussies in the audience that keep me from coming here on a regular basis. I can't cross enemy lines, or Mama would have my ass in a sling—literally.

"All rise for the family," Daddy says as Tre's family makes their way down the aisle, followed by everyone else. I notice Misty, KJ, Mickey, and Nigel walk down the aisle and sit in the back. I wave at Nigel and he nods "what's up" to me. He looks good, aside from the sling his arm is in. I wonder if his parents know he's here. I guess if they did, Mickey wouldn't be right behind him like she is now. This is going to be an interesting reunion for us all.

"Lord, we gather here today to send this young brother home to you," Daddy begins. With all of the wailing going on I can tell this is going to be a long afternoon.

The services went on without too much drama. There was a brief moment of tension when Tre's fellow gang members filed into the sanctuary like soldiers in an army, but Daddy's used to presiding over funerals in the hood and knows they mean no harm. Everyone has a right to mourn. Daddy even allowed them to speak their peace, bringing everyone in the place to tears.

"Would anyone else like to say a few words before we depart?" Daddy asks. I look around and see no one's hands raised and figure there's no time like the present to represent Mama.

"I would, Daddy," I say, taking the small Mason jar half full of water out of my purse and walking up to the altar where Tre's picture is. The floral arrangement is stunning and provides the perfect place for me to pour the libation. When I reach the front of the main sanctuary, I begin pouring and praying, not worried about the many eyes on me, including Misty's. She looks like she wants to kill me right here and now.

"Omi tutu, ona tutu, ile tutu, tutu Laroye, tutu egun. Mo juba Queen Califia, mo juba Maman Marie, mo juba to all of the ancestors whose names are known and unknown, mo juba Trevon," I say, reciting the prayers just like Mama would if she were here.

At the mention of Tre's name, three of his boys take out their bottles of Vodka, beer, and Hennessey and pour out a little liquor with me, the rest of their crew following suit. If they only knew how far back this tradition goes. As they salute with me I continue my prayers.

"We thank you for your protection, your blessings, and your love. Ashe, ashe, ashe o." I pour the remaining water into the flowers and end the prayer. I look up at Daddy, who gives me a stern smile. On one hand I'm sure he's proud of me. But I know he wishes I would come back to the church. I close the jar tightly and walk back down the aisle of the quiet church with all eyes on me.

Rah smiles at me when I reach our row. He hugs me tightly when I return to my seat next to him. I'm not sure if it's because of the service or what, but he's got tears in his eyes and so do I. I love that we feel each other, no matter how much it hurts sometimes. True love is worth all of the pain that comes with it, and so is our friendship.

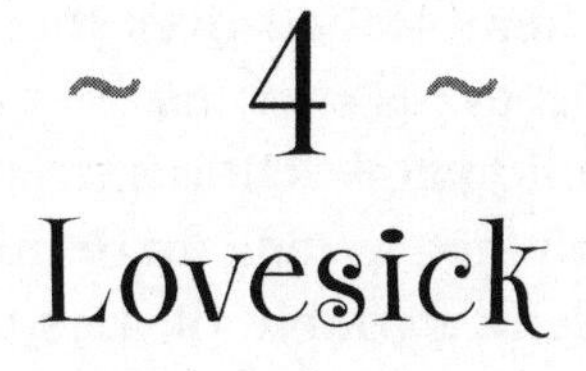

~ 4 ~ Lovesick

"It ain't all roses, flowers and posing/
It ain't all candy, this love stuff is demanding."

—MARY J. BLIGE

In the true tradition of the black church, there's plenty of eating and socializing after every event. Most of the church members have turned out to prepare the food and get the dining hall ready to host the large crowd. I can't believe Mama used to ever do this kind of work. I was a young child when Mama left the church. I remember sitting in the first pew with her, wearing my Sunday dress with gloves and shiny black shoes to match. But our experience was always dictated by the eyes on us and not by the sermon.

The church hasn't changed much over the years. It even smells like the same mixture of Pledge and Pine-Sol I remember as a child. The women of First Compton New African Methodist Episcopal Church keep this place spotless. There are still a few Christmas decorations lining the walls. It feels like the holidays were months ago, but the remnants of the drama they always bring still linger in the cool air.

Whoever said the holidays are the happiest times of the year lied. The past three months have been nothing but misfortune for me and my friends. Ever since Homecoming, Nellie has been tortured by her desire to be a rich bitch, Mickey and Nigel have managed to almost get themselves—and everyone around them—killed over their tainted love, and Rah lost his baby girl to his crazy ex.

I miss Rahima and I know Rah is sick with worry about his daughter. We didn't get to talk in-depth about it, but he talked to Sandy briefly a couple of days ago. She won't give up her location and Rah has no idea where to look.

Rah's doing a good job of holding it together for today. Nigel's the one who needs our support right now, as he faces his own mortality again. We could've just as easily been here for his funeral today. The somber look on Nigel's face says that he's thinking the same thing.

"I've missed hanging with y'all," Nigel says, while devouring one of the five dinner rolls on his plate. We're all eating well, even under the sad circumstances. "Y'all know y'all are family to me, no bull." I guess getting shot can bring a brother's sensitive side out.

"The feeling's mutual," I say. Mickey looks at me and rolls her eyes like she knows what I'm thinking, and she's right: it is her fault our crew's not together anymore. It hurts that I don't have her, Nigel, Chance, and Nellie to hang with anymore. When Nigel gets back I'm sure he'll be busy trying to get back on his game, so who does that leave me with? Mickey's a mile away at the continuation school, and even if she was on the main campus I wouldn't want to chill with her right now anyway.

"My moms and pops have me on lock-down for real." When Nigel swallows the last of his roll, Mickey kisses him hard on the lips, church be damned. This is the first time they've seen each other since the shooting, and she's not wasting a moment making up for lost time. On the other hand, Mickey and I haven't spoken a word.

"So when will you be back at school?" I ask. I look past Nigel and Mickey to see Misty and KJ talking to our neighbor

Brandy across the room. Misty looks back at me cold and hard, forcing me to stare down. What the hell? She thinks she's got powerful eyes like Mama and Esmeralda, but she's only got what Esmeralda lends her, and that's not real power. Misty put this curse on me because she blames me for everything bad in her life, including the death of Tre, her first love. I shouldn't feel sorry for Misty, but I can't help myself. Anyone so desperate for love and attention that they'd accept it from a crazy-ass lady like Esmeralda needs some pity.

"I'll be back on Monday. My shoulder's healing slowly, but the doctors say I should make a full recovery. I have to see about playing the rest of the football season. I'm not sure when they'll let me back on the field, but I hope it's soon. I can't stand sitting still for too much longer."

"You won't be still if I have anything to say about it," Mickey says, kissing him again. The two of them are starting to make me ill in the worst way. This is the bull that got us here in the first place. If they'd never gone behind Mickey's man's back with their secret love affair in the first place, none of this would've ever happened. Nigel looks around and notices the church elders staring and whispering at him and Mickey. Obviously embarrassed, Nigel backs away from Mickey's tongue and resumes eating his food, much to Mickey's disliking.

"Why did you stop? Does my breath smell like ham or something?" Mickey asks, taking another bite of her dinner roll and leaving the meat alone. She shouldn't eat swine anyway, but I don't tell people how to eat. Me and that baby of hers will have to do some serious bonding once it makes its grand entrance. Someone has to provide a different female energy because the baby's mama is always tripping.

"No. It's just a little disrespectful for us to be all over each other in a church, don't you think?" Mickey looks at Nigel like he's lost his mind. "And it's a memorial service for the brotha that got shot with me, but I'm the one who survived. The least I can do is be respectful." Well said.

"Who are you?" Mickey asks, taking a sip of her grape Kool-Aid before continuing. She only stopped eating to kiss Nigel, and now I see that's going to be replaced by going off. "I mean, really. We've been more affectionate than this in the aisle at the grocery market. Since when do you care what people think?"

"Since me not caring got three niggas shot—one of which was me—in case you forgot," Nigel says, wiping his mouth with his free hand and rising from the table. He looks down at Mickey, throws his napkin on his plate of half-eaten food, and exhales deeply. I guess he's had a lot of time to think about things since he's been laid up for over a week. "I'm going to pay my respects to Tre's family and then I need to take a walk."

"I'll come with you, baby," Mickey says to Nigel's back, not taking the hint. Nigel turns around with his free fist balled up like he wants to hit someone.

"Alone," Nigel says, making his wishes crystal clear. Rah and I look at each other and then at Mickey, waiting for her response. She looks like she wants to cry and run after Nigel, but he's already in the main sanctuary. I know she's not going back in there without an escort. With all of the trouble Mickey's caused, she's liable to blow up without some spiritual protection by her side.

"What did I do?" Mickey asks. Rah and I look at my girl in amazement. She still doesn't get it.

"I think it's more like what you didn't do," Rah says in between bites. He's never really had too much to say to Mickey since he knows her ex-man and therefore chooses not to get to know her that well. But her actions have affected two people he loves, and he can no longer remain neutral where Mickey's concerned.

"I don't know what you're talking about. I do everything just fine," she says, pulling down her black miniskirt before readjusting herself in her seat. Mickey looks like she's going to the club instead of a memorial service, and talking like it, too. Even if I don't attend church anymore, I still know how to behave when I'm in one. Mama would slap me silly if I acted like Mickey. Hell, she'd slap Mickey if she were here to witness this shit. It's bad enough she was never faithful to her ex-boyfriend, but for Nigel to get shot by him is a bit much.

"If you're the one pregnant, why am I the one who suddenly feels nauseated?" I ask, causing Rah to laugh with a mouth full of food. But the broad formerly known as my homegirl looks less than amused.

"Very funny, Jayd, but I wasn't talking to you."

"But you were talking to me, and I feel the same way," Rah says. "How can you be so self-centered all of the time? I mean, don't you get tired of it? It's got to wear you out at some point, because I know I get tired of the shit and I don't even see you every day." Mickey's jaw drops as Rah continues to clown her without missing a beat from eating his dinner. "Jayd, don't you get tired of hearing about Mickey and her drama?"

"Yes, I do. Can you pass the salt, please?" I ask Rah, who promptly hands me the shaker. Mickey looks like she's going to flip the table over she's so pissed.

"You know if I didn't know better I'd say she and Sandy were related. They both do what they want when they want, forget who gets shot in the crossfire—no pun intended." Rah's on a roll this afternoon. I know most of his frustration is because of his baby mama, but Mickey's just as wrong in her actions as Sandy is, and I'm glad someone other than myself is finally calling her out.

"All of y'all are tripping around here. Nigel's missing this opportunity to be with me and his baby for the first time in a week, and you two have the nerve to sit here and judge me like you're so high and mighty," Mickey says, turning red. That can't be good for the baby. "Does Rah still get his from Trish, or have you decided to take that stick out of your ass and give it up?"

"Mickey, shut the hell up. As usual, you've gone too far in the wrong direction," I say, even if she's right about Trish and Rah. I really don't know what's going on between the two of them these days and I don't care to ask. Rah and Sandy's drama is enough for me to deal with. I don't need Mickey throwing more salt in my fresh wound.

"I don't have to take this shit," she says, waddling her way back out of her seat and picking up her plate and purse simultaneously. "Tell Nigel I'll holla at him later." Mickey walks away, seething, and that's just fine with me. Maybe pissing her off will shake her into an understanding of the severe consequences of her decisions.

"I hate to upset a pregnant chick, but she deserved it," I say. I would continue eating my dinner but I've suddenly lost my appetite.

"Yes, she did," Rah agrees. If Mickey doesn't respect her pregnancy, someone has to fight for her baby—and who better than her friends or the friends of her maybe baby daddy? Misty walks in as Mickey walks out, almost running into Mickey and her growing belly. Misty looks around the room and catches my eye. She smiles big, like she just got a present she's been asking for forever.

I would say I missed hanging out with her at school, but just like Nellie, Mickey's unrecognizable now. What happened to my girls? This was the fist time in a long time I'd rather be at home and bored out of mind than at school hanging with my friends. Being at school's going to be uncomfortable come Monday, unless I find a way to change the circumstances over the weekend. And with me sleepwalking and carrying on I doubt I'll be able to help anyone else until I help myself.

"I'm surprised you had the nerve to show up here," Misty says, walking up to our table like she's got some sort of authority. Mama has this thing about people standing over her head and I feel her. Misty's so short she would be eye level with anyone sitting, but she seems to have grown a bit since I last saw her. I look down at her feet and see her three-inch black stilettos. She never used to wear high heels. A lot has changed about my nemesis in the past month or so, and it's gone straight to her curly head.

"I'm surprised you had the nerve to walk over here and face me. I know what you're up to, Misty, and take my word for it, it isn't working." I look at her and focus in on her eyes. She's wearing blue contacts similar to the ones Mickey likes to sport every once in a while. Misty may have changed up her entire stylo since hanging out with KJ, but her attitude still sucks.

"Wow, Jayd, I haven't seen bags like the ones you're wearing since I went shopping at Macy's last weekend. Sleeping much lately?" Misty smiles deviously and it's taking all of my strength to stay seated and not slap that smirk off of her face.

"Cool head, little girl. You know you can't afford to lose any more of your ashe right now, Jayd. Ignore her. She's air," my mom says, mentally reminding me of one of Mama's favorite lessons. I know she's right, but it would feel so good to feel the heat of Misty's cheek in the palm of my hand. Maybe kicking her ass is just what I need to get a good night's rest.

"No, it isn't, but I will make you a tea when you get over here, and that should help. Say bye to your little friends and come on. It's getting late and you should really get away from Misty before it gets dark. Your ashe is too vulnerable to be out at night, especially around your enemies."

Noticing the tense vibe, KJ walks over to stand behind Misty and to glare at Rah and me. Rah puts his fork down and stands up behind me, returning KJ's move. If this were a chessboard I'd feel like a pawn. I'd better stand up and stop this before it goes any further.

"Actually, no, I haven't been sleeping well at all. But you wouldn't know anything about that, now would you, Misty?" I look from her to KJ and lock onto his stare. I know he's starting to feel as if there's something Misty's not telling him, but I know if she can influence my head then she's working Esmeralda's magic on him, too.

"You're just jealous because you don't have any friends to boss around anymore," Misty says, crossing her arms across her tight black sweater.

My grandfather walks into the buzzing hall and catches my attention. Two women walk in behind him, both carrying more trays of food. One looks flushed in the cheeks and guilty of something. Daddy looks at me looking at her and his face carries the same look as the sistah behind him. I don't even want to guess what's going on between the two of them. Just the thought of them kissing or doing whatever in his office behind the sanctuary is enough to make my stomach turn.

"It's time to go," I say to Rah, who's right behind me. "It was lovely as always," I say, passing Misty and KJ by as we head toward the exit to the parking lot. If necessary, Rah would have gladly kicked KJ's ass. He's been anxious to repeat the whipping he served KJ on the basketball court a couple of months ago, but now is not the time, and my grandfather's church is definitely not the place.

Once we make a successful escape from the crowded parking lot, we relax in Rah's car and exhale the edgy experience. Misty knows how to rattle my tail feathers and so does Mickey.

"I love that you're you, no matter what," Rah says, turning out of the parking lot and onto Alondra Boulevard. We see Bryan walking down the street to work. Miracle Market is on the next block, which is on the way to Mama's house. If we'd known we were leaving the service early, he could've gotten a ride.

"Do you really?" I ask as Rah stops at the sign. It'll only take us a minute to get back to the house. We could've walked, like my uncle, if I were feeling up to it. But I've done enough walking the past few nights to win the LA Marathon in my sleep—literally.

"Yeah, I do. Look at how you went up to the pulpit and did your thang, girl. You're going to be a bad-ass priestess one day, no joke." I look at the smile in his eyes and know he's telling the truth about that. "It also get on my nerves sometimes, no joke," he says.

"The feeling's mutual." I can see why my mom was so shocked to find out Rah and I haven't had sex yet. The way he treats me when we're together has "serious relationship" written all over it, but I'm not going there yet.

"Huh," he says, turning up the music's already thick bassline. "Then I guess this is our song." We listen to The Roots and Erykah Badu sing about the woes of being in a relationship, and Rah and I can relate fully to the lyrics. "You know you got me, right? No matter if we get angry and don't talk for a week or whatever, I'll always come back to center if I know you're standing in the middle with me." Rah claims my left hand in his right and raises it to his lips, softly kissing each of my knuckles. Damn, his lips feel good.

"I wish it were that easy," I say as we pull up to Mama's house. My eyesight is now fully back after the good cry we all had at the service, so I should be able to drive to Inglewood on my own. But Rah's going to follow me to my mom's apartment anyway, just in case. I already put my backpack and weekend bag in the car, and I know Mama's at Netta's shop working in the back, which is where I would normally be on a Friday evening. But until I get Esmeralda's curse off my back or get some solid sleep, I'm not allowed to touch anyone's head or the hair products. This curse is costing me both sleep and money, and I need both to keep it moving in my world.

"It can be as long as we agree to have faith in us. I love you, girl, even if I did blame you at first for Sandy taking off with my baby. I know it's not your fault and I'm sorry I reacted so strongly." I admit I feel a little responsible for giving her the keys, but Rah chose to be with Sandy in the first place, and her crazy behavior is a consequence of that choice.

"I know, Rah. I know. I just wish we could have a normal relationship, where you bring me candy and flowers and take me out on a date." He puts the car in park and reaches into the glove compartment, pulling out a box of Tic Tacs and a deodorizing tree for his car.

"Would you settle for some mints and an air freshener?" he asks, passing the items to me. I can't help but smile at Rah's silly self.

"I guess it'll have to do for now," I say, surrendering to the moment.

When I get to my mom's, she is supposed to help me make a tea to help me rest, and I'm looking forward to a good night's sleep. My body is starting to feel the effects of sleepwalking and I can't think about anything else right now. Rah looks like he hasn't slept a peaceful night since Rahima disappeared either. I know he's feeling me right now.

"I'll always be here for you, queen." Rah does go above and beyond for me when I need him, like following me to my mom's house, even though I know he's as tired as I am. Who said chivalry was dead?

* * *

When I finally arrive at my mom's apartment, it's dark and vacant, as usual. I turn the lights in the living room on and drop my bags on the floor by the door. I guess she and Karl had plans. I miss hanging with my mom on the weekends, but I understand how being in love can be. All I really want is the tea she promised and to go to sleep.

I take the large bottle of horse-sized pills Dr. Whitmore gave me out of my weekend bag, and immediately decide against taking them tonight. It's just something about swallowing these large things that makes my stomach turn in the worst way. Besides, I don't want to mix the tea my mom mentioned with the doctor's medicine. But since my mom isn't here to make her concoction, maybe I can find the recipe in her spirit notebook.

"Now, do you think I'd leave my baby hanging like that? When you get settled, your tea is in the pot on the stove. Don't add anything to it. Karl and I have a tennis match tonight and a tournament this weekend. I'll check in with you tomorrow. Sleep well, baby."

"Thank you. I'm going to drinking this now so that by the time I'm ready to go to sleep I can just fall out," I say aloud. My mom needs a pet, because when she's not here I have no one to talk to. I don't want the neighbors to think I'm crazy. I walk into the kitchen and take a mug out of the dish strainer and fill it with the warm, fragrant brew on the stove. I wonder what's on television tonight. There must be a *Girlfriends* marathon on or something to keep me company.

The couch looks so inviting, with all of the fluffy pillows and the velvet throw draped across it. I'll make it up into my bed later. Right now I just want to sit down and unwind. I could sleep in my mom's bed when she's not here, but I feel like I can't hear everything if I'm in the bedroom—not that I want to hear too much of anything tonight. If this elixir does the trick I should be down for the count soon, tired feet and all. My cream pumps have been pinching my feet since I got in my mom's car to come here. I guess my Kenneth Coles don't agree with pressing on a clutch.

" *'Cause I'm a boss, boss, boss,"* Kelis sings, announcing a text message as I sip on my drink. It's Jeremy, wanting to know if I'm all right. I guess not seeing me for two days has made him miss me a little bit. Good. He needs to miss what he could've had if he'd acted right. Both he and Rah have a tendency to take me for granted, and that's changing as we speak.

As soon as I'm back on my A game, they both won't know what hit them, because Miss Nice is about to be replaced by a new and improved Jayd Jackson—no nickname needed, even if my license plates will read LADY J when they arrive. Rah and I already applied for them when we registered my old hoopty. I just have to get the registration transferred from that vehicle to my mom's, if she decides to let me take it over completely. It all depends on how long Karl lets my mom roll his second ride. If things continue to go as smoothly between the two of them as they are now, I should be able to drive my mom's car indefinitely.

Speaking of taking over, my head is starting to feel heavy and the room is spinning slightly. Barely able to place the tea back down on the coffee table, I look down at my half-empty cup and lean back into the couch pillows. What's in this stuff? I'm feeling overwhelmed by my tiredness all of a sudden, so I'll have to worry about researching the ingredients tomorrow. Tonight I'm going to surrender to this feeling and let it lull me to sleep.

"And for my beautiful girls," my dad says, passing my mom a red box with a large gold bow on top. They're seated by the Christmas tree, which is next to the fireplace. My fa-

ther still puts up the tree in the same place to this day. Even the couch and other furniture in the living room are the same. My mom was right: when she left all she took was me and her cast iron skillets. Everything else my father held onto out of spite, or so my mom says. But Mama says he held on to my mom's stuff because he still loves her and that's his only way of both getting back at her and keeping some of her ashe around.

"Oh, Carter," my mom says, opening the box to find a gold, heart-shaped locket hanging on a gold chain. My daddy takes the necklace out of the box and puts it over my mother's head. She moves her long, black hair out of his way and my father kisses her neck gently before closing the clasp. Once secure around her neck, she opens it to see a picture of my dad inside. Her face is less than thrilled at the sight. "You shouldn't have."

"I'm going to get the camera, especially since this day almost didn't happen. I'll be right back," my dad says, exiting the living room and heading to their bedroom. And according to everything I've ever heard from my mom and Mama, he's right. They weren't even together when I was conceived.

Waiting for my dad to come back, my mom warms herself by the fireplace. She looks into the glowing fire and truly appears to be happy and calm.

Interrupting her peace, the phone rings and my mom picks it up from the end table next to the couch. She's not as big as I pictured her at six months pregnant, and moves easily from one position to another.

"Merry Christmas," my mom says into the receiver, but her face looks anything but jolly. "No. Who is this?" she repeats into the phone. Oh, this can't be good. I think I remember this incident from when I was in her womb. And if I recall correctly, it didn't end so well. "You called my house. Who the hell are you?" Oh shit, I know that conversa-

tion all too well. It must be one of my daddy's side hoes calling to wish him a happy holiday. I bet you she'll think twice next time before calling this house.

"Who's on the phone?" my father asks, the camera in hand. My mom looks up at my father and throws the cordless phone at his face, breaking the skin above his eyebrow before he catches the falling phone.

"Damn it, Lynn Marie. What's gotten into you?" My dad returns the phone to its base without speaking into it. He then touches the blood dripping from his head. So that's how he got that scar. The phone rings again and neither one of them answers it.

"I knew I should have never listened to you. I'm out," my mom says, making her way out of the living room and to the back bedroom he just left, going to pack up her things to leave—again.

"You can't leave. That's my baby in there, girl. You can never leave me." If I could wake up right now, I would. Before I can see what happens next, my dream shifts to a different scene and I'm forced to follow. Damn, I wish I could choose what I want to see and when, instead of being an unwilling passenger on this ride down memory lane.

"You bastard!" my mom shouts at my dad. "You gave me the same heart necklace for Christmas. You think you're slick but you're not. What you are is busted." My mom stands up in the crowded restaurant and throws his glass of red wine in his face. Rubbing her very pregnant stomach, she picks up her purse from the back of the chair and gets ready to leave him sitting there, embarrassed. From the red-and-white heart-shaped balloons everywhere, I'd say they're celebrating Valentine's Day.

"You gave her my necklace?" the waitress asks. "How could you, Carter?"

"He can do it because he's nothing but a cheating jackass. Mama was right about you from jump street. Do you know how mad it makes me to have to admit that?" My dad looks like he wants to answer but he's afraid of saying the wrong thing.

"I thought when I left your ass on Christmas you had learned your lesson, but I see you'll never change." My mom looks from my dad to his mistress and then at the bottle of red wine on the table. "A toast to your new fool, because I'm done playing." She takes the bottle and pours the remaining wine over my father's head. "Bye," she says, looking victorious as she turns around to walk out of the restaurant. His side trick picks up the napkins on the table and hands them to my father. Before my mom can make her way out of the now silent place, she doubles over in pain, holding her stomach.

"Lynn Marie, are you okay?" my dad asks, throwing down his napkin and running over to my mom, who's now balled up on the floor in a fetal position. "Call an ambulance, now," he says to the hostess, who promptly dials the phone at her booth. His broad walks over with a handful of napkins, but it doesn't look like she wants to help.

"Lynn Marie, Lynn Mae Williams' daughter?" I see she's heard of our lineage, and by the way she's now trembling, she's heard enough to be scared, and rightfully so. "I heard she's into that voodoo mess. Why didn't you warn me you were married to a witch?" My dad looks at his scary-ass side skank and shakes his head as if to say "not now," but the dumb broad doesn't take the hint.

"Ahhh," my mom groans in pain. I remember feeling frustrated in the womb and I feel the same feeling now in my dream.

"I didn't know you were his wife, you have to believe

me," the woman says to my mom, who's now panting heavily, like she's in labor. My mom looks at the young sistah, her jade eyes glowing—she's so pissed.

"I'm not worried about you right now, trick!" my mom screams at her. She looks up at my father. He is trying to comfort her, but she doesn't want him to touch her. "And you, why don't you do me and my daughter a favor and leave. We have no use for you in our lives." My father looks sincerely hurt by my mom's words, but doesn't budge from his stance by her side.

"No matter what happens between me and you, Lynn Marie, that's my baby you're carrying and I intend to stay right here." How sweet. Too bad he doesn't feel the same way now.

"Are you sure she's yours?" my mom says, catching him completely off guard. What little color is left in my dad's face drains at my mom's venomous retort. I know she's only playing with his head, but wouldn't it be something if my mom had somebody on the side like he did? It would serve his ass right after all he put her through.

"You're just saying that because you're angry," my dad says, again trying to touch my mother's stomach, but she's not having it. The other couples in the restaurant look on as they wait to see how this dramatic scene will end.

"You're damned right I'm angry, Carter. I hate you for making me believe you loved me when the only person you really love is yourself. How could I be so stupid?"

"Lynn Marie, please calm down. It's not good for the baby," he says, talking to her quietly, which pisses my mom off even more.

"Shut the hell up, talking to me like you're my daddy, you short-ass punk," my mom yells, scaring his trick even more. The girl's trembling and looks frozen in place. She hasn't even seen a small fraction of how live my mom can

get, especially where my dad is concerned. "I hate you with every bone in my body."

I read about a curse in the spirit book that talks about using the word "hate" in conjunction with the phrase "bones in the body." It's supposed to weaken whoever the intended victim is. That's why Mama always warns against using such strong words haphazardly. There's a lot of power in the spoken word, especially when an angry sistah with ashe spits them out.

"You don't mean that," my dad says, looking around at all the eyes focused on the three of them. Even the restaurant manager's into the holiday soap opera they've created.

"The hell I don't. If I weren't in so much pain I'd kick both of your asses right where you stand." Before my dad can respond, Mama walks in through the front door with Daddy right behind her. If it has anything to do with her children—grandchildren included—Mama doesn't need a phone call to tell her something's wrong: she just knows it. And when I was in my mother's womb, Mama and I were even more connected than we are now. She could always communicate with me like no one else, and she could tell when I was in distress, like now.

"Get away from my daughter," Mama says to my dad and the girl who looks like she's seen a ghost. Daddy rushes over to my mother lying on the floor, while Mama looks around the place, her green eyes shining brightly. I wonder what she sees through those things?

"You're going to be okay, baby. We're here now," Daddy says to my mom, kissing her on her forehead and nodding at my dad to greet him; unlike Mama, who ignores my father's presence altogether. Mama kneels down next to her daughter and husband and touches my mom's belly, instantly calming my mom and me down. My mother's breathing returns to normal and her cramps dissipate,

shocking everyone present. No wonder the people in the neighborhood are both afraid of, and respectful of, Mama's powers. After seeing her work, who wouldn't be?

"Mama, I'm sorry I didn't listen to you," my mom says, allowing Mama to embrace her. The paramedics arrive but they're sent away.

"I know, baby, I know," Mama says. *"You can get up now. Everything's going to be fine."*

As Mama speaks, I'm forced out of my dream and back to the silent apartment I fell asleep in. I'm just glad I'm in the same place and not wandering around outside somewhere, sleepwalking.

"Damn, what the hell was that?" I ask aloud in the quiet living room. I can hear my neighbor's television downstairs, but nothing's on in here. I guess I never got a chance to turn on the television. My entire body is dripping with sweat and I feel like I've been asleep for hours. My church clothes are glued to my body and my hair is completely sweated out. I should change into my sweats and a shirt anyway, so I might as well get up.

I grab my phone from underneath my pillow and check the time. I wasn't even out for a full hour, and there's still more tea left in my mug. I also notice I've missed a phone call from Jeremy. I guess he's really worried about me, but he'll have to wait until tomorrow for a return call. I need more sleep, and I want to get back into my dream world. It's been so long since I had a normal one that I forgot just how much I need them to sleep well.

Without getting up from the couch, I reach down and grab my weekend bag and find my nightclothes inside. Unlike at Mama's house, I don't have to go in the bathroom to change. I miss this freedom every time I leave my mom's house.

"I hope I can't overdose on this stuff. Well, here goes nothing," I say before swallowing the rest of my herbal remedy. There's still another serving in the pot on the stove, but I don't think it'll be necessary for tonight. Maybe seeing more of my mom's relationship path will help me to deal with both of my dudes. Lord knows, I don't want to repeat my mom's mistakes in love.

"It wasn't all that bad, was it?" my mom asks, invading my thoughts before I drift off again. *"And no, you can't overdose. Had you taken the entire portion I made for you, you'd still be asleep."*

"It was all bad from what I saw," I think back to her, readjusting myself on the couch and returning my phone to its spot under my pillow.

"Jayd, there's always pain in love. Mind you, your daddy caused me more pain than necessary. But ultimately I should've known better, especially as many times as Mama warned me. All I can say is, learn from my mistakes, baby. True love takes time to develop, and you can't give up. Luckily you're young and you have a lot of time to fall in and out of love. Sweet dreams, baby."

From my mom's lips to God's ears, and I hope she's listening. I need more sweetness in my life these days, and that can start with me getting some more sleep. I'll worry about the love part later.

~ 5 ~
Sweet Hearts

"You own my heart and mind/
I truly adore you."

—PRINCE

After finishing the rest of my tea last night, I returned to my slumber and straight into another dream that I can't recall at the moment. I again had no control over when I fell asleep, which is unusual when I'm as tired as I was last night. I admit I've never lost this much sleep before. But still, there was something in that tea that made me literally lose my head.

Other than my first wicked dream, I slept better than I have since this whole curse thing started. Seeing my mom and dad at each other's throats at the Christmas before my birth and again on Valentine's Day, where she almost went into premature labor because she was so pissed off, was a bit much to handle. But at least I witnessed for myself how it all went down. To have been married once upon a time, my parents sure did—and still do—hate each other. I guess familiarity truly does breed contempt. And my parents are the poster couple for the truth of that theory.

What's really bugged out is that my dad had the nerve to give his wife and his mistress the same gift, even if it was for two different holidays. Maybe the jewelry store he purchased the necklaces from had a two-for-one special going on, or maybe they had the same sale for both Christmas and Valentine's Day, since those are the most popular holidays to give gifts of love, supposedly. When I think about it, there's really not much difference between the two holidays. They both make you think love is what it's all about, when that's the biggest load of bull ever sold legally to the masses.

If my parents, grandparents, friends, and personal experiences have taught me anything, it's that love is a shot in the dark. And the person who does the most loving is usually the one who gets their heart broken. All I know is that I'm tired of being in the line of fire, and more than that, I'm sick of watching everyone go down because of this thing called love. All of this drama is messing with my health and my money, since I still can't do anyone's hair until I get my own issues in check. At this point I could care less about the love shit. I just need my finances straight and I'll be as happy as any girl I've ever seen when a dude says he loves her.

It's been a quiet morning around here. Shawntrese is pissed that I can't do her hair today. I told her I wasn't feeling well and should be back on the job by next weekend. For both our sakes I hope I told the truth. I miss working and making money. There are only three weeks until Valentine's Day, and I know sistahs will be getting their hair done at Netta's and around the way that entire week. Sleep or no sleep, a sistah's got to get in on that money.

"She's got her own thing, that's why I love her," Ne-Yo sings, announcing a phone call. I've put everyone on this "Miss Independent" ring because being independent is one of my anthems, no matter whose name pops up on the caller ID. I pick up the slim cell and flip it open to find Jeremy's name in the window.

"Good morning," I say, cozying back into my spot on the comfortable couch that doubles as my weekend bed. I forgot to turn the heater on when I came in last night and it's chilly.

"Good morning, stranger." I see Jeremy has early morning jokes for a sistah. I take off the scarf that's wrapped around my head and scratch my oily scalp. I need to hook my own hair up today in a real way. And my nails could use some love, too. Since I can't work on anyone else I might as well work on myself.

"Now you're getting it. I knew that tea would do you some good. Being sweet to others starts with being sweet to yourself. Enjoy your day, baby, and I'll check in with you later."

"Mom, can you ring a mental doorbell or something before you come in?" Sometimes my mom has bad timing.

"No, not anymore," she says, leaving as quickly as she appeared. But she's right. I need to take care of Jayd first and foremost. I'm looking forward to chilling all day today.

"Jayd, are you there?" Jeremy asks. I'm glad he can't see me because I completely zoned out while my mom was talking to me. I've been so off lately that even regular shit takes more effort to focus on.

"Yeah, I'm here. Sorry about that. I dropped the phone," I say, trying to play it off. I didn't plan on talking to him until much later. I wanted to call and check on Rah and Nigel. I haven't spoken to Rah since he followed me home last night, and there are no messages from him on my phone either. I wonder if he's talked to Nigel since he stormed off after the memorial service yesterday. I need to get Jeremy off the phone so I can get my day started. From doing my hair to checking in on my friends, he just wouldn't understand, nor do I feel like explaining it to him.

"So what's on your agenda this morning, Lady J?" I hear footsteps walking up the stairs, which are on the other side of the living room wall I'm lying up against. We can hear each other's thoughts, the walls are so thin in this building.

"I missed you at school the past couple of days. Thought

I'd come and check up on you personally just to make sure you're still alive," Jeremy says. I can hear his laugh both through the cell and through the front door. No, this fool didn't do a pop-up on me. What the hell?

"Where are you?" I ask, rising from the couch and looking through the peephole in the front door to see Jeremy's blue eyeball staring back at me. He's so crazy.

"You can't answer a question with a question, Miss Jackson," he says, backing away from the door and letting me open it, allowing him and the cold air in. We simultaneously hang up our phones.

"Well, isn't this a surprise," I say, tightening my mom's thick, red Victoria's Secret robe around my body. With my Pink sweat pants and tank top on, and my mom's house slippers to match, I could be one of the catalogue models for the company.

"Yes, it is, and a very cute one, I might add," he says, kissing me on the cheek before taking his coat off and hanging it on the rack next to the door. Jeremy looks around my mom's apartment as if he's expecting to see someone else in the room with me. Little does he know my mom's always wherever I am, just like my ancestors.

"What's that in your hand?" I ask while resecuring the front locks. My mom likes to keep it like Fort Knox in here and I can't blame her, as many times as we've been broken into. It's just another fact of life in the hood.

"Breakfast. I thought you might be hungry," he says, placing the two paper bags full of food on the coffee table. "Sourdough breakfast sandwich, no bacon, right?"

"Jack in the Box. Oh Jeremy, you shouldn't have," I say sarcastically, joining him on the small couch, ready to dig into our fast-food feast. Sitting this close to Jeremy brings back nostalgic memories of the first time he came over here. And like then, Jeremy smells like fresh Irish Spring and good enough to eat. From the wet curls framing the back of his neck, I'd say he just got out of the shower—just how I like him.

"Only the best for a lady," he says, making me smile. Jeremy can be so silly sometimes. "And here's your orange juice and hash browns."

"Wow, a value meal. You must've really missed me, huh?" I bite into one of the hot potatoes, ready for my egg-and-cheese sandwich. I haven't had anything to eat since dinner at the church yesterday, and even then I didn't eat a lot. I'm so hungry I could eat both our value meals.

"I did miss you, girl. Where have you been hiding out?" Jeremy takes his food out of his bag and I notice he got the same thing for himself, just doubled. He then unwraps both of his sandwiches and smashes them together before digging in. Damn, dudes can eat.

"I wish I were hiding," I say, devouring my own breakfast. All that dreaming I did last night contributed to my hunger and I didn't even realize it. "I've been having some sleep issues since the shooting." Jeremy puts his mega sandwich down and lifts my chin with his right index finger. He looks deep into my eyes and I catch my reflection in his pretty blues. Man, I really need to do my hair.

"Physically you look fine to me, as always." Jeremy resumes eating his breakfast but not before I can smack some of the food out of his hands.

"Physically? What the hell is that supposed to mean?" I ask, only hearing half of his comment. Flattery will get Jeremy nowhere this morning.

"All I'm saying is that I know a great psychiatrist if you need one. He's a friend of the family," Jeremy says, as serious as a heart attack. What is it with white folks and their shrinks? I like to watch *Frasier* reruns as much as anybody else, but I'll be damned if I do a live reenactment of the television show myself. Dr. Whitmore's alternative medicine is more than enough for a sistah to handle.

"No, I'm good. But thank you for the referral." We continue eating in silence. I guess our appetites have gotten the best of us both, or so I think.

"I didn't mean anything by that, you know. I'm just saying that tragedy can be hard to get through sometimes. And I know I don't always say the right things, but I do want to help you in my own way, if you let me."

"That's so sweet, Jeremy. But really, I've got this one on my own." He doesn't need to know that as a priestess in training, I never walk alone. My ancestors and orisha are always with me, whether anyone else can see them or not. Sometimes I feel alone, but I never forget who I am or why I'm here. No shrink needs to tell me shit I already know.

"You don't always have to be so big and bad, you know." This reminds me of one the first conversations we had. Jeremy told me to break down some of the emotional walls I put around my heart and let him in. I see where that's gotten me, and I'm not so sure I want to keep going down this path. Between him and Rah I'm surprised I'm still standing up as it is. "You always have your guard up."

"Jeremy, it's not that simple." If he only knew how off about me he really is. If I'd had my guard up all along, Misty would have never been able to get to me and I wouldn't be in this mess to begin with. But I know Jeremy's not talking about that. Even with him, if I'd stayed on point and kept Jeremy at a distance, I wouldn't have been hurt by ex-trick Tania having his lovechild, no matter how far away she might be now.

"Well, then make it that simple," he says, sounding a lot like Rah did yesterday concerning his rationale about our relationship. Both Rah and Jeremy can be sweethearts when they want to be, especially on days when I'm feeling down, like I have been lately. But it's how they react every other day of the year that concerns me.

"Jeremy, some things you'll just never understand." I pick up the remote control and turn on the television to drown out some of the silence in between Jeremy's reasoning. Maybe Snoop Dogg and his family drama will distract me from the soap opera we've got going on right here. It doesn't look like Jeremy agrees with my attempted diversion.

"Why can't I understand? Because I'm white and you're black?" he asks, devouring the last bite of his sandwich before moving on to the hash browns still on the table. "No shit, Jayd."

"Uh, no, but thank you for reminding me," I say, taking a sip of my orange juice. I forget how salty this food is when I haven't eaten it for a while, just like this conversation. Whenever Jeremy and I talk about race it's not a good thing. I wish I could afford the luxury of being curious about other cultures when it's convenient and in denial when it's uncomfortable. But as a sistah, I never have that comfort.

"I don't think you ever forget." And he's damn right. "Sounds like you have some race issues to deal with, Miss Jackson."

"Say what?" Ignoring my shock, Jeremy picks up the television remote and begins flipping through the channels like I'm arguing with myself all of a sudden. This fool is tripping if he thinks he can throw out an ignorant comment like that and keep eating his food like he didn't just say the stupidest thing ever. "Did you just call me a racist?"

"No. You came to that conclusion all on your own." Jeremy finishes the last of his orange juice and sits back likes he's got the itis, but we both know that's not the case.

"You can't be serious. I tell you something is more complicated than you make it out to be and you jump to the conclusion that I'm a racist. What the hell type of reasoning is that?" I'm so vexed that I've lost my appetite for the time being. Maybe it'll come back once Jeremy leaves, which will be sooner than later if he keeps going on like this.

"Look, Jayd, you can't sleep because your friend was murdered and your other friend got caught in the crossfire because he's messing with another friend of yours who happens to be the girlfriend of a gangster. Am I missing anything here?" Jeremy's smart-ass smirk is about to get slapped off of his pretty face if he keeps messing with me.

"What's your point?" He's got the gist of the details without the depth, as usual. That's usually how the black gossip floats to the white side of campus. I didn't have to tell Jeremy much of anything about why I've been absent from school, with Nigel getting shot and being out for a week. When the star quarterback misses even one game it's everyone's business why he's not present. And in Jeremy's eyes, Nigel's business coincides with my business, making it indirectly his business. I would be flattered but I have enough faulty daddies in my life to deal with. The last thing I need is another one.

"My point is that you think I don't understand because I'm white, when race isn't the issue here at all. I understand all too well, and have for a long time, that you might want to consider a different crew to hang out with. And by the way, Maggie and her gangster boyfriend shouldn't be your fallback option."

"Damn, Jeremy. Do you think you're my daddy or what?"

"All I'm saying is that you can alleviate a lot of the drama in your life by making better choices. That's what I mean by it being simple."

"What, are you watching who I hang with now? But that would require you to actually be present at school on a regular basis." Just because the fool brought me breakfast doesn't mean he has the right to tell me who I should roll with. "Most people told me that I should have left you alone when we first starting kicking it but I didn't listen to them then. I'm not listening to you now."

"Jayd, come on. This is completely different," Jeremy says, taking the rest of my hash browns from the table and eating them, since I'm obviously done. "I don't want you making one bad decision after the next. I'm just saying I care about you and your safety."

"Yeah, you care enough to judge who I choose to associate with. Sounds to me like you have some control issues, Mr. Weiner," I say, snatching my blanket from under the pillow on my side of the couch and curling up like a cat. Jeremy laughs at my emotional response. He thinks it's adorable when I get mad, but I'm not feeling cute at all right now. I feel like if I could pick his six-foot ass up I'd throw him off of my mom's balcony.

"Miss Independent, that's why I love her." Thank God for my cell ringing, because Jeremy's definitely saved by the bell right now. It's Rah, and right on time, too.

"Excuse me. I need to take this," I say, going into the bathroom and shutting the door.

"We're not through, Lady J," Jeremy yells back. How did he become such a cocky jackass in a matter of minutes? He's too much for me to deal with sometimes.

"Hello," I say, ignoring Jeremy's response and trying to shield Rah from hearing him. I close and lock the bathroom door to make sure I don't get a surprise visit from my unexpected guest in the living room.

"I have someone here who wants to say hello to you," Rah says. I sit on the closed toilet seat waiting for my surprise.

"Hi," the sweet little voice says through the phone, instantly melting my frustration and making me smile. How is it that babies can make even the worst situation better?

"Hi, Rahima," I say in my sweetest voice. "How are you, baby girl?"

"Fine," she says. I can't believe she's saying another word. It's only been a couple of weeks and already her vocabulary has grown. I can see why Rah doesn't want to miss another moment with her.

"Okay, she's gone. Elmo's on and you know you can't compete with a little red monster," Rah says, reclaiming the phone from his daughter. His voice sounds happier than it has in a while, and I'm glad for it.

"I know that's right. So where's Sandy?" I ask, not that I really care. I'm just glad Rahima's back safe and sound, her mama be damned.

"She's in jail," Rah says. Well, I didn't literally mean she can be damned but it looks like the universe granted my request anyway.

"Jail? What happened?" I want to laugh out loud, the shit's so ridiculous, but I know this isn't the right time for it. Besides, I don't want Jeremy to overhear my conversation in any way, shape, or form. Who knows what wannabe sage advice he'll come up with next?

"She got pulled over in Pomona last night while driving a stolen vehicle, that's what happened. I told the bitch not to mess with me. Now she's really done it." And I know how far Rah can go when he gets really pissed.

"Damn, that's rough. Was Rahima in the car with her?"

"Nah. Rahima was at her great-grandparents' house. But Sandy did have some nigga in the car who had a warrant and got caught up with her. Oh well." My sentiments exactly.

"So what happens now?" I hope Rahima doesn't have to go back to Pomona until this mess is straightened out. Knowing Sandy, she'll try to drag this out in court as long as possible and in the process find a way to blame it on Rah.

"Well, for now I've got my daughter back and that's all I really care about. I'm sure Sandy's grandparents will bail her out eventually. And I still have to go get my grandfather's car from the impound and bring it back down here, but I don't want to take Rahima with me if I can help it."

"I'll keep her if you want," I say before I can even think about it.

"Jayd, you'd better not. That isn't your responsibility," my mom says all up in my conversation. Even if I can't tune her out I can still ignore her.

"I wouldn't ask you to do that, Jayd. Besides, I know you haven't been feeling well and I don't want to put you out like that," Rah says.

"Exactly. You have enough to deal with and you need to be resting. Ignore me all you want to, little miss, but you know I'm right." My mom momentarily gives up on her mission and let's me finish my conversation.

"You better bring that baby to me," I say, rising from my seat and glancing at myself in the bathroom mirror. I look a mess, but fortunately Rah has seen me look worse.

"Jayd, are you okay in there? You need a magazine or something?" Jeremy says through the closed door. I almost forgot he was in the living room. I push the mute button on my phone before Rah can hear my guest.

"No, thank you. I'll be out in a minute," I say, flushing the toilet for dramatic effect. Thank goodness I'm in drama class, because I can act my ass out of certain situations, especially when trying to throw the two of these dudes off each other's scent.

"Who was that?" Rah asks. Damn, he heard Jeremy. Does he have canine hearing or something?

"Oh, just my neighbor from downstairs," I say, trying to cover my tracks.

"What's he doing there? I thought you couldn't do anyone's hair until you were feeling better."

"Yeah, I just broke the news to him and he's a bit irritated, but oh well. So are you bringing baby girl over here or what?" I continue. I hate lying to Rah, but I don't want to hear his mouth about me and Jeremy this morning. It's bad enough Jeremy's getting up my ass about the company I keep. I don't need Rah grilling me, too.

"Are you sure you don't mind? I feel bad leaving a toddler with you after all you've been through." Yesterday I couldn't see and today I'm hung over from dramatic dreams, not to mention my sleepwalking episodes. I get his apprehension but I know I can handle this.

"It's very sweet of you to be concerned, but I think I can handle little mama without breaking down completely." Now all I have to do is figure out how to get Jeremy out of here before Rah arrives. His house is only ten minutes away from my mom's apartment, and getting Jeremy out of the way before then won't be an easy task.

"Alright, we'll be there in a few minutes. Thanks, baby," he says before hanging up. I open the door and step into the hallway leading to the living room to see Jeremy comfortably spread across the couch, ready to chill for a while. I've got ten minutes and counting to get him up and out.

"Sorry about that. Jack in the Box always runs right through me," I say, holding my stomach and feigning discomfort. "I think I'm going to lie back down."

"Okay. You want me to make you some tea or get you some medicine or something?" Oh God, now Jeremy wants to be sweet again, making me feel even guiltier. But he did just pop up on me, like I don't have a life of my own. He assumed I didn't have other plans and it's true, I didn't at the time. But I still don't like drop-ins, and I'm sure he'd feel the same way if I did that to him.

"No, I think I just need to rest. Thank you for breakfast and the lively conversation this morning. It's been real," I say, gesturing toward the front door while making myself comfortable on the couch again. Maybe if I feign illness he'll leave without contesting too much.

"You can't kick me out. I just got here, and I haven't seen you in days," Jeremy says, looking genuinely hurt. He rubs my leg affectionately. I glance at the wall clock and notice a minute has already gone by. Nine and counting. "I know you're not really mad at me because of what I said, are you?" This would be a perfect opportunity to ease my way out of this conversation and use my emotions as an excuse, but that's not my stylo. Picking a fight is the best way to get rid of someone, but I'm not going out like that.

"Jeremy, I'm just tired and I need to chill alone. That's all. I'll call you later if I'm feeling better and we can continue our argument," I say, patting his very comfortable hand still present on my thigh. "Besides, it's not fair if one opponent is off her game. It gives the other an advantage and that's not a good fight." We both smile at each other's stubbornness. Jeremy reluctantly rises from his cozy seat, picking me up in a bear hug with him, making me momentarily forget that I'm waiting for Rah and that I haven't showered yet.

"I don't want to fight with you. I've got nothing but love for you, Jayd. I hope you know that." I know he thinks that, but I'm not so sure if I'd call Jeremy's feelings for me love.

"Yeah, whatever." We both laugh at my mockery of the old school rap song before saying good-bye. Still in his arms, I look down at him as he lowers my feet back to the ground, but not before he kisses my lips gently and I instinctively return the gesture.

"Bye, Lady J. I'll check in with you later. Call me if you need anything."

"I will. Bye, Jeremy," I say, opening the door and handing him his coat from the coatrack.

"How's that new jacket working out?" he asks, referring to

the expensive Christmas gift he laid on me a few weeks ago, which is hanging on the coatrack. It's hard to believe the holidays have come and gone as they do every year, leaving behind all of the drama they bring with them.

"Lovely," I say. I caress the soft, pink fabric. This North Face jacket is the warmest one I've ever had and I'm grateful for his thoughtfulness. That still doesn't excuse Jeremy's daddy-like behavior on the regular.

"Good. By the way, if you don't already have plans, I'd like to be your date for Valentine's Day—well, night, really."

"Really? I thought you don't do holidays?" I tease as I glance at the second hand on his Tag Heuer wristwatch. Five minutes to go before I hear Rah's Acura pull up.

"I gave you a Christmas gift, didn't I? Now, you know I'm not going to the dance, but I could do dinner if you'll let me take you out."

"I'll think about it. Being a racist and all, I don't know if I should be seen in public with a white dude," I say sarcastically. Jeremy looks down at me and kisses my nose before heading down the stairs.

"We're going to work on all of that. I'm praying for you, girl," he says over his head. I know my nosey neighbors just heard that. I'm surprised Shawntrese didn't poke her head out to see who I'm talking to.

"Oh, now you believe in God, too? You are full of surprises this morning, aren't you?"

"I'll believe in whatever I have to if it'll get you to have a little more faith in me." Jeremy turns the corner and takes the last word with him. I shake my head in frustration and pleasure as I think about having an actual date on Valentine's Day. The last time I celebrated that wack-ass holiday was with Rah two years ago and it was horrible. We were supposed to go to the movies and then have pizza afterward, but as soon as we got to the theater Sandy was there to cause trouble for us. And that was the last time I spoke to him until he found me, via Nigel, at South Bay High. This year will be different, regardless of who I end up spending the day with.

I close the door and check the wall clock. I now have less than five minutes to shower and brush my teeth before Rah and Rahima arrive, and Lord knows I need to do both. I can't wait to see the little princess. My hair will have to wait until nap time. I'm going to spend the day playing with baby girl, and hopefully her daddy will be able to kick it with us later.

By the time Rah and his daughter arrive, I'm ready for the baby action. I moved the coffee table to the other side of the living room so we can have the couch and floor free to play. There's not much space in this small apartment, but what little room we have needs to be baby-proofed to keep the potential for accidents down to a minimum.

"Look who's here," Rah says, passing Rahima to me. We smile at each other and she jumps from her daddy's arms into mine, instantly melting my heart. I've missed this little girl.

"Hey, sweetie," I say to her. Both of her chocolate dimples look good enough to eat. She begins to play peekaboo with me, picking up where we left off last time I saw her. Damn Sandy for being such a fool.

"She's as happy to see you as I am," Rah says, putting the diaper bag and car seat down on the floor next to the couch and kissing me on the cheek. Man, babies come with a lot of stuff.

"Yes, and most of it isn't material," my mom says, adding her two cents. Will she ever get out of my head?

"Is that right?" I put Rahima on my back and give Rah a hug. Rahima puts her arms around my neck, ready to play horse for a while. "You have someone to ride with you to the impound garage?"

"Yeah, my homie's waiting in the car now. I'll check in

with you when we're on our way back." Since he's not being specific, I assume his homie must be Trish's brother, also known as his main supplier. Rah really had no choice since Nigel can't drive until his shoulder heals and I'm watching baby girl. I think Rah needs to meet some more people, but at least it isn't Trish escorting him on the hour-and-a-half drive.

"I'll be glad when you get some new friends," I say, letting him know that I know who the homie is and I'm not happy with the arrangement—but what can I really say?

"Jayd, I'll be back in a little while. Don't worry, it's just business." Rah bends down and kisses me on the lips and then kisses his daughter on the forehead.

"Yeah, yeah," I say, looking back at Rahima, who is ready to play. And I'm ready to be entertained.

"I'll see my girls later." His girls. As sweet as that sounds, it's only half true. I haven't been Rah's girl in a minute, and I'm not really looking to pledge that sorority again anytime soon. He's lucky I love his daughter. Otherwise he'd have a much harder time pulling at my heartstrings. But this little girl can pull all she wants. This time I'm not letting her go.

After playing with Rahima all day long, both the apartment and I are whipped. I never got a chance to do my hair or work on my spirit work. Having a baby full-time is no joke. I wonder if Mickey really knows what she's gotten herself into. Rahima wouldn't take a nap and keeps eating like she hasn't had any food in days, which may not be too far from the truth. Sandy doesn't cook, and prefers potato chips over the chicken pasta salad I made for us to eat. Rahima's eating my food like a champ. My phone vibrates on the coffee table and Rahima reaches for it. She must know it's her daddy.

"How's it going?" Rah asks as soon as I answer. "Y'all need anything?"

"No, we're cool. We're just eating some dinner now. Did you get the Regal back in one piece?"

"Yeah, everything's all good. It looks like she's got a couple of scratches on her but it's nothing I can't handle." As Rah and I talk, Rahima finally slows down and falls asleep on the blanket I spread out on the floor. Finally, some quiet time. I thought she'd never settle down.

"I'm glad you got your grandfather's car back, Rah. I know he'll be happy to see it," I say, turning off the cartoons and changing the channel. If I hear another kiddie television show I'm going to pull my hair out. At least then I wouldn't have to worry about washing it.

"Well, I guess. It was originally for me to drive so you could roll my ride, but it all worked out how it was supposed to, I guess." I know Rah was trying to help and it all went to hell once Sandy arrived, which is the usual when she comes around. Much like Misty, that girl is a force to be avoided at all costs because there's no reckoning with her.

"I have a run to make. I'll come and get Rahima now if you're too tired. I know you need your rest, especially now." I look over at Rahima, laid flat out like a butterfly. Her baby-pink and yellow *Dora the Explorer* blanket is draped across her chocolate skin. She looks so peaceful I'd hate for her to be disturbed.

"No, just let her sleep. She's probably out for the night anyway. Maybe you can pick up a movie and y'all can just sleep over here tonight."

"Sounds good, boo. I'll be there as soon as I can. And Jayd, thanks again. I really appreciate you, girl. I hope you know that."

"No problem, Rah. I know you do," I say before hanging up.

"No problem. Are you serious?"

"Mom, why are you up in my head again? You've been on

my case all day, it seems," I say aloud. I'm too exhausted to communicate via mental telepathy. This little girl has made even my brain tired.

"I'm up in your head because I can't believe what I just heard. Are you really going to watch Raheem's daughter while he goes out and plays? Jayd, don't be a doormat. As nice as it sounds to be sweet and gracious to fools we love, it's always the nice girl that gets walked on."

"Mom, he's working, not going out," I say, cuddling up on the small couch, ready to let the *Half and Half* reruns on TV One lull me to sleep.

"Same difference. Then let him figure the babysitting out on his own. As cute as that baby is, she's not your responsibility."

"But I'd help out any of my friends who needed it, not just Rah," I say, imagining myself watching Mickey's daughter. I'm sure there will be plenty of times I'll babysit her.

"Well, that's your choice. But I'm telling you, Jayd. Nice girls never win."

"There's nothing wrong with being nice, Mom. Mama Oshune is over all things nice and sweet, remember?" I say, gently reminding her of the spirit lessons she gave up a long time ago.

"Yes, but Mama Oshune is also a warrior woman, and she's no one's doormat. That's for damned sure."

"You're right," I think back, too tired to argue. It's been a long day, and I'm going to join Rahima in sleep land as soon as I can get my mom to be quiet. I wish I could put her on time-out sometimes.

"You have a sweet heart, and because of that it'll always get stomped on if you allow it to, baby girl. When are you going to learn that lesson? Mama's told you all of your life not to wear your heart on your sleeve because people will take advantage of you, but you just don't listen, Jayd. And

you need to. It's the only way to protect your ashe. You'll learn the hard way if you don't take our advice."

"You're right. I need to listen better," I say, trying to appease her so I can get a nap in before Rah gets here. "Good night, mom. I'll see you tomorrow."

"I love you, baby. And listen carefully to what I'm saying, Jayd. It's for your own good. Sleep tight." Something about my mother's tone makes me think twice for a minute about her advice.

Shifting my pillow comfortably under my head, my scarf accidentally falls to the side of my neck. I touch the top of my head and remember the *rogacion de cabeza*—or head cleansing—Mama and Netta gave me on Tuesday, and the sacrifice to the river I made a few weeks ago. When I looked in the water I felt sucked into the reflection. That same feeling of surrender is how I've been feeling lately in my dreams, and it feels that way with Rah lately, too. Maybe guarding my ashe a little more would help me get some good rest instead of allowing myself to be sucked into other people's realities.

I don't want to sleep too hard even if I do need it because Rah should be here sooner than later. I have a little bit of the tea left from last night and it should be just enough to help me nod off. I don't want to pass out as hard as I did last night, especially not with the baby here. Maybe if I only take half of the remaining portion it won't hit me so hard. I'll take what's left when it's time to sleep for the rest of the night.

"Young brides are the prettiest," Netta says, primping my hair as I stare into the mirror's reflection. "You're even prettier than your mother was when she married your father. I wish you nothing but the best, Jayd." Netta smiles as she kisses the top of my head. But behind the smile her eyes are filled with sadness. I look beyond her at the room's reflec-

tion. It looks like we're in someone's bedroom. She touches my shoulder-length tresses again, smoothing wayward strands down with the palm of her hand. "The bells are ringing," she says, looking toward the open door. "It's time. Close your eyes." I can feel her place something on my head and then she gives me something to hold.

Netta takes me by both hands and directs me to rise from my seat at the vanity. She leads me out of the room and I find myself apprehensive about being led with my eyes closed. The ringing bells get louder the more steps we take. I don't know where we're going but now I can feel myself walking slowly down a spiral staircase to avoid tripping over my long dress with my bare feet. Curious about where it leads, I continue moving downward even though I can't see the next step. I trust that it's there and just keep walking.

"At last, my love has come along," Etta James sings as I continue walking. The music is coming from the speakers located at the bottom of the staircase. When I get to the bottom I open my eyes and see various people standing around what looks to be a living room, watching me walk toward the center of the cramped space. I catch a glimpse of myself in the mirror and notice I'm dressed in all white, veil and all. I'm the bride and these people are here to see me get married, but to who?

"They were high school sweethearts, you know," I hear someone whisper to another faceless observer.

"Actually, junior high. You know he was her first love, kiss, and everything else," they whisper, snickering as I continue my procession. Rah and I are getting married? Why is there a screaming newborn in the living room? What the hell is really going on here?

"That baby knows there's trouble coming their way and no ring is going to be able to fix that," I hear one of them

say. We have a child together and before we get married? That's definitely not the way I envisioned my life turning out.

"Oh, doesn't she look beautiful? And how romantic, having the wedding on Valentine's Day. You can't even tell Jayd just had a baby less then two months ago. Little baby Destiny is so beautiful." I look down at my body and notice the little pooch in my belly like the one Mickey will have soon after her baby's born. I named my baby Destiny? That's not a bad name, but I just knew if Rah and I had a baby we would give her an African name. Why do I feel so different? I need to wake up from this dream now because I have a bad feeling about this one.

"Yeah, being born on Christmas sucks. Holiday babies never get their fair share of gifts."

"Neither does a project twin. Can you believe Raheem had another baby with that girl, and that Jayd's forgiving him, again? You'd think he'd have learned his lesson the first time around."

"I thought she'd learned her lesson. She was on her way to being such a powerful young priestess. But she got drawn into the spell, and you know she could only go down from there."

"Yeah, when these little girls think they're in love you can't tell them shit. And what could she do? By the time she found out that hussie was pregnant again, Jayd and Raheem had already announced their engagement and everyone knew the girl was expecting." I look at the elders present in the room and they're all looking at the floor, ashamed of me, I assume. But I don't seem to care about what anyone's saying or feeling. I'm on a mission and I'm determined to make it to my destination.

I look around and see Raheem waiting for me near the back door. He looks nice in a white linen suit. Mama,

Daddy, and my mom and dad are standing on one side of him, while his mother is on the other side. The conscious part of me wants to stop walking, but I can't keep my feet from moving forward. Before I reach my husband-to-be, Sandy bursts through the room with another newborn in her arms. I guess this is the project twin for our newborn that the bystanders were referring to. This is definitely one of my worst nightmares come true.

"You are not seriously marrying this trick after all we've been through." Sandy stands in my spot like she's the one about to say "I do."

"Trick? I got your trick," I say, hurling the small bouquet in my hands at her before I can stop myself. She dodges the flying roses and charges ahead, baby in her arms and all.

"Ladies, please," Daddy says. Mama, who's said nothing in this dream, looks at me and smiles. Her green eyes glisten in the afternoon sun's reflection shining through the window behind her.

"You can't stop what we've got, Jayd," Sandy says as Rah and my grandfather escort her from the room. "We are destined to be together. That's why we named our baby Fate."

"You named that baby. I didn't have anything to do with it," Rah says, manhandling the other mother of his other children. What the hell's gotten into him? No matter how upset he's ever been with Sandy, Rah's never put his hands on her.

"Oh, you had something to do with it, for sure," she says seductively, embarrassing me and my family, not to mention herself. Why would Rah deal with this heffa again after he knows what kind of trouble she brings? But the better question is, why am I still dealing with this foolishness?

"Because you didn't listen, just like your mother," Mama says from her mind to mine. My mom looks at me with glowing eyes, like she's in on the conversation, too. "You lost

all of your powers dealing with Rah and his drama, and now you can't help anyone, not even yourself or your baby."

Just then, Misty rears her big head in the crowd, smiling deviously at what I'm sure is partially her work. She's getting too powerful for my own good.

"You can't get away from me," I hear a shrill voice say. Immediately my head begins to pound hard, just like when Esmeralda, our evil neighbor and Misty's spiritual godmother, locked on to me with her evil blue eyes. I look out the window, past Mama's head, and notice a woman in all black with a veil on. It is Esmeralda. She lifts her veil and looks dead at me. My headache immediately worsens and I can't take it anymore.

"I have to get out of here," I scream.

"Jayd, no. Come back," Rah yells after me. He tries to catch me but the crowd is too dense and the elders aren't moving out of his way quick enough to let him by. I run outside barefoot and keep moving away from the drama. My baby is crying and I want to go back for her, but I can't focus on anything but the fierce pounding in my head.

"Jayd, what are you doing outside at this time of night without any shoes on? Have you been smoking that stuff again?" Shawntrese asks, making light of my situation as her boyfriend pulls out of the driveway. I look around and realize I'm no longer dreaming, even though I still feel asleep.

"I'm outside," I say. When I snap completely out of my dream, the first thing I notice is how cold my feet are. I have on nothing but a T-shirt and sweats, my usual night gear. How did I get outside? I must've been sleepwalking again. Damn it. I know Mama's going to have a conniption fit when she finds out I had another episode. I know she's going to partially blame it on the fact that I didn't take Dr. Whitmore's pills today. If Shawntrese hadn't stopped me I could've wandered out into the street, leaving the front door wide open and Rahima all alone.

"Jayd, are you okay?" she asks again, this time more concerned. My head is pounding and I can't hear her words very well. I want to respond but all I can hear now is Rahima's crying.

"Oh no. The baby," I say, running back upstairs to Rahima. I climb the concrete steps two at a time until I reach my mom's apartment. I'll never forgive myself if something happens to Rahima on my watch. Here I am, judging her mother for neglecting her, when I can't even be trusted to watch Rahima for one night.

"What baby? What the hell is going on around here?" Shawntrese says, following me up the stairs on the way to her mother's apartment across the hall. She knows I've got issues, but she has no idea the full extent of my drama. This sleepwalking is making it a little harder to keep my cover.

"Rah's daughter. I'm babysitting." I walk in to find Rahima lying in the same spot I left her, but tossing and moaning with her eyes closed. She must be having a bad dream too because she's still asleep, thank God.

"Jayd, how babysitting usually works is that the baby sits and you sit with her. What the hell are you doing downstairs when she's upstairs?" I look around the apartment, making sure everything is still intact. I have no idea how long I was out or, truthfully, if I'm even really awake now. I could still be dreaming for all I know.

"If I knew I'd tell you myself." What time is it, and where is Rah? He needs to get here soon because I don't trust myself to fall asleep around Rahima until I get my dream world under control.

"Thank goodness she's okay. Remind me never to let you watch one of my babies," Shawntrese says playfully, but she did just hurt my feelings, and I can't really blame her for feeling that way. Misty and Esmeralda have got my mind on lock. I've got to find a way out of this mess before someone ends up getting hurt.

"Good night," I say wearily. I'm more tired now than I was when I first lay down. Shawntrese and I close our doors at the same time, and I resecure the various locks on my mom's front door. How did I unlock all of these bolts while sleeping? Without Mama here to catch me I don't feel safe sleeping, but I know I need it. I look at the wall clock and notice it's almost two in the morning. I think I was out for about three hours. I wonder how many of those hours were spent walking around?

Rah's drama is getting me into trouble, yet I feel like I can't escape, even if I truly wanted to. It's like he's got me under some sort of spell. Speaking of which, Esmeralda crept her way into my dream, bringing back my headache from hell with her. How did she do that, and how can I get rid of this pounding? Where are my mom and Mama when I need them? And more importantly right now, where the hell is Rah?

~ 6 ~

A Spiral Spell

"Tainted love, don't touch me please/
I cannot stand the way you tease."

—SOFT CELL

After downing the maximum amount of Extra Strength Tylenol I can take in one dose, I call Rah's phone, which is off at the moment. Damn it. I know he gets lost in his music when he's in the studio, but now that he's primarily responsible for his daughter I think he should consider changing how he conducts his business.

When his voice mail picks up I decide to leave a message.

"Rah, call me, please. Did you forget we had plans? You haven't checked on me or your daughter all night, and we need you. Bye." I know I sounded more than a little pissed and I am, especially now that I remember we had plans to chill once he was done with his so-called business. Maybe my mom was right. I'm sitting here, stuck watching Rahima, while he's out playing. What's wrong with this picture?

Rahima's stirring in her sleep, but looks peaceful. I wish I could sleep like her. Before I can get more vexed, my cell rings with a call from Rah.

"What's up with you?" I ask, trying not to bite into him too hard off the rip. I'll ease into cussing him out given the fact his daughter is close by.

"Nothing much. Sorry I lost track of time," he says, sounding distracted.

"You did more than that. You stood me up, or did you forget we were supposed to hang out this evening?"

"Jayd, I told you I had business to handle. I'm wrapping it up now." I wonder what else he's wrapping up.

"That doesn't excuse your apparently broken fingers. You couldn't call a sistah and let me know you were running late or not going to make it at all? What the hell, Rah?"

"Jayd, I don't know why you're so upset. You've got my seed right there with you, so you know I'm coming back there."

"Rah, that's not the damn point," I say. My head's getting hotter and my voice louder with each passing moment. The Tylenol can't help the psychic booming going on in my head, but it's taking the edge off. And talking to this fool is bringing it back to full force.

"Jayd, we can sit here and argue or I can hang up and finish my work."

"Where are you, anyway?" I glance at Rahima, who hasn't moved an inch. When babies sleep they sleep hard.

"I'm at the studio, but I'll be done sooner than later if you let me go." I can hear a female laughing in the background and it sounds like Trish. I have half a mind to go over there right now with his baby on my hip like I'm his wifey, but that would just be too ghetto. And I'm not letting this fool push me that far, no matter what my last dream predicted.

"It doesn't sound like you were getting much work done anyway." I've been in the studio with Rah enough to know when he's working and when he's just chilling. My mom was right. I am basically serving as Rah's babysitter.

"You know how it is. I got caught up."

"Caught up with Trish?"

"No, her brother. He wanted to lay down some tracks while they were fresh in his head." Almost every other brotha I know thinks he's either a rapper or ballplayer. Why can't they just do whatever it is they came here to do well, instead of playing hood karaoke all night?

"So you're his producer now?" And Rah thinks he's David Banner, always trying to record someone's song. First it was just his and Nigel's thing. But after he and Rah revamped Rah's garage and turned it into a professional studio, with the microphone booth in it and all, Rah's now renting it—and his skills—out by the hour. Why his high-priced trick is there is another thing altogether.

"Jayd, you know that's what I do. If a nigga's good and he's coming to me with dough to rent my studio space and my time, that's what it's all about. Not all of us are born into money, you know."

"Of course I know that. Why would you say something like that to me?"

"I'm just saying, you think I want to give up my entire night and morning dealing with someone else's shit? I do this shit because I have to, unlike them white boys you dealing with at that punk-ass school of yours. I thought you understood my flow."

"I do, and don't try and turn this around on me. You know what the hell I'm not understanding. It's that chick being a part of your flow. Don't play with me, Rah." I hear Trish laughing again in the background like the cackling crow she is. She sounds as high as a kite. Maybe that's why Rah lets her stay around, because she's fun in a stuck-up sort of way.

"Calm yourself down, Jayd. I'll be there as soon as I can."

"Whatever," I say before hanging up the cell and tossing it on the other end of the couch. If it weren't for his daughter being here, I'd tell him not to bother coming this way. What will it take for Rah to understand that he can't take advantage of my time?

"He'll stop when you stop letting him," my mom says. For

once today, I'm glad to hear her in my head. *"And what are you doing up? Shouldn't you be sleeping?"*

"Bad dream," I think back. I don't want to relive my most recent sleepwalking incident right now. I just want to focus on Rah getting back here so I can tell his ass off in person.

"Jayd, you've got to listen to me, baby. If you don't get your sleep issues under control, your whole life will start to unravel. You've got to stop taking on other people's issues and focus on your own shit."

"Okay, Mom. I know you're right. But it's easier said than done."

"It's only difficult if you make it that way. Give Rah his pretty little girl and send them home. You need space and time to heal, Jayd."

"Mom, I don't have a cold." Even if the pressure in my head feels slightly like congestion.

"Sick is sick, Jayd. And with us, being psychically ill is just as bad, if not worse, than any other type of ailment out there. When Esmeralda started her mental attacks on me I felt like I had the flu for weeks. People at school thought I had pneumonia at first, then they thought I had something else, as weak as I was. Don't let your defenses down for a minute. Mom out." My mom knows more about my dream than she's saying.

"But wait," I say aloud before she mentally checks out. I know I'll see my mom tomorrow before I go back to Mama's, but I need her help dealing with Rah right now.

"Yes? I want to get some sleep too, Jayd, and your little nightmare woke me up." See, I knew she was holding back.

"What do I do about Rah?"

"I already told you. As long as you let him get away with giving you crap, he will. Men can't help it, especially men with mama issues like your boy. Rah is as sweet as he wants to be, but he's also inconsiderate and self-centered, which is

a bad combination in any relationship. I love him like a son, but I'd beat his ass if he ever left me waiting, and with his baby, too? Oh hell, no, girl. You'd better nip this one in the bud right now before it gets out of control. Bye."

"I love you, Mom, and thank you for checking in." Which is more than I can say for Rah.

"I love you too, Jayd. Now make sure you protect yourself and get some solid sleep." Rather than go back into a dream world I can't control, I think I'll watch television until Rah rears his ugly head.

By the time Rah gets here I'm going to be too pissed to be rational. He was supposed to come back sooner than later. He didn't even answer his phone the three times I tried calling since our conversation a couple of hours ago. That can only mean one thing: he's still caught up with Trish.

When I finally hear his Timberlands stomping up the stairs, I'm steaming. It's damn near four in the morning, and he's got the nerve to smile when I let him through the front door.

"So, where were you, really?" I ask, trying not to get too loud. I don't want to wake Rahima, nor do I want the neighbors to hear us with their nosy asses.

"I had to hustle, Jayd. You know how I do."

"Why was Trish involved in your late night hustling? You have her out working the corners or something?" I ask. I know that was a bit bitchy, even for me dealing with Trish. But he deserved it, especially for that smart-ass remark he made about being born with money. I know that was a stab at Jeremy. You'd think he would know how down-to-earth Jeremy is by now, unlike his ice princess with the high price tag.

"Jayd, you know you don't have anything to worry about. I love you, I trust you, and I would never do anything to violate your love and trust for me again." As Rah stands in front of me ready to plead his sorry case, the room becomes hazy, like I'm in a dream state. The floor appears warped and the lights and everything else around us start to sway like things do when an earthquake happens. What the hell? I feel like I've been drinking, or what I imagine it to feel like. I've never taken more than a sip of champagne at a wedding, and don't really want to. From the way my friends act after a drink or two, I want no part of being drunk.

"Whatever. I know you and Sandy have been creeping around," I blurt out. Now my headache from Esmeralda has returned to full force, edge included. Rah continues to justify his actions, completely unaware of my issues. The pounding in my head gets louder as Rah talks to me. I see his lips moving but can barely hear his words, which I should be glad for. Everything's getting hazier and I'm losing control of my feet underneath me. I sit back down on the couch, holding my head in my hands. Am I dreaming or awake?

"What the hell are you talking about? Sandy's in jail, Jayd, remember?" I look up into Rah's confused eyes and catch my reflection. I look tore up in the worst way. Oh no, it's starting. Esmeralda's getting to me like she got to my mom, and this fool's presence is weakening what little defenses I've got left. This whole situation is turning me into a jealous, angry girl, and I don't want to be that type of female, but I also can't simply calm down.

"I meant Trish," I say, trying to clean up my paranoia. "I know she still wants you and since I'm not giving you any you've got to get it from somewhere." I feel like my mom must've felt when she caught my daddy cheating on her: like kicking this fool's ass.

"Jayd, please. I know you're not that insecure. You know me and Trish hang out sometimes, nothing more." I look down at the floor where Rahima's shifting in her sleep.

Everything's still fuzzy and the clock on the wall's seemingly moving backward. I really need to get some sleep. I feel like I'm losing my grip on reality. I can't let this go on for too long, but he needs to feel me.

"Please don't tell me I just babysat for you while you and Trish went out on a date." I glance at Rah and momentarily I'm back in my nightmare, walking down the aisle to Rah. But instead of our baby Destiny screaming, it's Rahima. Just then Rahima screams out in her sleep just like she just did in my vision. I hope my nightmares aren't contagious, but I know that was no coincidence.

"Jayd, now you know it's not like that at all. Her brother and I had to take care of some business and yes, she was there, but no, we were not on a date. It's complicated, baby, you know that."

"It's only as complicated as you make it." I can't believe I just said that. After the hell I gave Jeremy this morning for saying the same thing, I should be ashamed of myself for using his reasoning. But truth is truth.

"Look, you know the deal between me and Trish. If her brother weren't my supplier we'd have no reason to see each other, ever. Otherwise I wouldn't be asking you out for Valentine's Day, now would I?" I guess Rah expects me to melt at his invitation, but he's a day late and a dollar short.

"So, does Trish get you the night before, or do we have to split custody of you?" He doesn't need to know that I already have an offer on the table. I don't care if Jeremy did ask me out already, Rah should've beat him to the punch. And as a girlfriend to neither one of them, I refuse to put all my eggs into one basket. If I did they'd all be rotten by now, if it were left up to Rah doing the right thing.

"Jayd, don't be like this, please. I've got my baby girl back, and we're working it out. Please, let's just stay in the moment. I just asked you out, girl."

"If we stay in this moment I'm going to end up kicking your ass. Damn the date, Rah."

"Jayd, you're tripping, you know that, right? First accusing me of being with Sandy, now Trish. What's up with you tonight?" I would tell him about the dream I had earlier, but I don't want to fuel his fire. Rah has a way of turning things around when it's convenient. Rather than let him win this argument—because I know I'm right—I'll do the next best thing. I choose to retreat.

"You can have the couch. I'll sleep in my mom's room," I say, throwing the pillows and blankets from the small couch at him. "And you don't need to wake me when you leave in the morning. I'm sure you can see your way out." I look over my shoulder at Rahima sleeping quietly. She's not having a nightmare anymore, and for that I'm grateful. I can't help but feel guilty about her feeling my negative psychic energy, not to mention leaving her in the apartment alone. He doesn't need to know about that part, either.

Passing up a shocked Rah, I go into the kitchen and swallow the remaining drops of my mom's sleep tea. I hope I have better luck sleeping soundly than I did earlier. I walk back into the living room and Rah's stretched himself out on the floor next to his daughter. I guess he's too tall to sleep on the same couch that fits me perfectly.

"Jayd, I think you're being unreasonable, but I still love you and appreciate you watching my girl for me." He reaches his hand up and pulls me down next to him before I can protest. Rah looks me in the eyes and comes closer for the kiss that'll never happen.

"Look, I'm not going to be one of your side chicks anymore. You can have Destiny and Fate and whatever other project twins you want to have with someone else. I'm out," I say, pulling myself back up. I wish I could get louder, but it's late and I don't want to wake Rahima up. I know my neighbors have been listening the whole time. They can't resist a juicy fight.

"Project twins? Jayd, what the hell are you talking about?" Rah asks, looking as confused as I feel. Rahima's image is shifting between the two-year-old toddler sleeping on the blanket, to a slighter older Rahima like the image in my last dream. Rah himself is also shifting between the one I know and love, to the baby daddy he was in my dream. Crazy isn't a good look for me.

"I'm talking about your tendencies, Rah. And one of them happens to be taking my love for you for granted. Another one is recruiting ghetto girls as your baby mamas and I'm not going out like that." I look past Rah and catch my reflection in the mirror hanging on the dining room wall. I look like the tired, scared bride in my dream, white veil and all. My head is throbbing and I can't get a grasp on reality. I've got to get some sleep.

"Jayd, come on," Rah says, reaching for my arm, but I back away before he can make contact.

"Come on where? We have no place else to go. Good night, Rah." I'm so sick of playing games with him. It wouldn't be so bad if he could just be honest about his shit, but who am I to talk? He doesn't know about Jeremy and me hanging out as much as we do, but his shit is different. It's like Rah and I are addicted to each other and the drama that comes along with the craving. How do I rid myself of this shit, for real? There's got to be a way to reverse our bad luck in love, and we need to do it before the entire friendship is poisoned as a result of our bad decisions. Maybe the morning will bring some clarity to the situation.

When I wake up the house is completely silent. I peel the plush red comforter back and instinctively reach for my robe at the foot of the queen-sized bed. Living in a house full of men Monday through Friday has taught me to always be ready to cover up. There's nothing like running to the bathroom in the middle of the night without a robe on and being caught by Mama, who would promptly smack me for not covering myself. That's one of the main reasons I'm grateful to have my mom's ladies-only apartment to escape to on the weekends.

My mom's bed is comfortable and warm, but I can only sleep in her room when there's someone sleeping in the living room. Otherwise I feel much more secure sleeping in the front of the apartment, just in case someone tries to break in. I could hear a perpetrator at first contact, allowing me more time to call the police or get the hell out if need be. I swing my feet out of the bed, staring back at myself in the mirror hanging on the back of the closet door. I look like a truck hit me, but I did sleep hard. Maybe sleeping in a comfortable, spacious bed made the difference. I should sleep in here more often.

As I make my way from the bedroom into the living room I see that Rah and Rahima are nowhere to be found. The pounding in my head has subsided slightly, allowing me to feel some of the benefits of a good night's rest. I guess he took me seriously when I told him not to wake me and I appreciate Rah finally honoring one of my requests.

There's breakfast with a note attached waiting for me on the dining room table. Wow, free breakfast two mornings in a row. So this is how it feels to be treated well. Let's see what this fool has to say about leaving me and his daughter alone at night without him, when I'm not feeling well and he should've been home hours before. If that nightmare in motion I had last night was a glimpse of being his wife, I'll have no part of it.

"Hey, baby. I know you haven't been feeling well because of your personal sleep issues and whatnot. I love you, I'm here for you, and I can take whatever you

throw at a nigga, so bring it on. Love, your boy. P.S. Rahima says bye-bye."

In some other world with some other girl Rah's almost-sweet understanding might fly, but not here. He might as well have said that it's my time of the month and he excuses my irrational behavior. This fool must be close friends of Tattoo's because Rah's straight up living on *Fantasy Island* if he thinks I'm to blame for this one.

"Miss Independent," Ne-Yo sings, announcing my first call of the morning, and surprisingly it's not from Rah or Jeremy. Instead it's Mickey. What the hell does she want this early in the morning?

"Hello," I say groggily into the phone. The only thing about taking my mom's concoction is that it leaves me with what I imagine a hangover feels like. I take a seat at the table and open the McDonald's bag, taking out the hash browns to nibble on first. I'll tear into the Egg McMuffin as soon as I get Mickey off the phone.

"What's up, Jayd? What are you doing today?" Mickey asks, like I haven't been pissed at her for the past couple of days and she knows it. The nerve of some people, I swear.

"Schoolwork and other stuff. Why?" I can't help but entertain her. I'm curious to see where this conversation is going. I finish the greasy potatoes and take out the warm sandwich and check for meat; there is none. I know Rah wouldn't forget to order it the way I like it, but sometimes this hood's McDonald's neglects to get the order right. I also notice a smaller bag inside with a donut for me. Rah must've felt really bad to make two stops for my breakfast. Good, because he has a lot of groveling to do.

"Well, I know Nigel's parents are away at a church conference this weekend and that he's home all alone. So, I was wondering if you wanted to go over there and kick it."

"Mickey, why would you need to call me to go over your man's house? That makes absolutely no sense at all," I say, snacking on my Krispy Kreme donut. Is Rah trying to fatten a sistah up, or what?

"Jayd, look, I know you're still mad at me or whatever, and so is Nigel. I need some backup, and you're all I've got, so please get over it. My baby will be here before we know it and I don't have time for this shit." In Mickey's twisted world that was an apology, and as her friend I'm inclined to accept it, no matter how sorry it is.

"Fine, Mickey. But how do you know he wants you over there if he's still mad at you?" I'm trying not to smack but I'm hungry, and I can't stand cold fast food unless it's pizza. My mom never got into the whole microwave thing, and neither did Mama. We have toaster ovens around here, and I'm not about to go through all of that to eat this morning. I'm hungry now.

"I talked to him last night and he told me I could come by if I wanted to." Mickey's living on the same mystical island as Rah does, a place where you can screw up other people's lives without permanent repercussions. And as friends we're just supposed to ignore their foul behavior. They both need to wake up and smell the funk they've created.

"So he didn't ask you to drop by?" I can see this girl's not going to let me out of this conversation quick enough, so she'll just have to deal with me eating in her ear. I put my cell on speaker and dig into the rest of my breakfast.

"No, he didn't, but he gave me the green light and that means go. I just don't want to roll over there without a buffer, so finish your food, get up, and get dressed. I'll meet you over there at noon, Jayd. Bye." Damn. No thank you or nothing. Mickey's so demanding and full of herself: a lethal combination for any person to be made up of. I'd better call

Rah so he can give his boy a heads-up on our itinerary and to say thank you for the morning treat.

I wipe my greasy hands on a napkin, take a sip from the miniature carton of orange juice and pick up my cell, ready to dial. The picture of Rahima and me is still my wallpaper. I smile every time I see it. Why does her daddy have to be such a jackass sometimes?

"What up?" Rah asks, like he was expecting my call. I can hear Rahima playing in the background. I miss her already.

"Thank you for the breakfast," I say, taking the last bite of my food before finishing the juice. I'm stuffed. That meal should last me until dinnertime. Hopefully when I get back to Mama's later she'll have something good cooking. "Y'all left awfully early," I say, glancing at the clock on the wall. It's barely nine and I know he doesn't like to wake up before noon, baby or not.

"Oh yeah, Rahima ran out of diapers and she wasn't smelling too good when she got up, so we had to roll out real quick. But I came back and dropped you off something sweet just to say thank you for watching baby girl yesterday, and to say I'm sorry for staying out so late."

"Yeah, yeah," I say, not fully accepting his apology, but I'm getting there. I gather my trash and walk over to the kitchen to throw it away. I have to clean the house before I leave today. I also need to get in this head of mine and hook myself up. That's the only thing about doing hair for a living: my own do becomes less of a priority, and that has to end.

"For real though, Jayd, I don't want you to think I'm taking advantage of you because I'm not. I would never risk messing up what we've got again, ever." I want to believe him, but actions speak louder than words. And right now, I can't read anyone's actions clearly. I'm still not over the fact that I sleepwalked again last night and left his baby alone up here. And then the image stayed with me until I woke up this morning. I feel better, but not completely. I know Mama will want to hear all about this recent experience. I just hope she doesn't revoke my freedom to do hair for too long. I need to make money like anyone else, sleep or not.

"I got you, Rah," I say unconvincingly. I want him to sweat this time around. "So what are y'all up to today?"

"Well, little miss here is going to spend the day with my grandparents. They are missing her like crazy and I was going to go hang with my boy for a min. Why? What's up with you today?"

"Apparently I'm going over Nigel's house too, with Mickey later on, or so I've been told." Rah's silence through the phone speaks volumes, but I don't know exactly what it's saying.

"Really? Does Nigel know?" Rah asks. I had the same concern, but Rah's tone is a little more suspicious than I'd like to hear. What's he hiding? It better not have anything to do with Trish, or I'm going to hang up right in his trifling face.

"Really. Is there a reason we shouldn't go?" Rah takes a deep breath and pauses before answering. Now I know he's keeping something on the low, and as a part of their unspoken boy's code, I know better than to expect him to give me a straight answer.

"Nah, not that I can think of. But I should call him and give him a heads-up, just in case."

"Just in case what? I know Nigel's not creeping on Mickey, is he?" Rah's silent again before responding and that's not a good sign. Mickey's the one used to doing the creeping, not the other way around. I know this isn't going to sit well with her at all. She's already feeling insecure about her and Nigel's relationship. If she can't come over, and I'm the one to warn her about it, it'll send her into a whole other realm of miscommunication that I don't have the time or energy to be a part of.

"That's my other line, Jayd. I've got to take this call." Speaking of creeping, I know that was probably one of his broads now. "But for real, don't go over Nigel's until I call you back. In a minute," he says, clicking over. I hang up the phone, not knowing what to do. Should I text Mickey, or call her and break the news? Whichever way it goes I'm going to have to hear her mouth, and I'm not up for it this morning. I'll just wait for Rah to get back at me before making a move. In the meantime I can shower and wash my hair. A little me time is definitely in order.

By the time I get out of the shower with the conditioner still setting in my wet hair, I have three text messages from Mickey and one voice mail from Rah. Mickey's worried about what to wear and whether or not she should bring Nigel something to eat. I'll have to hit her back after I listen to Rah's message. I wouldn't want her to go out of her way for nothing.

After listening to the voice mail, I have to figure out how to break the news to Mickey that now's not a good time to visit Nigel. According to Rah, Nigel's parents are back from their retreat and Mickey knows she's not welcome when they're home. At least I won't have to rush now. I can take my time and do my nails, too, before going back to Compton. I've been working so much I've forgotten how good it feels to pamper myself.

I scroll down my contact list and push Mickey's name and the send button. The conditioner is dripping down the sides of my face so I can't stay on the phone too long.

"Hey, Jayd. Did you get my messages? I don't know if I should wear something bright and cheery or flashy and sexy. What do you think?"

"I think you should wear something warm and comfortable because you're staying home today, girl." I use the towel around my neck to wipe away the dripping conditioner. I love the smell of Pantene almost as much as I love Herbal Essence, both of which Mama would have a fit if she knew I was using instead of her and Netta's products. I ran out about a week ago and forgot to restock my personal inventory. But I'll have to remember to hook myself up this week when I go to work. I also need to stock up on my own line of braid products too, so I can get back to my hustle.

"Very funny, Jayd, but I'm serious."

"So am I, Mickey. According to Rah, Nigel's parents came home early." I glance at the clock, timing my conditioner. If I leave it on for too long my hair will become limp and hard to curl after I flat-iron it, so I only have a small window of time to hear Mickey bitch about her and Nigel, for real. The lavender essential oil I added to the conditioner is also making me feel too relaxed to listen to her talk for much longer.

"That's bull, Jayd, and you and I both know it. Nigel told me they weren't coming back until late tonight."

"People change plans, Mickey." Another minute has gone by and I can feel my hair losing body as we speak. I've got to wrap up this conversation right now.

"The hell they do. He's still avoiding me and I don't know what to do about it."

"Mickey, I would love to help you, but I've got to go now. I'll call you back later, okay? And don't worry about Nigel. I'm sure everything's okay," I say, lying to my friend. Truth be told, I didn't buy Rah's explanation either. I'll grill him more about it later. He said he's going to drop by on his way back from his grandparents' house this afternoon.

"Whatever, Jayd. Bye," Mickey says, abruptly hanging up. Whatever is right. I'm so sick of her rude behavior. And I've had it with my friends' drama and them involving me in it.

Even when I try to help they're unappreciative of my effort, which really irritates the hell out of me. I've got enough of my own shit to deal with. Hopefully by the time I'm finished with my hair and nails I'll feel better about it all. I'm going to study my spirit book too and look for something to help me out of this mess before I lose myself in it.

It's early afternoon and I'm really enjoying the day alone. Rah should be here any moment to steal my solitude, but I feel stronger than I have in days. I thumb through my mom's old spirit notebook, but it's no help. The spirit book has only limited accounts of sleepwalking, which seems to be unique to my path of our collective ancestry. My powers lie in my dreams rather than in my eyes, like my predecessors' visions. Our visions are equally powerful, just different for me. Before I can go any deeper into my studies, Rah knocks on the door, disturbing my peace.

"Hey," I say, opening the front door and letting him in.

"What's up with you?" Rah asks, kissing me on the cheek before sitting down on the couch. "Your hair smells good." I reclaim my spot next to him, ready to grill him about what's going on with Nigel. We'll get back to our own issues in a minute.

"Thank you," I say, running my hands over the smooth ponytail I just put my freshly pressed hair in. I'll cornrow it later this week. "So what's up with your boy not wanting to kick it with Mickey today?" Compliments won't charm his way out of being interrogated.

"It's complicated, Jayd. But we need to give Nigel some space right now. He's been through a lot in the past few weeks and is still processing it all."

"I know he is," I say, recalling the drama with him and Mickey getting busted for ditching at school, the shooting, and everything else in between. I bet part of him wishes he'd stayed at Westingle instead of transferring to South Bay High. We don't call it Drama High for nothing, that's for sure.

"We've always had bad holidays, especially this past Christmas." Rah's right. The expectations are always set so high at Christmas and on Valentine's Day that there's no possible way we could ever meet them. There's a reason why these two holidays are also the loneliest times of year for millions of people. Every time Rah and I try to have good celebrations they end up ruined somehow. If I could change that fact I would. But there's no going back in time.

"Or is there," my mom chimes in. She's supposed to be enjoying an all-inclusive spa day with her boo, but I guess she still has time to butt into my business.

"Mom, not now. Rah and I are having a serious conversation," I relay back to her. Rah looks at me, waiting for a response, but this ain't like walking and chewing bubblegum. I can only concentrate on one conversation at a time.

"Don't you think so, Jayd?" Rah asks. I can barely nod my head in agreement as my mother continues her chatter in my head. Rah looks at the look on my face and acknowledges the transformation. It may take him a little while but he can always tell when my mom's in my head. I'm glad at least one of my friends is familiar with my lineage and all the idiosyncrasies that come with it.

"Jayd, I'm serious. If you really want to solve the issues that you, Rah, and your friends experienced during the holidays, there's a punch recipe in the spirit book that can handle that. And it tastes good, too." Ever since we found out that my mom's powers are only in effect to help mine grow, she's been anxious to relive her teenage days of conjuring, through me.

"Bye mom," I say, devoting my attention to Rah and Rah alone.

"I'm sorry about that, but I plan on making up this Valentine's Day to you in a real way." If he knew that Jeremy has already asked me out for that night he'd be so pissed. But what he doesn't know won't hurt him. And I still need a date to the dance if we're going at all.

"What do you have in mind?" I'm glad I tuned back into the conversation, right in time to hear this. After all of the drama we've been through lately, having a regular date like a regular couple will be nice. Now that he has his baby full-time, we're going to have to account for her, too.

"She's not your baby, Jayd. I already told you about that, girl. Don't end up being a teenage stepmama like I was. Rahima is Rah's responsibility. Let him figure it out," my mom says, giving her last two cents before she's finally out.

"Well, I was thinking we could go out that night. What do you think?" I just knew he would want to take me to the dance and skip the personal celebration, especially with our history on that day. The three we spent together as a couple over the years didn't turn out so well, and I doubt this year will be any different.

"Don't you want to go to the dance? I'm sure Nigel's taking Mickey, isn't he?" If we all go together maybe there will be less tension when we see Nellie. I know she'll be there, sporting her new crew and boyfriend.

"I don't know about that one, boo. He's not really in the mood."

"But they have to go. Nigel's still on the football team, hurt or not, and I know they're going to want him to at least make an appearance."

"Jayd, it's not that simple," Rah says. I can hear the hesitation in Rah's voice. What's he holding back?

"What's going on with Nigel? What aren't you telling me, Rah, other than what you and Trish really got into last night." I know we're not talking about us, but I want him to know I ain't over that shit—not yet. I believe him when he says she was only there because of her brother, but completely trusting Rah is still a work in progress.

"Jayd, they are thinking of throwing Nigel off the team and sending him back to Westingle."

"What?" Ah hell, no. This isn't good for anyone. "How can they do that when he was an innocent bystander who got shot? Their star quarterback could've been killed, and this is how they're treating him?" Being black in a mostly white school is never any fun, not even for the school's best football player.

"The administration and the coaches in particular don't see it that way. They think Nigel is in a gang and brought this on himself, especially since he was involved with a gangbanger's girl and got her pregnant within his first month being there. Not to mention the fact that he was accused of ditching on a regular basis before this all happened. Basically they say he's dragging down the South Bay High name and he needs to pay for his actions."

"So he's their sacrificial lamb? If they want to make an example out of someone why does it have to be him? Nigel needs to play ball and he needs to be with Mickey and their baby."

"Mickey's baby, *maybe* his," Rah corrected.

"Wait a minute. I thought you were all for Nigel claiming this baby with or without a paternity test." After that long-ass lecture he gave me about him just knowing he was Sandy's baby daddy, I know he's not tripping about Nigel feeling the same way.

"I'm for whatever my boy's for," Rah says, breathing deeply. I know he's in a tough spot being both my and Nigel's friend. "And right now my boy's for saving his ass, and I don't blame him. I mean, if it's his baby he's going to take care of it, no doubt. But Mickey and her drama wasn't in the plan."

"Well, Nigel should've thought about his plan before he slept with Mickey. She never lied about her situation. That boy knew what he was getting into," I say, pissed for Mickey, who I know is going to be beside herself once she finds out about all of this. She's not stupid. Mickey knows something's wrong, but she has no idea it's this serious.

"Yeah, I feel you, girl. But this isn't really our business, and we have to let Nigel deal with this shit in his own way. Besides, his mom and dad are all up in his ear too, so he's got a lot to deal with right now, and Mickey pressuring him isn't going to help."

"I know you're right about that, Rah, but still. He can't leave Mickey hanging like this. She's about to split a wig trying to get to him, especially after he walked away from her on Friday. She's worried about the baby, Rah."

"He's got his career to think about, Jayd, and that's part of taking care of his seed, too. Just tell her to back off for now, please. It's the only thing she can do, really." Well, I guess that's that. Nigel thought he could handle being with a gangster girl but he's bitten off more than he could chew. There's no going back, so what he's going to do now is the real question.

~ 7 ~
Misty Morning

"Don't jump in the water if you can't swim."

—BOB MARLEY

I hate these types of mornings and so does my hair. There's not enough moisture to justify keeping my windshield wipers on, but there's just enough mist in the air to limit my visibility. When I stepped outside of Mama's house a few moments ago my straight ponytail turned into a huge fuzz ball before I even made it to my mom's car. Luckily it was a national holiday yesterday, and because of Dr. Martin Luther King's sacrifices, I got to say home and catch up on my homework, since I took Sunday to work on me. But all of my sweat is a distant memory now. I guess that's how Misty got her name, because she's every bit as annoying as the morning mist in the air.

Even though I made the effort to walk out of the back door this morning, as usual, I'm parked in front of the house, well within Esmeralda's evil visual range. If I could immediately take off I would, but I have to sit here for a few more minutes while the car warms up. Rah said it's about time for the car to have an oil change, the first one on my watch. My mom says while I'm driving her vehicle it's my responsibility to keep up with the maintenance. I'm just glad she let me roll her ride until I get my own, since my daddy's of no real help.

I haven't talked to my father since I left the raggedy car he bought me in his driveway without telling him. I'm sure he's still pissed at me. I probably won't hear from him until my birthday or the next holiday. I'm sure he's feeling a little embarrassed that the gift he bought to show off at his family Christmas Eve dinner ended up broken down in his driveway the very next week. At least I left the keys in it so he could move it, if it even starts. If he had listened to me and had the car checked out properly, my first car would've made a great Christmas gift. But instead the bucket he bought from my driving instructor only added to my holiday hell.

"Jayd, can a brotha get a ride to work? It's cold out here. Open up," Bryan says, knocking on the passenger's window. I push the automatic door locks to let my favorite uncle in. With me getting up a half hour later because I don't have to catch the bus, I don't always get to see him in the mornings; he's usually gone by now. I know he misses our morning chats and so do I. If it weren't for him and Jay, I wouldn't have any male allies in our house, since the rest of my uncles are trifling. What did Mama do in a house full of men before I was born?

"Drive me crazy," my mom says while Bryan throws his backpack in the backseat and settles in. *"She would call me every day when I lived with your daddy. And if I didn't answer she'd have someone drop her off. I'm so glad I had you."*

"What's up with you, little J?" Bryan looks at my distant gaze and, like Rah, recognizes the dazed look on my face. "Oh, tell my big sis I said what's up and that she needs to get a radio in this bitch."

"Tell that fool not to call my car out of her name," my mom says, all up in the conversation. *"Bye, baby. Have a good day."*

"My mom said not to call her car a bitch," I say, relaying the message. "Why are you late this morning?" I put the stick shift in first gear, ready to get on with my day. Miracle Market is in the opposite direction I usually drive to get to school, but it's only around the corner. Besides, out of all six of my uncles, Bryan's the only one who would do the same thing for me.

"Man, me and Tarek were on a roll at the radio station last night for King Day. First, he deejayed during my show, and then I turned around and did the same shit for him. I didn't get in until three o'clock this morning." Bryan loves working at the public access radio station. He needs to see if he can turn it into a paid gig and quit his hustle at the market since music is his true love.

"You're going to run yourself ragged if you keep going like this."

"You're one to talk, sleepwalking and scaring niggas and shit. By the way, how's that going? If Mama took you to see Dr. Whitmore I know it must be serious. That dude is no joke." All of Mama's children have been seen at one time or another by our family doctor. None of the boys care for him too much and Dr. Whitmore doesn't like them much either. I don't know what that's all about. It must be a man thing.

"I slept okay again last night, but I wasn't able to remember my dream again. Mama says not remembering my dreams isn't as bad as sleepwalking, but it's pretty close because that's where my visual power lies." I pull up in front of Miracle Market, ready to drop my uncle off and get a move on.

"Whatever you do, try not to do that shit again. That scared me for real, Jayd. Brothas can't take feeling out of control, and I felt helpless that night. Whatever they tell you to do to stop that, please do it. Don't be your usual hard-headed self on this one. Peace," Bryan says, exiting my mom's little ride and walking around the back of the building to enter through the side door.

When I turn the car around to head toward Redondo

Beach, I notice Dr. Whitmore walking into his office next door to the small store. I never did call him to let him know how the pills were working. I guess I should continue taking them, but I'll have to smash them down or something. I can't see ingesting the huge pills on a daily basis, and two of them at that. I'll work on it when I get home. Right now I have to focus on getting through my day at Drama High.

Today's the first day back for me since I missed two days of school last week because of my blinding sleepwalking episode. It's also the first day back since we attended the memorial service for Tre. According to Rah, Nigel still isn't talking to Mickey and he's supposed to be coming back today as well. I can't wait to see how that's going to go down. He can only avoid Mickey for so long, even if she's technically attending class off-campus now.

I haven't spoken to Mickey since she abruptly hung up on our conversation Sunday. And to tell the truth, I really don't have too much to say to her. I don't take too kindly to her mixing me and our friends up in her mess and then acting like a brat when the shit hit the fan. Mickey's lucky I haven't slapped her ass by now. But her luck is running out.

By the time I arrive on campus there's a line around the corner to get into the main parking lot, as usual. Rather than wait with the rest of the crowd, I decide to park on one of the residential streets near campus. I check the parking signs to make sure I won't get a ticket. The last thing I need is to get cited on my mother's car and have to hear her mouth about me being irresponsible with her vehicle. I'd never live that one down.

As I exit the car I notice one of the neighbors eyeing me as she walks her small, fluffy dog down the block. She knows I don't belong in her neighborhood. I wish I could ease her mind and inform her that I'm not here to steal her precious poodle, or her son if she has one, but I don't want to be as rude as she's being right now. Never letting go of her gaze on me, she bends down and picks up the fresh dog shit with a plastic bag. And she thinks I'm beneath her. As my grandfather would say, white folks have some serious issues. Why can't they designate a spot in their yards for their dogs to shit, like we do for Lexi?

Even with the rude-ass rich neighbors, I enjoy walking around Redondo Beach. It's a beautiful neighborhood and you can see the ocean from almost every angle, including from where I'm standing now. I wish that I didn't have to cross the street, but I must face my inevitable school day. Hopefully I can get through Spanish and English class without too much drama, especially since they are my quietest periods of the day. It's a nice way to get the morning started. Because after my fist two classes it's all downhill from there.

It feels strange being in class this morning after all I've been through recently. Sometimes I drift off into my own thoughts while the teachers are talking, especially in my second period English class. We read this short story about a woman who thought the wallpaper in her bedroom was talking to her. Turns out she was severely depressed after having a baby. I didn't have a baby, but I did have a dream about having one, and I can see how someone could lose their mind if the situation isn't right.

"Jayd," Mickey says as I approach my locker to change out my books for my next two classes. The day is moving quickly and I'm glad for it. But with Mickey intruding on my nutrition break, I'm sure it's about to get longer. The main hall is beginning to fill up with students and staff alike, giving the brisk Tuesday morning air a warm energy. School wouldn't be so bad if it didn't come with so much bull, as I'm sure Mickey's going to help shovel my way now. "We need to talk."

"Good morning to you too, Mickey," I say with hella attitude. I hope she feels my energy because next to Misty and Nellie, Mickey's the last person I want to see.

"Look, Jayd, you've got to help me with Nigel. He won't take my calls, answer my e-mails, my texts, nothing. What am I supposed to do?"

"Well, you could've started by not lying to him and your man before all of this shit went down. I don't think getting shot felt too good to Nigel," I say, switching out my English and Spanish textbooks and folders and retrieving my materials for my government and debate classes. I can't believe I have a class with Misty and the rest of her crew fourth period. At least there's beautiful eye candy to look forward to seeing. I love knowing I'm going to be around Mr. Adewale every day.

"Jayd, sometimes lying is a necessary evil. And I can't go back in time and change anything. If I could, I would have done some things differently, but we still have to deal with the present, and I need Nigel in order to do that." Mickey is as jaded as they come.

"Oh what a tangled web we weave, when first we practice to deceive," I say to Mickey, but Sir Walter Scott's words are way over her head.

"Jayd, enough. I don't have time for your philosophy on living right now. This is serious. There's got to be something you can do to help me get my man back. We're about to have a baby. We don't have time for your strange sayings and shit."

"Oh, but you have time for me to supposedly cast a spell or something like that, right?" Mickey looks at me as if to say *well, isn't that what you do?* I'm tempted to tell her off again, but she waddled her way up to the main campus to apologize to me and ask for my help, so I'll give her some mercy, but not too much.

"Jayd, please. You know Nigel better than anyone up here.

I know you can be persuasive in your own way." She's right about that. I do know him better than anyone, and I'm glad she's finally coming to that realization. And because I know him, I know when to put on the pressure and when to leave him be, like now.

"Mickey, Nigel is really having a hard time with all that's going on right now. He asked for space. Honor that," I say to Mickey, who's not hearing me, as usual.

"We don't have time for space, Jayd. I need him right here, right now." Just as the words come out of her mouth, Misty's there to catch them. It's enough I have to deal with her at home and school, but having her in fourth period is just too much to bear.

"Aren't you supposed to be a little farther south of the lunch area these days?" Misty says to Mickey, who's already overemotional as it is. Misty ignores me completely, and she'd better keep that behavior up if she knows what's good for her. Mama says she and Esmeralda are still working their mischief and for me to stay as far away from her as possible, much to my delight. It's not going to be easy to avoid her, with the broad in my face all of the time.

"Misty, step," Mickey says, and Misty takes the hint. I know Misty doesn't want to push Mickey too far, no matter how bad she thinks she is.

"If it's magic you want, go ask Misty to help you, because we don't work like that. Like I said before, I can help you better yourself and help Nigel do the same if he asks me to. But I can't do any work for him without his permission—period. I have to get to class now, Mickey. I'll talk to you later."

"If it's not to help me, then don't bother. Maybe I will ask Misty, since she seems to be on her game these days, unlike someone else I know." I know Mickey didn't just give Misty a compliment, even if it was a weak attempt to gain my sympathy. She's really bugging if that's the case.

"Mickey, how many friends do you have? Better yet, how many do you know would put up with your rude, selfish behavior?" Mickey looks shocked that I'm fronting her on the spot like this, but I've had enough. Some students stare at me and my girl without slowing down their quick pace. "Exactly. I recommend you check all of that attitude at the door and recognize your true friends before you lose the few you've got left." Without a comeback, she walks out of the main hall, steaming. I don't know what's gotten into her, but if she keeps this madness up she's going to end up on my shit list. I slam my locker shut and head to third period.

"Esmeralda's working all of your friends through Misty. I hope you know that," my mom quickly relays before the bell rings above my head. Jeremy walks into class right behind me, nodding what's up as he heads to his desk right next to mine.

"Please take your seats so we can begin," Mrs. Peterson says. Before I can make it to my seat, Laura and her snobby followers walk through the open door with Nellie not far behind them. What's she doing in our class? Doesn't she have her own third period to attend?

"Uhmm, excuse me, young lady. I don't see a new student's name on the roster," Mrs. Peterson says. With the new semester, some classes take a couple of weeks to fill. But I know Nellie didn't change to the AP track. Not because she's not intelligent enough, but because it's too much work for her. This visit must be purely social. "May I help you?"

"Oh, this is our fellow ASB member, Nellie, and she's been assigned to visit the class this period for research purposes," Laura says, like she's Nellie's official spokesperson.

"Here's the note from Mr. Wilkins, my history teacher." Nellie passes the note to Mrs. Peterson, who's eyeing it like it's a counterfeit bill. She then looks from Laura to Nellie and nods her head in approval. White folks can get away with anything around here. Let me try to bring Mickey up in here for a visit. Note or no note, she'd be out on her ass.

"Fine. Please take a seat so we can begin." The girls head to the back where Laura usually sits, but not before Nellie can throw some hater rays my way.

"Cute sweatshirt. Did I miss the sale at the Salvation Army?" What did this trick just say? Nellie must really be smelling herself these days to go there with me.

"Nellie, please. If you're going to waste what few brain cells you've got left under that horse hair, use them to say something more clever than that."

"Ouch," the boys sitting behind me say in unison. Other students laugh at the intrusive episode in our class, which is usually dry as sandpaper. I might be grateful for the interruption if it weren't at my expense.

"You're just jealous because I've got everything you could never have."

"Nellie, I do hair, remember? I'm sure I could put a few tracks in my head if I wanted to."

"Damn, she's not letting up on your weave, dude," Sam, one of the class clowns, says to a steaming Nellie. Truthfully, that's all I would say about her because I don't want be too mean to her. I don't like to get too ugly with anyone, especially not someone who used to be a good friend of mine.

"Well, Chance doesn't seem to mind my hair or anything else about me." Nellie puts her hands on her hips and rolls her neck at me. When did she get all that sass? She then sticks her nonexistent breasts out like she's somebody's mama. What's gotten into this girl?

"That's because Chance is a nice guy. What he sees in you is beyond me."

"He sees that I'm a real woman and whoever he was attracted to before was a little girl."

"Okay, ladies, that's enough," Mrs. Peterson growls from her desk.

"What do you mean, a real woman, Nellie? You're a sixteen-year-old girl last time I checked, just like me, fool."

"Some of us mature faster than others." Nellie continues her trek to the back of the class where the queen bitch has officially claimed her throne for the hour. I hope this girl didn't give it up to Chance. And I hope Chance didn't give it up to her either. He's liable to be more hurt from this relationship, the way Nellie's acting these days. I'll have to talk to him about this new development. I would ask Jeremy, but he looks as curious about Nellie's revelation as I am. Maybe I can catch him before fourth period, since I usually see him walking to class. It's a simple yes or no question, no long conversation needed.

By the time we get to fourth period the classroom is already packed with students. I haven't seen Chance yet. I guess I'll try to catch him later. I scan the room to see who's arrived before I take my seat. There's one student in particular who has caught my eye. It's the new student who had eyes for me last week. I don't know where he came from, but I'm sure glad for the new energy in the room.

"My name is Emilio," he says in the sexiest damned accent I've ever heard. Where is this brother from, and can I go back there with him? Jeremy looks at me, and the rest of the girls salivate over the new student. He can't talk; I've seen him eye plenty of asses since we've been dating.

"Are you from Mexico or something?" Shae asks, sucking on her Blow Pop a little too suggestively. I think he's cute too, but does she really have to be so crude with it?

"No, I'm from a small village in Venezuela, originally." He smiles at me as I sit down at my assigned desk. Mr. Adewale has made it perfectly clear he means business and I definitely want to stay on his good side.

"Okay, class, we have a lot to go over in this short period, so let's get to it."

I'm glad today is an early day. When I get to Netta's after school, hopefully they'll give me the clearance to do hair again. I need to make some money sooner than later. And it's boring only having school and my spirit work to focus on. Hair is my therapy. Tomorrow I will be back on my grind and thankful for it.

I can't believe it's already Wednesday. I was so busy at Netta's shop yesterday I came home last night and crashed, which is unfortunate because that means tonight and tomorrow night will be spent catching up on homework. But at least they temporarily gave me the okay to do hair again.

Mrs. Bennett has decided to reinstate our mandatory AP meetings at break and lunch on Wednesdays because she says we need the help. I'll be so glad to graduate next year that I'm counting the days.

"Buenos días, Señorita Jayd," Emilio says. I smile my biggest smile and return the greeting.

"Buenos días. Como estas?" He smiles at my wack-ass Spanish accent, but at least I got the words right.

"Bien, y tu?" Damn, Emilio's not letting the Spanish go. It'll be cool to have another friend to practice my chosen foreign language with. Maggie and I go back and forth sometimes, but she mixes Spanish and English like that's another language all its own. We call it Spanglish in the hood, but like Ebonics, I don't think it'll ever show up on the AP exams.

"Así así." Now we're both cheesing. It's been a long time since I met someone who could make me blush. Jeremy had that effect on me until our madness began. And Rah never

really made me blush. All of the heat in my body rises when I'm around Rah, not just in my cheeks. I wish it weren't true, especially now when it's so hard loving Rah, but I can't lie to myself. I'm confused about dealing with Rah and all of his baby-mama drama. But he's not here right now and Emilio's fine self is a pleasant distraction.

"Bien." He looks at me, his hazel eyes hypnotizing me for just a moment. But the noisy hall snaps me back into the present moment. I've spent enough time off in another world lately.

"Okay, that's all the Spanish I know comfortably. English, please." We begin our walk down the main hall toward the language hall. It's another foggy morning, and according to the dark clouds outside, it looks like it's going to stay that way. I watched The Weather Channel last night and it said the rest of the week would be sunny. So much for that theory.

"So, Jayd, tell me about yourself. What do you like to do, where do you live, how many brothers and sisters do you have?" Emilio's more interested in me than the Census Bureau.

"Well, I like to make money and chill, I live in Compton and I'm an only child from my mother, and I have a brother and a sister from my daddy. How about you?"

"Wow, you only have two siblings? I have ten," he says, turning the corner behind me, now directly in front of my first period classroom. Too bad he's a sophomore. If he were a year older, I'd eat him up like a piece of chocolate cake.

"Well, I live with seven other people in a small house, so I feel like I have ten siblings." Emilio laughs at me and I love seeing his pretty smile.

"As you already know, I'm an exchange student from South America, I'm staying in Redondo Beach, and I like to play chess, read, and dance. Do you like salsa?"

"Yes, I love it. My favorite is the spicy kind, although mild is good on tacos." Emilio laughs hysterically at my comment. What's so funny about dip?

"No, not the food. The music, salsa. I love to dance," he says, putting one hand in the air and the other out in front of him like he's holding a girl's waist. "We should get together sometime. I'll show you how." As the warning bell rings above our heads, Mr. Adewale turns the corner and smiles at me.

"Good morning to you both," Mr. A says. He passes us by and goes into the classroom ahead of me. I guess Mr. Donald is out today. I thought that since Mr. A has his own class now he was off of sub duty, but apparently not.

"I'll see you in third period, *Señorita* Jayd. *Hasta luego,*" Emilio says before I have the chance to grill him some more.

"Okay class, quiet down," Mr. Adewale says, writing our assignment on the board. "I'm going to be taking over your Spanish class for the remainder of the semester and it's going to be very different from what you're used to." Mr. Adewale just made my morning with his presence, but crushed it with his announcement. If I know anything about him, it's that he doesn't play when it comes to academics. My first period was the one class I could count on being easy. Now all that's going to change.

"Ah, hell no, man. Where's Mr. Donald? He was supposed to change my grade to an A last week, but I think he forgot," Chad says, one of the potheads who hangs out at the back of the classroom with my in-class homegirl, China, and the rest of their crew. They are used to being able to cut up and ditch class at will, like Jeremy. But not anymore. Mr. Adewale has little tolerance for any type of disrespectful behavior.

"Back to your new assignment," Mr. Adewale continues, ignoring Chad's outburst. "You'll find your new syllabus online, which is also where your additional classwork will be housed. This class now has its own website where you can post your work every week."

"Dude, I don't have a computer," Chad says, further antagonizing Mr. A, who has obviously lost patience with the high white boy. Mr. Adewale's chiseled cheekbones tighten and his hazel-green eyes are now glaring. They almost look red from where I'm sitting.

"That's why your school invested in a million-dollar multimedia system. Use it." The stern tone in Mr. Adewale's voice silences the entire class. If anyone was going to challenge Mr. A about anything else, I'm sure they've changed their mind by now. "Today's class will focus on Spanish verbs. Once you memorize them, the rest of the language will come relatively easily. Please turn to page seven in your textbooks and read chapter one. Your homework is on the board. And please don't try to rush through the chapter and do your homework in class. If you do, I guarantee you will flunk tomorrow's quiz."

Damn, Mr. A is on fire this morning. He seemed like he was in a good mood outside. Maybe it's just because he's new to taking over the course. Hopefully he'll lighten up as the semester progresses. All I need is another reason to dread coming to school. Between my girls tripping and the rest of the frenemies present on this campus, the last thing I need is another hard-core teacher to make my school experience completely dreadful. With AP meetings all day and spirit work waiting on me when I get home this afternoon, I won't have any time to myself today. Hopefully the day will go by fast. At least that way I'll be one more day closer to Friday.

~ 8 ~
Punch Drunk

"My friends wonder what is wrong with me/
Well I'm in a daze from your love, you see."

—BOBBY CALDWELL

By the time I make it back to Compton I'm starving and I already know Mama didn't make dinner. Today was one of those days I had no time to eat. I've been in such a daze, dealing with my own shit, that I've lost my stride with my schoolwork. It's been kicking my ass and today's no exception.

"Let's see what I can eat real quick," I say aloud. I walk into the kitchen, put my things down and wash my hands. I look around the bleak yellow kitchen and see years of grease stains on the walls. Mama must be in the backhouse cooking, because I smell something good coming from the spirit room. I'd better not take too long because I know Mama knows that I'm here. I glance at the old stove and wish I could change it into a new one for Mama just by looking at it.

"Cornflakes will have to do for now," I say, reaching for the large box of cereal on the top of the refrigerator. Sometimes being five feet tall ain't really that cute.

"Damn, you're short," Jay says, coming into the kitchen, reaching over my head and snatching the cereal box down like it's easy. I don't understand how he and his mom clear six feet just like Daddy, and me and my mom barely hit five.

We are closer to Mama's five-eight frame, but still con the runts of the family gene pool when it comes to hei

"Give me that," I say, reaching for the box. "I'm too gry to play with you, boy."

"Aren't you supposed to be out back with Mama, killi chickens or something?" he says, finally giving me the cerea I put it on the counter, get a bowl and spoon from the dish strainer, and pour the cereal into the bowl.

"Maybe, maybe not. If we do decided to kill one I'm sure you'll have no problem eating it when we fry it up," I say, returning the box to its place before opening the refrigerator to retrieve the milk, which isn't there. "Damn it."

"Ha! I could've told you we were out of milk. That's what you get for being a smart-ass," Jay says, leaving the kitchen to go back into the room he shares with Bryan and Daddy. He cherishes what little privacy he can get when his roommates are gone, and I don't blame him.

"Whatever, fool," I call after him. I can't eat cornflakes with no milk. It just ain't right. Maybe Mama has some milk in the spirit room I could use.

I take my bowl and the rest of my things and head out the back door. Lexi, Mama's most trusted companion, wags her tail as I walk down the steps leading to the garage and backyard.

"I would pet you, girl, but my hands are full." Lexi follows me to the small house attached to the garage, where Mama does some of her best work. The sweet smell of sugar and cinnamon lures me in, almost making me forget about my milk-less bowl of cereal.

"Hey, Mama," I say, opening the screen door. "Do you have any milk back here? There's none in the house kitchen, and I need to eat my cereal before I drop dead from hunger." I drop my backpack and purse in the corner, careful not to

e ground. Mama has a thing about
She says if you want Legba to
best place to leave it for him.
in the refrigerator. You're welcome
sing condensed milk on my cereal al-
nate using powdered milk, but at least it
d I'm too hungry to complain.

u," I say, reaching for the small can she hands to
ouring its contents on the thirsty flakes.

aven't talked to you about last Friday's service. How
Tre's memorial, baby?" Mama asks. Time's flying. It's al-
eady the end of January and I'm not ready for any more holiday drama. If I see another damned cupid or heart-shaped poster at school I'm going to throw up all over it.

"It was okay." Mama's been extra busy making all kinds of love potions for her clients. Next to Christmas and Halloween, Valentine's Day is her busiest money-making holiday. After this she'll have a break until Mother's Day.

"Did you pour the libation to the ancestors?" Mama asks, returning to her post at the kitchen table.

"Yes, and so did some of Tre's homies." I would tell her about the hussies that helped Daddy out, but no need in me being the bearer of bad news, especially when Mama already knows how Daddy gets down. "What really got me was the fact that out of all those supposedly spiritual folks in that church, the gangsters were the ones pouring libation to the ancestors with me."

"The youth are closer to the creator than old fools with closed minds, no matter how misguided they might be," Mama says, raising my chin and checking me out.

"Yeah, I was shocked. But the service was good." I don't want to talk too much about Daddy's job, but he's good at what he does and I know Mama misses having that connection with him.

"You know why I was so smitten with your grandfather when I first met him? His charisma. He was on fire for his god and me for mine. When I first saw your grandfather walking down the streets of New Orleans, with his congregation behind him singing and carrying on, I was mesmerized. Much like Maman was when she first saw my daddy preaching too, although it was a completely different congregation he spoke to."

"Daddy was on one up at the pulpit. He had everybody on their feet." We couldn't help but feel moved by Daddy's sermon.

"That is his job, isn't it?" Mama's tone is saltier than a potato chip. "I had faith in the black church of the past. It was a revolutionary place to be. People wanted the truth; they wanted justice with or without peace most of the time. I thought we could make a change in the world, and we did. But as time passed, people got comfortable and greedy. They got forgetful and allowed fear to replace hope. And I got sick of the drama."

"I hear you, Mama. It was nothing but haters up in that place." I won't tell her about the women giving me the evil eye, because I know that'll just upset her more.

"Haters are everywhere. Speaking of which, how are your little friends doing?"

"Don't ask," I say, not ready to deal with my broken crew.

"I already did."

"Well, Nigel's not talking to Mickey and neither am I. Rah and I are talking again, but it's still a little tense where Sandy and Trish are concerned. And Jeremy doesn't get any of it. Oh, and Nellie's still tripping. That about sums it all up in a nutshell."

"Oh, Jayd, I'm sorry your friends are having so many issues. Have you asked your ancestors for their help?"

"Not really." Other than my morning prayers, which I usually say in the shower, I don't really commune with my ancestors or my orisha like Mama does. She's always got one foot in this world and the other in the spiritual realm. I guess that's why she only has one friend in her crew who rolls pretty much the same way that she does. Netta's a true ride-or-die homegirl.

"Well, what are you waiting for? All hell to break loose?"

"Hasn't that already happened? Once I started walking around in my sleep I figured Armageddon was on its way." Mama laughs at my silliness, but I'm serious. I feel like the world as I know it is gone and all of my friends along with it.

"Speaking of which, how are your dreams? Have you been taking your prescription from Dr. Whitmore?"

"Well, not exactly." Mama looks at me sideways like she wants to smack me, but manages to restrain herself at least long enough to hear the rest of my answer. "Mama, they're too much. He couldn't give me a tiny pill like an aspirin or something?"

"Girl, stop whining. I don't care how you get that medicine in you, but you'd better do it. Here, start smashing," Mama says, handing me the brown bottle with two spoons. She knows all about my aversion to taking pills and came prepared. I knew she'd count the pills if I left them on the nightstand, which I did by accident last night. I'm really slipping on my game these days.

After smashing two of the pills up with water and swallowing the bitter medicine, we sit in silence for a few moments, waiting to see if I feel any different. Mama continues her cooking and I'm still hungry, even with the lingering nastiness still present on my tongue.

"Your mama told me she made you some tea to help you sleep," Mama says, changing the subject. If I'm forced to take one more damned thing I'm going to give up on this dream thing altogether.

"And that it did. I had crazy dreams, one in which you were picking my mom up off the floor in a restaurant. She had just found out my daddy was cheating on her with one of the waitresses—again."

"Oh, I remember that day vividly. I was so upset at your father I could've killed him where he stood," Mama says, beating the eggs harder than necessary. If she keeps it up she's going to end up liquefying the meringue instead of whipping it for the banana pudding she's preparing, one of my favorite treats. But this is no ordinary dessert. Mama's making this special pudding for one of her favorite clients. The girl can't cook worth shit, and she's trying to snag a ring from her boyfriend this Valentine's Day. Mama agreed to help her out. I'm sure she's also agreed to put a little something extra in it to give the sweetness a boost, unlike this bowl of cereal I can't force myself to down no matter how hungry I am.

"Mama, you couldn't kill a fly," I say, snacking on one of the vanilla wafers that's going into the banana pudding, straight out of the box, and irritating Mama to no end. She hates it when I eat out of the container no matter what it is.

"What have I told you about that, girl? Children of Oshune do not eat leftovers, and by eating out of the box you're making your next serving a leftover." When it comes to taboos, Mama doesn't make allowances. Mama and her logic. It's not leftover to me yet, but who I am to argue with her?

"Yes, ma'am," I say, reaching to the counter behind me and grabbing the roll of paper towels. I pour a few of the wafers out of the box and snack on my portion. I wish I could roll my eyes without getting smacked.

"Now, back to your crazy dreams. Have you had any more?" I didn't want to get into it with Mama about my sleepwalking incident with Rahima, but I can't help it. She's going to find out anyway, and it would be better coming directly from me the first time around.

"Well, I had another sleepwalking incident while dreaming about Rah and me getting married. We also had a baby. It was freaky." Mama stops what she's doing and looks at me sternly, probing for what, I don't know. I continue to snack on my cookies and let her look away.

"Did you tell Rah about it?" Mama asks. She returns to her meringue, ready to put on the final layer of cookies, custard, and bananas before putting the fluffy sweetness on top, making the perfect pudding. I hope her client knows how lucky she is to have Mama in her corner. Her man won't have a chance once he tastes Mama's homemade goodness.

"No. I didn't really have a chance since I was going off on him about something else. I didn't think I should, especially since I was watching Rahima at the time."

"Watching Rahima? Where the hell was he?" Mama puts the finishing touches on the dessert and pushes it to the side of the kitchen table, ready to start on the next creation. Valentine's Day keeps a sistah extra busy, I see. It could probably be a very profitable holiday for me too, if I weren't busy going crazy.

"Working," I say, with extra bitterness on my tongue, and it's not from the pills. I'm going to be sour about this one for a long, long time.

"Mmmhmm," Mama utters. "Don't get pimped, Jayd."

"Dang, Mama, why you gotta say it like that?"

"Because that's how I mean it, young lady. I know Rah's a good young man, but he's still a man and sometimes they just can't help themselves. They do stupid shit even when they know better. And Rah is not immune to the stupidity prevalent in his genes."

"I hear you, loud and clear." Unfortunately I agree with her one hundred percent. I'm just glad she said it and I didn't. It makes me feel better knowing someone else is having the same thought that I am.

"And where was Rahima while you were walking around? Please tell me she was asleep too, and somewhere safe."

"She was knocked out on the floor of my mom's living room. I, on the other hand, woke up outside at the bottom of the stairs."

"You were outside?" Mama asks, alarmed. I know it scares her to think about it. I was scared, too. If Shawntrese hadn't been there to wake me up, who knows where I would have ended up.

"Yeah, luckily one of the neighbors came home late and woke me up. But it was still a bit much, especially with a baby upstairs I was supposed to be watching out for." I shake my head at the thought of something happening to Rah's baby girl.

"Was Rahima in the dream?" Mama takes a few small vials from one of the many cabinets lining the walls of the tiny house and places them on the kitchen table. She then opens them and sprinkles their contents on her sweets.

"Yeah, but she was a couple of years older. And Rah and I had a newborn. Weird, I know." When I think about it, that was only a couple of years from now.

"Not really. You love him and his daughter very much. It's only natural that you'd dream about them," Mama says, mixing batter in the large, metal bowl. It looks like she's making cupcakes now.

"If that's the case then why were Esmeralda and Misty there? I have no love for them."

"There how?" Mama asks, glancing in the direction of Esmeralda's house next door. Her forehead crinkles up like she's worried about something. She then whispers under her breath and returns to her work.

"For starters, Esmeralda looked at me while I was walking down the aisle toward Rah and gave me back my headache." Just thinking about it makes my head hurt.

"I see," Mama says, almost breaking the wooden spoon in her hand. Something else must've happened that she's not telling me about and I'm not sure I want to know. "Take your pills, Jayd, and try to focus on staying cool in your dreams, no matter what happens. Our enemies are working every angle they can to get to you, which is why you shouldn't be alone with that baby anymore until this is all over."

"But Mama, I would never hurt Rahima. You know that." Not intentionally, but I know she's right.

"Of course I know that, baby. And I'm not worried about the child; I'm worried about you. Children are very close to the ancestors and bring them into the world with them when they're born. The younger the child the closer they are to the source, and Rahima has that protection all around her, like you did when you were a baby. We want you to take care of yourself fully before you take care of anyone else, children included."

"But what about Rahima? Are you saying I can't see her anymore?" Mama pauses before answering my question. She looks like she's choosing her words very carefully for my sake.

"It's like when you're on a plane and they tell you to put the oxygen mask on your face before strapping it onto anyone else's. How can you protect another individual if you yourself need protecting?"

"I get that. I don't like it, but I get it." I look at the bottle of pills on the counter and pray that whatever's in them works. With every passing day I feel myself slipping away, and everyone that I love right along with me.

"The Williams' legacy has always been tainted by one weakness, which is also our greatest strength—love—and our enemies know this. Esmeralda knows your weak spot, Jayd, and she's not above using any and every opportunity that presents itself to exploit it. The door is wide open as long as your focus is distracted. Unfortunately, Rah and his daughter are big distractions. And so are your other friends. Don't make it so easy for her to get to you through them."

"But if she can get at me from every angle, how can I keep her from hurting me? This is too much for me to handle alone." Tears well up in my eyes and I want to break down, but I know that won't help. Mama reaches her left hand across the table and pats my right one. She then takes some of the flour in the canister on the table and pours it onto the wooden surface, like she's about to roll dough over it. She reclaims my hand and sticks out my index finger, using it to draw a pattern in the flour that begins to look familiar.

"You have everything you need inside of you at all times," she says as the symbol for Legba becomes clear on the table. "How easily we forget all of the power we were born with once the world gets a hold of us. And the older you get, the harder it will become to remember these lessons."

"But you remember," I say. I wish Mama would just cast a spell of her own and make this entire experience disappear.

"I can only do so much for you, chile," she says as if she heard my request. "You have to finish this madness by yourself. Of course I'll help you as much as I can. But some battles are more personal than others."

"Why would the orisha allow all of this mess to happen to me?" I know I sound naïve, but I don't understand the point of receiving a gift to then be tortured with it. What kind of blessing is that?

"No orisha is good or bad, including Legba. He's the opener/closer, as my godfather used to say. He will open a door and you, as the seeker, have to make the choice whether or not to go through it. You've allowed several things to open up, making yourself vulnerable to what energy ends up coming through after you. Like I said before, don't make it so easy for your enemies to get to you." She takes the cupcake pan out from under the sink and places it on the table. "And as far as your dreams go, you will have to go through several past experiences and a future one to figure out exactly how to change your present, or immediate past in this case." This sounds like some fairy-tale shit to me. Mama finishes the cupcake batter and returns her attention to layering the pudding.

"But, Mama, if I recall correctly, in the Christmas episode of one of my favorite television shows, *Vegas,* the fine black dude only went through one past, present, and future experience. Why do I have to go through more past experiences than he did?" Completely frustrated with my naïveté, Mama drops her spatula down in the bowl and rolls her eyes at me.

"First of all, little girl, *A Christmas Carol* is the original name of the story that show was based off of. And second, that was them and this is you." Mama looks at the small, fluffy cloud of egg whites and sugar, and decides she needs more meringue for the top of the pudding. She gently cracks the eggs, carefully separating the yolk from the white. She glances across the kitchen table at the sugar and sifter. "Pass me the sugar, Jayd," she says as I instinctively hand the items to her before she can finish her request.

"Here you go," I say, watching Mama work her magic. I hope this client appreciates Mama's work as much as I do. This pudding looks like it's going to be good. "But Mama, I'm serious. Why do I have to see all of the stuff that happened before I was born? What does that have to do with what's going on now?"

"Now I know you didn't just ask me that." My past and the past of my ancestors are linked in more ways than one.

"Yes, I did. I mean, what's the point of finally getting some real sleep and having dreams, if they only turn out to be nightmares about the doomed love lives of all the women in our lineage? Who wants to have dreams like that every night? I might never sleep well again."

"Didn't you learn something from the vision we shared with Maman? You learned what can happen when jealousy takes over. Now you have to do the same thing with these dreams. They're your lessons, Jayd. Learn from them."

"I'd rather sleepwalk," I say, listening to my stomach growl. I'm in no mood for a history lesson right now.

"You don't mean that and I know it. Besides, this is only phase one of your transformation. I know how Esmeralda works and she's a lot smarter than she acts."

"Phase one?" What the hell? "Do I look like *Blade*? I'm not trying to change into anything."

"Jayd, you don't have a choice. Esmeralda's curse is forcing us to move you ahead in your spirit lessons to save not only yourself but also our lineage. You have to master your powers sooner than later, and I'm here to make sure you do it right, uncomfortable dreams and all."

"But Mama," I whine. But she's not having it.

"Girl, don't test me. That shit didn't work when you were two years old and it isn't going to work now, so get over it. Here, drink this," she says, passing me a tall bottle of apple cider vinegar with some twigs floating around in it. What the hell is that?

"I'm actually full," I say. The very sight of the thick brew is making the few cornflakes I did digest turn in my stomach. The last thing I feel like doing is swallowing that shit.

"Did it sound like a choice?" Mama passes me a shot glass from the dish rack on the counter next to the sink, and continues spreading the meringue over the pudding. I twist off the bottle top and air escapes the strong concoction, causing bubbles to fizz at the top. I pour a small amount into the glass and Mama's eyes tell me to keep pouring. After the glass is full, I quickly take the shot to the head, swallowing the bitter drink down in one swift gulp.

"Yuck!" I exclaim. Mama laughs at my reaction, but is pleased that I took it. "What was that for?" I ask, twisting the top back on the bottle and pushing it across the table to Mama.

"It'll help thicken your blood and fortify your body in other ways, too." Mama puts the last of the meringue on the pudding, making my mouth water, especially with the bitter taste still fresh on my tongue.

"My blood is fine. It's my mouth that could use the help." Mama smiles at me, rising from her stool and replacing the bottle on the counter.

"Your mouth needs help in more ways than one." Mama can be sarcastic when she wants to, just like anyone else. She turns the dial on the stove to preheat the oven for baking.

"But Mama, isn't making this food and having your client do this ritual the same thing that Esmeralda and Misty did to me?"

"No, because I'd give this to my granddaughter," Mama says, rolling her eyes at my line of questioning.

"I'm just saying."

"Well, don't. Believe me, Jayd, Esmeralda doesn't want a taste of what she's dishing out to you through Misty. She's taking advantage of that girl, but Misty's mother left her vulnerable, and when her grandmother was alive she was no help either. You have to take care of yourself spiritually or you leave yourself vulnerable to anything. We fortify you, child. Your ancestors, your elders, your family. We give you support, and that's why I do what I do everyday. I do it so my lineage lives on."

"Okay, I get all of that. But doesn't your client's man have a right to know what he's eating?" Mama looks weary but continues with her explanation.

"That man is sleeping his future away. All my client wants to do is help him get a jumpstart on their life together. There's nothing wrong about helping someone to wake up from the living dead. Some people are out here just walking around asleep with their eyes wide open. They don't know who they are or why they are here. Those are voluntary zombies, as far as I'm concerned, and if I don't help to wake them up, someone else will. Speaking of which," Mama says, opening the oven and pulling out a mini pudding and handing it to me.

"So you do love me after all," I say, biting into the tasty treat. This tastes damn good. I love the fact that Mama whips her bananas smooth, unlike most banana puddings that have chunks in them.

"More than you know." Mama's eyes look into mine and I can see my reflection bouncing off the green glow. As I continue to look into Mama's eyes I see Maman's eyes inside of them, looking back at me. It's as if the energy of our ancestors is alive and recognizable in her eyes in a way that I've never seen before. "It's time for you to get inside, little Jayd."

Mama breaks our stare-down and concentrates on finishing her baking. I know she had to feel that connection as strongly as I just did. Maybe that's why, when I dreamt about my mom moving out of Mama's house, it was Maman who was in Mama's place. I don't know what was in that drink I just downed, but it's got me feeling a bit buzzed.

"As you already know, your head carries your Ori, which is your personal link to the creator. And the shrine is a representation of that connection. Here, take this with you and give it to your head," Mama says with a smile of recognition on her face. It's another personal-sized pudding for my head orisha, Oshune.

"I guess Oshune likes this dessert, too," I say, smelling the tasty treat. It's going to be hard to give this one up.

"Of course she does. She likes what you like, and vice versa. You are one and the same. The sooner you realize that, the quicker your powers will develop. Now run along. We've both got work to do."

I grab my school bag and purse and head out the door into the backyard. There's nothing in the house to eat, and my one little pudding didn't do anything to help end my hunger. Luckily my mom's ride can easily solve my involuntary hunger strike by taking me to get something to eat after I feed my orisha. I don't know what I'd do without my mom.

"Hey, sweety. I'm glad you think so, because I need for you to come to dinner with me at Karl's mom's house on Friday. Some family thing, and I'm going to need you there with me. Mothers always hate me."

"They don't like me much either, in case you've forgotten," I say, returning the thought. *"I don't know if I'd be much help."*

"The in-laws are usually easier on the new wife if they see she's a good mom. So you'll be there, right?"

"In-laws? Did I miss a step?"

"Not really, but I'm hopeful for Valentine's Day. Besides, wanting me to meet his family is a huge step, and you should be there to witness it. Come on, Jayd. When have I ever asked you for anything? Oh, and that reminds me, I'm going to need you to hook my hair up before we go, if you're feeling better. So, get on it, girl. We've got a ring to get and no future mother-in-law of mine is keeping it from my finger," my mom says, leaving my head just as quickly as she entered it. I could care less about Valentine's Day, but if she likes it I love it for her. But seriously, will these holidays ever end?

I'm so happy it's Friday, I don't know what to do. With the exception of my friends' drama it's been an okay week. I decided to leave Chance alone about him and Nellie consummating their relationship until I'm in better space to deal with the impending bell that's going to eventually ring. And ever since I informed Mickey that I couldn't help her deal with her relationship with Nigel through magic, she's been avoiding me like the plague.

It's not my fault Mickey doesn't understand how we get down in Mama's house. What's even stranger is that she and Misty seem to tolerate each other in public now, which is highly unusual. Although Mickey's attending the continuation school on the lower campus, which is on the other side of the football field, I guess she's still allowed to come up here for lunch, and she hasn't missed a day yet.

Nigel seems to be warming up to her a bit more, but they are not completely back to being all good, or so it looks to me from a distance. I know Nigel's dealing with a lot. Tonight's football game is the first one where he's actually going to sit on the bench and watch from the sidelines. Pissed doesn't begin to explain his current feelings toward the administration, and from what I'm hearing from Rah, he still blames Mickey for most of the shit.

Rah and I aren't back to normal either, but I have a little bit more sympathy for his ass than Nigel does for Mickey, and rightfully so. Rah has to go to Sandy's arraignment today and I know when it comes down to it he's not going to let the mother of his child stay in jail over charges he filed. He would expect the same loyalty from her, even if I doubt she'd be as generous.

"What's up, lady? Where's your head at this morning?" Jeremy asks. It's lunchtime and everyone's paired off or in a group except for me.

"In the clouds. What's up with you?" I ask, looking up at him from where I'm sitting under a tree next to the library. It's a great spot to sit and think when I don't want to be bothered by anyone. I noticed him, Matt, Seth, and Chance heading to the parking lot to do whatever it is they do, but I was too caught up in my own world to acknowledge them with more than a nod. Seeing Jeremy in third period last semester was enough. But now that I have him and the rest of the Too Live Crew that Misty rolls with in debate class, school has been overwhelming, to say the least.

"Nothing much. We were going to get some Mexican food if you want to roll with us." I haven't been off campus for lunch in a while, and if Jeremy's inviting me then he must be paying, too.

"What the hell. I haven't worked in a couple of weeks and could use the treat," I say, listening to my growling stomach second the motion.

"A little hungry?" Jeremy teases, reaching his hand out to help me up off the grass. "And cold." It's a nice day but still a bit chilly to be sitting outside. I didn't notice how cold my hands were until he said something.

"You're right," I say, zipping my North Face jacket up and handing him my backpack. We walk toward the rest of his waiting crew, only to see Nellie has joined them. What fun this is going to be.

"Ah, baby, I didn't know she was coming. Honest," Jeremy says, instantly aware of the tense vibe. It's sweet of him to be concerned about my comfort, but I think he's more concerned about me going off at the mouth in the restaurant and embarrassing him. Whatever the case, I intend on keeping a cool head no matter how hot I may want to become.

"No worries. I'm a big girl and I can handle her." I take Jeremy's hand as we walk down the steep hill toward the back parking lot near the theater. I can't wait until the next festival this spring. We haven't returned to our regular schedule in drama class yet, but we do know what our next play is going to be. Mrs. Sinclair's too wrapped up in the semester change, like most of the other teachers, to really care what we do this week. Thank God it's Friday, because I know next week all of the teachers will be back on their game, and that means I will have to be on mine, too.

"What's up with you, Jayd?" Chance says, choosing to give me the Obama fist bump instead of a hug. Wise choice.

"Nothing much. Hi, Nellie," I say, trying to make nice. But her rude ass chooses to play deaf and that's just fine with me. I wish she'd play invisible so we could have a diva-free lunch, but I doubt that'll happen. Where is her clique anyway? I'm surprised she's hanging with Chance and his friends. But I guess hanging with the rich potheads on campus is also good for her image.

"Last one to the restaurant pays for everyone's drinks." Matt's got jokes. If this were my crew rolling, that wouldn't even be funny. But with Jeremy and his friends, money's something to be gambled at will.

"So how do you like your new schedule?" Jeremy asks, opening the passenger's door and letting me in his classic ride. I miss rolling in the Mustang on a daily basis, but my mom's car is cool. And nothing beats being able to take myself in and out of any situation. I wish I could master that art with my dreams.

"It is what it is," I say when he joins me inside of the vehicle. He starts the car and we follow the caravan of students out of the crowded lot. "Different semester, same school."

"I feel you on that one," he says, catching up to Chance's Nova, the leader of the pack. Matt, Seth, and Nigel each rev their engines, ready to race the two miles to the burrito spot. These boys have way too much time on their hands. "What do you think about the debate class?" I know that's not his real question. What Jeremy wants to know is what do I think of Mr. Adewale. He already knows I think our new teacher is beautiful. But what he doesn't know is that we have an ancestral connection that supersedes the typical teacher/student relationship.

"I think it's interesting at the very least. We've got some characters in our class, that's for sure." With Misty and all of South Central as our classmates, I'm sure the debates will be hot topics every day. I just hope Mr. A can control it. But after the way he checked Del earlier this week, I think he's got it down.

"Yeah, I think it should be very interesting. I'm just glad I get to sit next to you in two classes back to back," he says, taking his right hand off of the leather steering wheel and placing it on my left thigh. I look up at Jeremy's olive complexion and notice he's sporting a five o'clock shadow. How sexy is that?

"Well, like I said, it should be interesting." I reach up and stroke the stubble growing on his cheek. The roughness feels good against the back of my hand. Jeremy stops my hand in mid-stroke. He takes my hand with the one that was formerly keeping my thigh company and kisses my knuckles.

"I miss you, Jayd," he confesses as we pull into the parking lot. Everyone's rushing to get inside first, as if paying for six drinks will break any of these fools. Jeremy turns off the engine and sits back in his seat. I guess we know who the loser's going to be.

"Did I go somewhere?"

"Yeah. Away from us. Why is that, by the way?"

"Jeremy, we've been through this. Besides, aren't you concerned about losing this bet y'all have got going on?" I reach over to open my door, but not before Jeremy can turn my face toward his and plant a big kiss on me. I allow his lips to mesh with mine, matching him move for move. I don't want to pull away but I feel like I should.

"Let's go," Nigel says, knocking on Jeremy's window and

interrupting our flow. I wish Nigel hadn't seen us kissing because I know he's going to give Rah a full report.

Once inside we all stare at the menu like we've never been here before. We each have our favorites and usually stick to the norm. Nellie and Chance order first with everyone else following suit. Jeremy orders last so all the drinks can be on his tab.

"At least he's a man of his word," Nigel whispers in my ear. "But he's still not a nigga, if you get me."

"Yeah, I get you loud and clear." When will Nigel get over the fact that I'm kicking it with a white boy? "I hope you realize that you're kicking it with white boys now, too." He looks at me like I just called him a bitch. He needs to get used to it. When in Rome, do as the Romans. Isn't that how the saying goes? I know this isn't Europe, but Redondo Beach is still a foreign country to us and we need to survive, white friends included.

When we get back to campus we have less than one minute before the bell rings. Luckily most of us have drama class, which is on the west end of the large campus, near where we're parked. If college campuses are any bigger than this property, I'm going to be one fit sistah by the time I graduate. Nellie and Jeremy are the only two who have to hike up the hill to their classes, but neither of them look too concerned about getting there on time. When Matt, Seth, and Nellie leave, Nigel says his good-byes, too.

"Hey, both of you are invited to my official pre–Super Bowl party tomorrow night," Nigel says to Chance and Jeremy. I never need an invitation. "Come with your cash in hand. There's a pool for each team." What is it with boys, sports, and losing all of their money betting on them? I'm sure Rah's in on this bet, too. I know Nigel's torn between his loyalty for Rah and his new friendship with Jeremy. But when it comes down to it, Nigel's my friend too, and I hope he remembers that before he goes blabbing to Rah about unnecessary shit.

"Hey, thanks, man," Chance says, giving him the nod of approval.

"Thanks, man, but I've already got plans tomorrow night. Next time though," Jeremy says. Plans? What kind of plans does he have on a Saturday night and with who?

"You want to hang out tonight, Lady J?" Jeremy asks with the sweetest look in his eyes.

"I'm sorry, but I already have plans." They may be with my mom, but he doesn't need the details.

"You sure have been busy lately. It's turning me on," he says, bending down and planting a kiss on me as the bell rings. "I'll call you later."

"Okay," I say, smiling from our lip lock. I have half a mind to tell my mom I can't make it this evening, but I can't let her down. Besides, if I stay home it's going to be to catch up on some much-needed sleep. Jeremy can wait until I'm back on my game.

When I get to my mom's house she's got clothes everywhere. It looks like a bebe tornado hit this place hard. I set my bags down and look for my mom amidst the destruction that is her bedroom.

"Mom, are you in here?" I ask, picking up skirts, dresses, and shoes off the floor and returning them to their place in the closet.

"Jayd, are you ready to do my hair? We've only got an hour before Karl gets here and I still have to do my nails." My mom's so nervous. I've never seen her like this before. "And get me a glass of wine, please. Oh, and don't let me forget the bottle of cognac for his father, on the table."

"Mom, calm down. It's just a family dinner. It's not like you're going to a hater's convention or something," I say, trying to make my mom laugh, but she's far from laughing.

"Jayd, the biggest hater a woman will have to deal with in life is the mother of the man she's going to marry. It's the oldest jealousy relationship in existence and it's not going anywhere anytime soon." I can tell that from the way both Rah and Jeremy's moms deal with me. They hate on me and I'm just a girlfriend. I can only imagine how they'd treat me if I married one of them fools.

"Well, in that case I think I'll sit this dinner out. I have enough hating of my own to deal with. Besides, I still need to catch up on my sleep," I say, yawning and stretching out on her bed. I managed to clear a spot for me to sit down among the designer clothes.

"Oh, baby, I'm sorry I didn't ask how you are. I've been so wrapped up in my own mess, I didn't consider you may be too tired to go with us. Have your friends starting acting right yet?" she asks, exiting her room, and I'm inclined to follow. She takes my hair bag out of the hall closet and walks into the dining room, ready for a quick press and curl.

"Nah. They're all tripping." I take out my tools and set up at the dining room table.

"You can still try the punch, you know. I made it for you anyway, just in case you needed it." She walks over and opens the refrigerator, taking out a clear pitcher with a thick liquid inside.

"Thanks, Mom." I plug in the miniature oven to warm up the hot combs. As soon as she leaves I'm going to pass out on the couch and not move until tomorrow afternoon, or at least I hope so.

"You'll love the results. It's like having a camcorder in your head. Try finding that at Best Buy," my mom says, stirring the red brew. She cuts up some lemon and puts in a dab of honey, for luck I guess. "Almost there," she says, tasting the punch with the wooden spoon. She then puts enough sugar in it for ten bags of Kool-Aid. "Perfect. Read up on it in my notes and you'll see the benefits of being able to walk in your friends' dreams. Now come on, I've got to get going. Karl will be here any minute." We'll see how this punch works at Nigel's party tomorrow. If all goes well, I should be able to fix some of what they've broken.

~ 9 ~
Santa Baby

"I really do believe in you/
Let's see if you believe in me."

—EARTHA KITT

By the time my mom left last night I was ready to pass out, and I did just that. I slept most of the day away too, only getting up to eat. When Rah picked me up a little while ago for Nigel's party I was more than ready to get out of the house. I'm also anxious to try out my mom's punch on the crew. It'll have to wait until we get inside and chill out. Right now, the boys are too busy showing off their toys.

"Hey man, Santa was real good to me this year, you hear me?" Chance says, bumping his sound system and shaking the entire block. The new bling slides down his arm as he waves his hands up in the air like he's at a T.I. concert. I wonder if that thing can still tell time with all of those diamonds in it.

"Yeah, I do. What kind of system you got in that joint, fool? And where's the old one?"

"Ah, man, you know this is Kenwood, baby. And I gave the other one to my little cousin. We don't mind hand-me-down gifts in my family, know what I'm saying?"

"I'm sure y'all don't," I say. I'm not a hater, but damn. How much extra money does one family need?

"Ah, Jayd, I told you I'll hook you up. Just say when," Chance says, putting his arms around my shoulders, instantly pissing both Rah and Nellie off. I'm glad Jeremy couldn't make it; otherwise I'd be catching his hater rays, too. Feeling the heat, Nigel switches the subject back to sports and food, two of any dude's favorite subjects.

"Come on, man. We can watch some college ball and get our grub on. I'm getting the munchies," Nigel says, leading the way into his house. We walk up the stairs and into his large room, ready to settle in for the evening.

"I brought some punch," I say, putting the container on the table while everyone gets comfortable. We all have issues with one another, but we're trying to keep the peace, for now.

"Is it spiked?" Nigel asks, checking the punch out from afar.

"If it was, do you think I'd give it to your pregnant girlfriend?" I look at Mickey, who follows suit. I hope this works. I need to change a few things in all of our actions over the past couple of months. And since we've had such an effect on one another I need to get into everyone's head tonight. I wish Misty were here, but she'll have to get the trickle-down effects of this spell. I pour everyone a cup and prepare to walk in their dreams.

"Tastes like Kool-Aid," Chance says, making him and Nigel laugh hard. I think it was mostly funny because they're high.

"How would you know?" Mickey asks, throwing punches at the white boy in the room. I guess she'll take cheap shots at Chance as a warm-up to roasting on Nellie for the rest of the evening, not that she needs warming up. Mickey's got plenty of ammunition, and with Nellie's new attitude and attire, I know Mickey's just waiting for the right moment to dig into Nellie's ass.

"Hey, we drink Kool-Aid at our house too," Chance says a little defensively. Ever since he landed Nellie after jocking her for many months, he's been a bit sensitive about being the token white boy in our crew. It's not like he didn't know what he was getting himself into when he started hanging out with us.

"Okay, y'all, be cool. We're supposed to be celebrating our boy getting the motion back in his shoulder," I say. I don't want the party to take a turn for the worse before I have a chance to see if this stuff works. We need to get our drink on and fast. I don't know how much longer we can all stay in a room together and keep the peace.

"And just being alive, nigga. On the real," Nigel says solemnly. Mickey gulps down her share, ready for seconds, but there are none. My mom made enough for everyone to get their fair share, plus some. I know Mickey feels guilty about Nigel's arm and wants to make it right, but she just doesn't know how. Nigel has barely spoken a word to her since she got here and she looks uncomfortable.

"Now I'll drink to that," Rah says, raising his glass to Nigel's. We all follow suit and finish the first round. Nigel takes the remote from the nightstand next to the futon where he's sitting and turns the music up. Nigel must be in quite a mood to play Sade all night. She's my uncle Bryan's favorite songstress and I love her, too. It's also the perfect music to help lay us all out.

"I used to have a copy of this CD but I think one of my brothers stole it," Mickey says, passing the freshly rolled blunt Nigel just gave her and officially starting the rotation. I hope smoking won't affect the punch.

"I hate it when that happens," I say. I'm probably the only other person in the room who can relate to what Mickey goes through on a daily basis, living in a house full of family. Everyone else in this room is either an only child—which I am from my mother—or has only one sibling to deal with. But being raised with my mother's brothers has not allowed me to ever truly feel like the only one.

"I love being the only child. I gets all of the attention,"

Chance says, putting his hands behind his head like he's big daddy. The long, embroidered sleeve of his new Sean Jean shirt slides back again, revealing his new diamond-encrusted watch.

"Damn, nigga, that's a lot of ice," Nigel says, peeping the shiny platinum timepiece from across the room. Nellie smiles at the sight of someone envying her man. She's turned into quite a trick.

"Yeah. It was a good holiday. I'm not complaining," he says, smiling big like he hit the jackpot this year. I'm glad one of us did. As soon as this punch settles in I can see what everyone else truly wants from Santa, even if he is hella late this year. But I guess it's better late than never.

"Man, what's in that blunt? I feel like passing out, and we didn't even get our munch on yet," Rah says, stretching out on the futon he and I are sitting on. We haven't seen each other since last weekend and we haven't talked about our plans for Valentine's Day, or Mickey and Nigel's issues, since then either. The only conversation we've had has been about the mundane daily shit. I wonder if Mickey even knows about Nigel possibly being transferred out of South Bay High if his shoulder doesn't heal? Probably not, since Nigel's barely speaking to her. He hasn't looked her in the eye since she's been here and she's feeling the neglect.

"Some of your shit, fool. What else?" The secret ingredient isn't wrapped up in that cigar paper but they don't need to know that. I casually take over hosting duties since Nigel and Rah look unable to help anyone out. Just as well. They need to relax and let it take over. The sooner I can get in their heads the quicker I can begin to unravel this hell we've created.

"More punch?" I ask, topping off everyone's cup except my own. The spirit book says I, as the seer, shouldn't have any. The more everyone else takes the deeper their dreams will be. I want to make sure everyone gets their fair share so we can get down to the root of our problems and solve them before Misty and Esmeralda completely destroy my crew.

Before I even finish pouring the second round Chance is knocked out and Rah isn't far behind.

"Man, I can see why Sade named this track 'Punch Drunk'," Nigel says, almost slurring his words he's so relaxed. "It makes you feel straight." I look at Mickey staring at Nigel and wonder what she's thinking. As I focus on her eyes, they begin to give in to their sleepiness and she and Nigel both fall into a quick slumber. Nellie's the only one who's resisting the urge to chill, but she can only hold out for so much longer. I focus on the rhythmic tones of the saxophone playing in the background, intent on Nellie falling asleep. I glance over at Rah, sleeping next to me. I can't wait to get in his head, but Chance is the first to invite me in.

"His mother's father was a black man and she had a rough time. I guess she thinks baby Chase will have a better chance at living a good life with someone else," the woman says, holding an infant Chance in her arms for the couple to see.

"Chance, that's his name. Chase is so common," Chance's adopted mother says, holding her arms out, ready to receive her son. The father, on the other hand, doesn't look so sure he's ready to accept the new arrival.

"Look, we wanted a son that would look like us. We don't necessarily want everyone knowing we adopted a child. Won't his other side start to show?" At least he's honest about his issues with black people, which is more than I can say for a lot of people I meet.

"No, not necessarily. I didn't know the mother was half black when I met her. She just looks like an average young white lady. I mean, can you tell this baby has any black blood?" They look down at the tiny infant swaddled in a blue blanket and their eyes melt at the precious sight.

"All I see is the perfect Christmas gift. Tom, write the lady a check. We're taking our son home." Wow. I wonder if Chance knows this is his true Christmas story? Does he even know he's adopted, let alone part black? That would explain a lot, but damn, I didn't ask to see all of this. I thought I was just supposed to see what they were wishing about, not shit they've been through and may not even remember.

"Oh, you can't control that, Jayd. Just relax and go with the flow. Whatever's there for you to see, you will observe. Don't worry about anything else," my mom says, quickly checking in and out. I know she's still recovering from her night of drunken bliss with Karl and his family. I'm glad they had a good time without me. *"Remember, you asked how to help your friends and this is the answer. It may not be what you expected, but it is what you asked for. Good night."*

"Later, Mom," I think back. Rah is still out cold and not making a sound, which means I can't get into his head yet. I can't seem to penetrate Nigel's dreams either. Maybe he didn't drink enough of my mother's concoction. I turn my attention to Nellie, who's not giving it up, either, even though she's now asleep, too.

"Remember, you have to be invited in when they start talking in their sleep," my mom says. And these three aren't saying a word. Mickey's the only one left. I hear her uttering something and that's all I need to jump in her head.

"I'm Nickey Shantae, your goddaughter. You don't recognize me?" the little girl in Mickey's dream asks me. There's a glow around her head that reminds me of being in my mother's womb. Mickey's daughter is a caul child? I wonder if Mickey is conscious of just how special this child really is. The little girl looks dead at me and I can see her clearly now. Unlike in Chance's dream, I'm not witnessing what hap-

pened in the past but rather I'm an active participant in this vision from the future.

"Hello. Earth to Jayd," Nickey Shantae says to me, but I'm still stuck on the fact that this child is talking to me through her mother's dream. *"Look, all I want for Christmas, my birthday, and any other holiday is for my mama and daddy to be together—end of story. And as my godmother you're supposed to make that happen."* Even if she weren't the spitting image of Mickey, I can tell it's her child by the way she talks. I'm definitely going to have to get myself together so I can be a steady influence in this child's life, because she's going to need it.

"Nickey, your birthday is not a holiday. And I'm not sure I can make that happen." Mostly because at this point no one knows for sure who her daddy is. But she doesn't need to know all of that.

"Why not? Because my mama's not sure my daddy's the real daddy?" I guess she can hear everything that's going on from the womb, just like I could. We caul kids really need to come together and form our own crew. We can have international chapters and all. *"Jayd, I wasn't born yesterday and neither were you. Our destinies were decided ages ago and mine doesn't stop here, you feel me?"* She hasn't been born at all, but who am I to tell her that?

"How old are you?" I ask the mini boss bitch. She's cute, but if she keeps rolling her neck at me, I'm going to check her, dream or not.

"Eight going on eighty," she says, like that's her real age. I'm sure by the time she's really eight she'll have heard that very thing time and time again.

"You sure are demanding for an eight year old."

"Wait until you meet me at sixteen. My mom's going to send me to live with you for a while. But that's another story. The point of this little visit is for you to make sure that

my mama and the man we are choosing to be my daddy stay together, you got it? I've got little brothers and sisters depending on this working out."

"Well, when you put it like that," I say, smiling at the mini Mickey. She is a cutie. Besides, I know she's really speaking on her mother's behalf. It is, after all, Mickey's dream. And I think I've had all I can take from her mind for one night.

I can understand Mickey's child coming to me on behalf of her parents, but how is knowing Chance is adopted and part black going to help me get my friends back together again? And how am I supposed to keep all of this to myself? Since no one else is inviting me in and the drink is now wearing off I think I'll catch some sleep with my friends. Lord knows I need it after what I just saw.

Last night's pre–Super Bowl party had all of us hung over today, some more than others. I'm still recovering from the dream sharing. By the time I woke up yesterday morning, Rah, Nigel, and I were the only ones left. If it weren't for Nigel's begging me to braid him up today I would still be in my cozy spot on my mother's couch. Instead, I'm out so early on a Sunday morning.

"Hey, watch where you're going," I say to the car in front of me. The driver can't hear me, but I know he heard my loud horn. It's too early to have road rage, but Crenshaw Boulevard's always packed, no matter what time of day it is. I turn my iPod up and try to focus on the road ahead, almost to Lafayette Square, one of the most exclusive neighborhoods for wealthy folks who still want to live near the hood.

Nigel's still not allowed to have any friends over—with his parents' knowledge—who got him caught up, me included. Rah's exempt because he's practically family, but I'm sure Mr. and Mrs. Esop aren't too happy with him, either. I know

Nigel's having me come over this early because his mom and dad are steady churchgoers, even if he says it's because the game party he and his family are going to is in the Hollywood Hills and they have to leave early. I'm not tripping. As long as I get paid the same money, I'm not sweating the small stuff.

Now that I know Mickey's baby is going to be my spiritual godchild, I've got to intervene in their tattered relationship. When Nigel called me this morning to ask me to braid his hair, I thought it would be the perfect way to get inside his head and see what he's really thinking about, since he didn't let me in last night. I don't care what he's going through. He can't just leave our girl and her baby out in the cold.

Brothers always think that when they're going through some madness the whole world should stop and pay homage. Whatever. Nigel's going to find out the world doesn't revolve around him, and that the baby takes precedence over everything now, funky attitudes included.

"What's up, Nigel," I say, entering the foyer of his classic home. If his parents weren't mad at me for the role they think I played in Mickey trapping their son, I might be able to kick it over here more often, which I wouldn't mind. I never really got to try out the game room. And it looks like it's complete, from what I can see through the open door to my right. I can hear someone fumbling around in the kitchen. Maybe it's the maid. I know his mom isn't the cleaning or cooking type.

"Jayd, thank you for coming over on such short notice. I've been meaning to get this head dealt with. I'm just glad it's you braiding it and not some stranger," Nigel says, leading me up the stairs to his private fortress.

"Me too," I say, thankful I can help. If Mama hadn't given me the psychic clearance to braid again it would be a stranger up in his head, and that's never a good thing when someone's trying to heal. And the dream-sharing with my friends really took a toll on me, but it was interesting, to say the least. I should've just stayed here, had I known he'd want me to come right back.

"Hey, Nigel," Tasha says, surprising us both—or so I think. Nigel doesn't look nearly as shocked as I think he should.

"Hey, girl," he says casually.

"I picked up your favorite snacks and the movies for tonight after the game. I'll be right back," she says, smiling at me as she walks out of the room without directly acknowledging me. Oh no, this trick isn't back in Nigel's life. What the hell's going on around here?

"I know what you're going to say," Nigel begins, but not before I can smack him in the head with my comb.

"Damn right you know what I'm thinking, because you should be thinking the same thing. What is your ex-girlfriend doing here when you have a pregnant girlfriend at home, crushed?"

"My mom called Tasha when I got shot, and she's been here almost every night, no drama included."

"Oh no, Nigel. Mickey is sprung on your ass and thinks you feel the same way about her."

"I did, until her man came after me and Rah with a gun. Besides, I don't even know if the baby's mine, and when that nigga gets out, I don't want to be anywhere around." I'm glad Nickey Shantae can't hear this.

"Well, you should have thought about that before, Nigel," I say, smacking him in the head harder than usual. "Have you lost your damn mind? Mickey's hard enough to deal with as it is, and now you're going to drop this shit on her?"

"Man, forget her. She wasn't thinking about me when she got us into this mess. Why should I care about what she's going through?" Tasha walks back into the room with a tray full of snacks, like she's been serving him all his life. I refuse to discuss this in front of her ass.

"How many braids do you want?" I ask, pulling his hair back hard.

"Ouch, girl," Nigel says.

"Is it your shoulder, baby?" Tasha asks, almost throwing the tray down on the table to rush to his side. What the hell?

"Baby?" They both look at me and I look at Nigel, who knows he's stepped over the line now. They're back sleeping together. I can feel it.

"I'm okay, Tasha. Would you mind getting my medicine from the kitchen? I think it's time for another dose." Tasha looks from Nigel to me and then back at Nigel, like she wants to say or do something but he won't let her. I wish the trick would step to me. It'll be the last time she steps in those shoes if she does.

When Tasha leaves the room Nigel begins his begging fest. We're cool, but I'm not his boy and he can't expect me to hold this information for him.

"You know you're tripping, right?"

"Come on, Jayd. I know you understand."

"The hell I do. I'm not your boy, lest you forget. And as I recall, Mickey didn't hold a gun to your head when y'all first met. So man up and take responsibility for your shit," I say, packing up my hair tools. "I can't braid in this environment. You'll have to come to me if you want your crown kept, no hussies allowed." I storm out of his room, down the stairs and out the front door. I'm so glad I have access to a car now, I don't know what to do.

Putting the key into the lock, my head starts pounding like another headache from hell. And with it comes the vision of Mickey's daughter talking to me through Mickey's dream. As her godmother I'm supposed to help her destiny manifest, and part of that destiny is making sure Nigel and Mickey stay together. I don't know how, but I've got to keep my friends together for the sake of their unborn child. But heffas sure can make that task more difficult than it already is.

~ 10 ~
5 Golden Rings

*"Looking like she is the queen of the Nile/
Like she wanna be the mother of my voodoo child."*

—BIG BABATUNDE

Yesterday was a quiet day once I got back to Compton and I caught up on my homework last night. This new semester has taken off regardless of our personal issues. Work still has to get done and I'm the only one who can do what I do. For a Monday it wasn't bad at all. My sleep has been improving and I'm glad for it. I took my bath and I'm ready to hit the sack. Thank God one school day is already behind me. Maybe the rest of the week will be just as quiet as today was, and it all starts with a good night's sleep.

"I'm so glad we had a daughter," the woman says, opening the baby blanket and revealing a pink-cheeked newborn child. "She's the best gift we could've asked for."

"I agree," the father says. He looks eerily familiar, and for some reason I feel I know this little girl, and not just because I'm her nanny in this vision. "I'm especially glad that she has your eyes. Here, darling, why don't you take little Judy and wash her up." Maman's lover passes the baby to me, and I instinctively take her in my arms. I can't believe my ancestors had to do this shit on a regular basis. If I had to care for someone's child and household for next to nothing I think I'd go crazy.

"And could you please run my bath water and fix my husband's evening drink. I'm just too tired to move," the woman says. What the hell has she done all day except order me—or whoever I'm supposed to be—around all day? "And would you be a dear and iron my laundry after you're done collecting the clothes from the line? And don't forget to wash the baby's diapers twice. I just hate it when they don't get completely clean. And don't forget we have to prepare the place settings for our guests. You know my Christmas Eve dinner is always to die for, and this year will be no exception." If she says "and" to me one more time I'm going to forget about why I'm really in this dream state and go after her, ghetto style, and whip her ass.

"Girl, do you hear my wife talking to you?" They both look at me as if I've forgotten to get dressed before coming outside. I look from Maman's lover's face to his wife's, almost forgetting to speak.

"Yes ma'am," I reluctantly whisper. They both look relieved that I've remembered my "place" and resume flattering each other's egos. I look down at the squirming infant in my arms and notice her eyes opening. At this age babies tend to sleep most of the day away, and this one's no exception. I walk out of the large bedroom and into the hallway. I catch a glimpse of myself in the mirror and see a young black girl looking back at me, but she looks like one of her parents belongs more to this family than her other side, which is obviously black.

"Shhh, I'm going to get you changed and all cleaned up in just a second. Don't boss me like your mama does." The little girl opens her eyes and looks up at me in recognition and I immediately recognize her as well. This baby is Jeremy's grandmother, which means Maman's lover is Jeremy's great-grandfather. I remember seeing a family collage of pictures from his mother's side of the family in

one of the rooms in their massive home. It's time to wake up from this dream, and now.

"Is there a problem?" I look up at Maman's lover and feel ashamed for my great-grandmother. I wonder if she knew about his family and, more importantly, about his treatment of other black women who weren't her.

"Jayd, can you give me a ride to work again? I need to catch a few more minutes of sleep before going in," Bryan says, waking me from my bizarre dream. At least I stayed in one place for this one. But Mama's still going to have to hear about it and provide some clarification on the subject. Jeremy's folks on his mother's side were definitely racist. This brings a whole new dimension to me and Jeremy's relationship, and he doesn't even know about it.

"You coming up with gas money?" I whisper, rubbing the sleep out of my eyes before I throw back my blankets and allow the morning chill to fully wake me up.

"Hell no, I'm not giving you any gas money. It's around the corner." I make my way out of my small bed and glance at Mama's bed, which is empty. Ever since this shit with my sleepwalking started, Mama's been up and out pretty early. I guess she's out back praying for some extra protection and I'm glad for it. I'll wait to tell her about my dream later, when we're at Netta's. It's her personal day to get her crown worked on, so she'll be in a good space to share her wisdom this afternoon.

"My time is worth something, fool." I grab my Apple Bottoms jeans and matching purple hoodie from the hook on the back of the bedroom door and make my way into the warm hallway. The heater's on full blast, warming the narrow space between Mama's room and the bathroom. If Daddy's door were open, he, Jay, and Bryan would get some good heat in there, too. But I'm glad they keep their door closed for the most part, because they all have gas at night and it can drift into our room, which isn't pleasant at all.

"Don't talk back to your elders, little girl," Bryan says, opening the door and snatching the scarf off of my freshly cornrowed head. When I left Nigel's house Sunday I came home and braided my own hair.

"Cut it out," I say, slapping his hand and snatching my scarf back. Daddy turns over in his sleep and Bryan and I scowl at each other for almost waking him up. "You've got thirty minutes, Bryan. And I want my five dollars." He should know by now how I roll. I don't work for free, and he's not going to milk rides from me every morning no matter how much I love him.

"Fine. You can add it to my hair tab. By the way, when can you hook me up? My braids need repair."

"They need a whole lot more than that, my brotha," I say, putting my clothes down on the overstuffed hamper in the bathroom before pushing him out of the way to claim my toiletries and other necessities from their bedroom closet. Next year I'm asking Santa for my own room—I don't care whose house it's in. And a dresser would be nice too, because my stuff being housed in these large garbage bags is getting really old. From my vision of the day she moved out, my mom had to do the same thing. I think it's time to break this tradition once and for all.

"Exactly. So pencil me in for one of these days, preferably in the evening. My lady likes it neat." Bryan can be so silly sometimes. He climbs back into his bottom bunk bed and goes back to sleep. I look up and see my cousin Jay is still knocked out, too. Between them and Daddy it looks like a slumber party up in here.

I thought when I got a car and subsequently started waking up later, all of the boys would be up and at it, but I see that's not a part of their daily routine. Some days they're up and out. Other days they choose to sleep in as late as possible. It must be nice. Having to drive thirty miles one-way to school doesn't afford me that option. Speaking of which, I'd better get a move on before I'm late.

I'm glad it's Tuesday and an early day at that. Thank God for teacher's meetings. Before I can get too happy Nigel comes around the corner, wiping the smile right off of my face. The first half of the day flew by. Now it's going in slow motion. We haven't spoken since I abruptly left his crib on Sunday when his ex-girlfriend interrupted our hair session. Now his do looks unloved and I feel a little bad for my boy.

"Jayd, please braid my hair. I can't stand it anymore," Nigel says, scratching his head like he's got lice. I feel bad for his hair, but I'm still not feeling his actions. Even if Mickey's not my favorite girl right now, in the long run she's still one of my best friends and I can't pretend like I don't know any better.

"Nigel, it's just hair. You'll live." As the words escape my mouth I feel like I've just violated a sacred oath me and my ancestors took eons ago; to do hair to the best of our abilities. I'm also reminded of how just a few weeks ago we were all in a situation where we might not have lived and one of us didn't. Maybe I should stop being so hard on my friend and at least hook his crown up. Maybe it'll help him act better if I work on his head.

"Come on. Let's get this over with," I say, leading him to the lunch area. I would tell Nigel to come check me at Netta's later, but I know she has a lot of make-up work for me to do since I've been pretty much out of commission for the past couple of weeks. Maybe one day my friends will come to the shop where I have more tools to hook them up. I wonder if Nigel would let me do a head-cleansing on him. Probably not. As close as Rah and I are, he still won't let me do anything like that. And I would never even approach Jeremy with something like that.

"Chica, I thought I was next?" Maggie says, walking past us on her way to her crew across the lunch quad. I guess she took her braids down over the weekend. Even if her hair is thick, cornrows still don't last long in her hair.

"I got you, girl. I can hook you up after school." I've already got three braids in Nigel's head and we still have over twenty minutes left in the lunch period. I can finish his hair and then hook Maggie up real quick after school, before I got to go to work. That's forty dollars I could leave with. Thank goodness, too, because a sistah's bank account is on low these days. I have a lot of money to make up for. Too bad we don't get sick days in my chosen profession.

"Okay, that sounds good. Later, you two," she says, sashaying her way across the grass. Mickey passes by Maggie on her way over to where Nigel and I are posted up. They roll their eyes at each other, which is their normal mutual greeting. How is it that I can get along with people from different backgrounds when some of my friends damn near hate each other for that very reason alone?

"So what's going on here?" Mickey asks, more antagonistic than necessary. What's gotten into her? "I can't come see you, but you can sit in between Jayd's legs and let her all up in your head?"

"I don't see how the two are related," Nigel says, cocking his head to the side so I can continue my job while he responds to his girl. I'm not even going to dignify her drama with a response because I know this ain't really about me.

"They're related because now that I'm not on campus anymore y'all think I'm not watching you, but I know what's really going on."

"Please do enlighten us. What's really going on?" Nigel can be a smart-ass when pushed, just like the rest of us. I bet

Mickey never thought she'd see the day Nigel turned on her. She's used to having boys under her thumb—but not my boy. I tried to warn her about the brothas from Westingle. They can be true players when they want to be.

"You're cheating on me with who I thought was my best friend," Mickey says. I look up from Nigel's scalp and see that she's dead serious. This girl must be high to think I'd do something like that.

"What the hell gave you that impression?" I ask, offended by her accusation. I know she's extra emotional because of her baby growing in her womb and all, but now she's lost her damned mind.

"People talk, Jayd, and they're talking about the two of you." She looks back at KJ, Shae, and the rest of South Central who are watching the dramatic scene unfold. Now I understand.

"If by people you mean Misty and her crew, I thought you knew better than to listen to anything they have to say," I say, continuing my work and choosing to make light of my girl's tirade.

"It was your choice not to attend school with the rest of us. Don't get mad if you're lonely on the lower campus." Nigel's still bitter from Mickey's decision to give in to the administration's pressure for her to attend the continuation school across the football field. Even if she can visit during lunch and after school, it's still not the same as being here with the rest of us. I wish she'd never made that decision, just like I wish Nellie would stop tripping.

"This isn't over." Mickey turns around and walks back toward the parking lot as the warning bell rings. The lunch period is just about over and she has to get back to the lower campus. I can't wait for this school day to end. I'm going to have to ask Mama and Netta how to navigate my way through this mess, since none of my friends are seeing straight.

* * *

As I turn the corner near Netta's Never Nappy Beauty Shop, I notice the Christmas tree and lights are still shining brightly for all to see. I'm with *Chelsea Lately* on this one: if your Christmas gear is still out and you need to wear sun block, you are way behind. It's definitely time for Netta to take down the tree if nothing else. That's a fire hazard. Maybe that's one of the many tasks she has set aside for her only assistant—better known as me—to do. I didn't realize how much she's come to depend on me until I was gone for a couple of weeks. It feels good to be back at our home away from home.

"There's our girl," Netta says, scrubbing away at Mama's hair in the washbowl. Mama slightly lifts her head to give me a wink before relaxing back in the chair. I walk over to the closets lining one of the walls and put my things away, ready to get to work. Maybe this will take my mind off of my school issues, especially where Mickey's concerned. If she keeps talking crazy to me like she did today, I'm going to end up smacking her whether she's carrying my godchild or not.

I haven't told Mama about me and my friends sharing dreams last weekend, and I'm not sure I want to just yet. I'll wait and see how she's feeling first before I divulge all of my confessions this afternoon.

"So how are your dreams coming along, little Miss?" Mama asks as Netta sits her head up straight while wrapping a towel around her wet tresses. Mama always looks refreshed after Netta washes her hair, even if her eyes tell how tired she really is. With Valentine's Day around the corner Mama has literally been burning the midnight oil.

"Oh, they're coming. At least I haven't moved around while sleeping, in the last couple of dreams I've had." I place my personalized apron over my head and close the closet doors.

"Amen to that," Netta says, slathering Mama's hair with some of their sweet strawberry leave-in conditioner. I walk over to one of the vacant sinks and wash my hands, ready to start my work for the day. I also have to remember to stock up on my hair supplies before I leave today. But first things first. And these Christmas decorations are definitely top priority. The sooner the holidays are completely behind us, the better.

"Anything interesting happen in the last one?" Mama looks over at me and I can tell she knows something's up. Netta leads Mama from the wash area to her station, ready to blow dry Mama's crown. Her hair seems to get longer each week.

"Actually, yes. The one I had last night was very interesting," I say, unplugging the tree lights before removing them. "This time Jeremy's grandmother was Maman's lover's daughter and I was the nanny. That was a whole lot of fun," I say sarcastically. Mama looks up from her reflection in the mirror and into my eyes.

"Are you sure, Jayd?"

"Your little white boy, Jeremy?" Netta asks, clamping the hot curlers hard three times before placing them in the miniature oven to heat. I guess Mama's getting a simple dry and curl today, no press needed for her soft hair.

"Yeah, positive." I place the lights in a plastic bag and continue un-decorating the dehydrated tree. Netta should be ashamed of herself for leaving this thing up here for so long. She's not the only one still stuck in Christmas past, but still. I expected more from her.

"Now isn't that a coincidence?" Netta says. She, like Mama and I, knows there are no coincidences in life. Jeremy and I being the descendants of ancestors who knew each other during the time when it wasn't even legal for white and black folks to drink from the same water fountain, is more than a fluke.

"It just goes to show you how planned out your destiny truly is," Mama says. That's what Mickey's baby said to me about our destinies almost verbatim. "Did you gain anything from the vision?"

"Just that I'm glad I'm living now and not back then. I'd hate to work for somebody and get treated with no respect."

"It wasn't easy for our ancestors, but they made it through," Netta says.

"Yes, they did. And so will you, Jayd. If you keep calling on them they will answer." Mama's words resonate deep inside of me. All the petty bull I go through on a daily basis is nothing compared to what I've seen Maman deal with and even what Mama went through in the sixties. They were both gangster with their shit.

"I hear that, Mama, but it seems like they're taking a long time to answer my call this time. I'm trying not to get a hot head about it, but Mickey's making it real hard for me to keep cool." Just thinking about Mickey rolling her neck at me during lunch makes my blood boil.

"Don't give up on the emotion, Jayd. Just do away with the pettiness. Emotions are how we navigate our feelings. If it doesn't feel right then you know to go in the opposite direction, and vice versa. Just get rid of the BS so we can move forward and get some work done."

"I know you're right, Mama," I say. I can't help but agree with every word. Had I listened to my first uneasy feeling about Misty and KJ being friends, back in the day, I wouldn't be in this mess right now.

"No matter how many times they try and take you out of your body, remember the shell cannot replace the self," Mama says, eyeing her fresh do in the mirror. She looks good with long hair, but I prefer it short and sassy.

"Exactly. As long as you can find your way back to center, little Jayd, you'll be okay." Netta's right, too. I just need to find my way back to the middle with all of my friends. I also need to find my balance within my powers. Once I get both of my worlds straight, with the help of my ancestors, I'm sure I'll feel a lot better.

After talking to Mama and Netta Tuesday, I feel a little better about my dreams coming back, even if they are still causing me to walk in the past. I'm not in the mood for anyone's madness, especially not Misty's or anyone else up here for that matter. It's been a long week and it only promises to get longer, especially with Valentine's Day next week. My mom's the only one I know who's happy about the stupid day. She's hoping for a big engagement ring, and I hope she gets exactly what her heart desires.

If my mom and Karl are going to get engaged I don't see why she needs his mother's approval. They should just do the damned thing. They're both grown, been married, and have children. If it were up to me I'd tell them to elope. But no, my mom has to go winning over the in-laws. I'm tired of being pulled both in and out of my sleep world, which at the moment seems saner to me than my reality.

"Secret valentine?" one of the lesser members of ASB says to me as I make my way through the main hall. I didn't get a chance to switch out my books at break so I have to do it now.

"No, thank you," I say, acknowledging the poor freshman. If she only knew what she was getting herself into with ASB. When Nellie started hanging with the school clique she basically sold her soul to the devil.

"Chica. Que paso?" Maggie asks with her entourage not too far behind. "You don't look so good, *Mami.* I know you're not still letting those *brujas* mess with you, are you?" She shouldn't even joke about witches because they're real. And I know Maggie knows it.

"Girl, you know how it is," I say, giving my friend a hug while continuing the trek to my locker. "Your hair still looks tight but bushy." I'm proud of my work, especially now that I've figured out a way to keep the braids in longer with my personal line of products. But touch-ups are inevitable with cornrows, and I'm thankful that they are. That will always keep a sistah in business as long as I stay on my game.

"Sí, Señorita. So when can you hook me up again? Me and my *papi* are going to take pictures next week and I want my hair to be extra flyy." Maggie's becoming one of my best clients and I am grateful for the steady side hustle.

"Well, maybe Monday after school. I've got to get to Inglewood this afternoon and hook my mom's crown up, otherwise I'd do it today."

"Maggie, Jayd, *vamanos,*" Mario calls after her. Her boyfriend smiles our way, giving me a nod to walk over with her and I oblige. It's been a while since I showed *mi hermanos* in El Barrio some love.

"Oh *chica, mi papi* told me you have a secret admirer," Maggie says like she's sharing the family crest with me.

"Oh, no. I don't need any more admirers, secret or otherwise," I say, as serious as a heart attack. "I have enough drama on my plate."

"But what if he's the one you've been waiting for your whole life? And what if he's super cute?" She sounds like she's seen *Cinderella* one too many times.

"Okay, Maggie, I can see it's not that secret so just tell me who he is. You know you want to." Maggie looks like she's going to pop if she doesn't spill the beans, but we reach her crew too quickly for me to get the full details. I'll get it on Monday when I get inside that head of hers.

"Hola, Mario, y adios," I say to Maggie and her crew. I don't mean to be rude, but I need to get to third period. We have a quiz today and I don't want to be late.

"Later, Jayd," Mario says. I give Maggie a quick hug and head to class. Besides, the sooner I get through government class, the quicker I can get to speech and let Mr. Adewale distract me until lunch.

Mrs. Peterson's quizzes always take up the entire period. I thought that was called a test, but whatever. I'm just glad it's over. Jeremy and I didn't get to speak much in third period and by the looks of it we won't have much time to catch up in fourth, either.

"Okay, class. Today's debate is going to center around the purpose of music in our lives. This entire section for the next few weeks is going to focus on the relevance of culture in our daily lives. We'll begin with the roots of hip-hop, since I know many of you listen to that genre. Then we'll venture into rock, alternative, and reggaeton as well as reggae, jazz, and the blues."

As the music begins to play, students start dancing and really feeling the vibe. I personally love Common. Jeremy looks at me and I him. We both love East Coast rap, and even though Common's from Chicago, he's still got that East Coast vibe.

"Want to dance?" Emilio, the new student, asks. I don't want to embarrass him but I was kind of hoping Jeremy would ask me. Jeremy smirks at the youngster's advance. What was I thinking—Jeremy would offer me a dance? I should know by now this is not his thing, but that doesn't have anything to do with me.

"Sure," I say, taking Emilio's hand and allowing him to lead me into a slow dance. He slips his right hand around my waist and moves me to the melodic beat. Mr. A watches us as we easily move to the music.

"You're pretty good," I say, acknowledging Emilio's skills. The boy can move.

"So are you," he says, blushing as he smiles down at me. I look at Jeremy, who's no longer smiling in that cocky way of his. He looks concerned now. Serves him right. He should've taken my hand when he had the chance.

"Okay, that's enough," Mr. A says, rolling his eyes at me as he stops the music. Why is he hating? "Now, how did the music make you feel? Jayd, let's start with your response." I haven't even had a chance to catch my breath yet and he wants to put me on the spot. Damn, I guess that's how it's going to be having him as my regular teacher in not one, but two of my classes this semester. Lucky me.

"Hot," I say, fanning myself like I'm in church. Before he can reply to my smart-ass answer Mickey shows up, interrupting the already excited classroom.

"May I help you?" Mr. A asks.

"Yeah. I came to get Nigel Esop. We have a doctor's appointment," Mickey says, rubbing her baby bump like it's a trophy. I see that's not the only reason she's ventured up to the main campus this afternoon.

"What's up, Jayd?" Mickey asks while Mr. A inspects the early pass from the office. Something about her tone isn't sitting well with me. We haven't seen each other since she accused me of trying to steal her man when I braided Nigel's hair the other day. I know she's not over that conspiracy theory so quickly.

"What's up?" I say. Mr. Adewale calls the main office to verify the pass and I don't blame him. With Mickey and Nigel's history of ditching, their faces should be posted across campus to let everyone know not to let them leave without triple-checking their notes.

"Me and Nigel made up, and just in time for Valentine's Day, too," Mickey says, sitting on Nigel's lap and claiming him like he's a puppy. I've never seen Mickey giddy before and I don't like it at all, especially not at my boy's expense.

"I'm happy for you." Even she has to know she's living in a dream world if she thinks she and Nigel are back to normal.

Nigel hasn't been himself since the shooting, and not playing football isn't helping the situation much at all. And neither is his keeping a girl on the side.

"You should be, especially with this bling," she says, holding up her ring finger and showing off the shiny diamond and gold engagement ring on it.

"What the hell?" I exclaim without thinking first. I look at Nigel, who has no response at all. It's like he's asleep or something. If I didn't know any better, I'd say that Mickey turned him into her personal zombie.

"Careful with that word. We know that's what they're trying to do," my mom says in my head, reminding me of the fact that Misty and her evil godmother are trying to make me their dream mule, even if we're not having it. And that goes for my friends becoming ones, too.

"That doesn't sound too happy at all," Mickey says, smiling at her conquest. I just talked to Nigel and he was anything but ready to propose. He wasn't even claiming her baby fully, and now they're engaged? Something's definitely not right with this picture.

"Oh, she's just mad because she couldn't get you the results that we did," Misty says. "You know haters can't help themselves." Mickey laughs at Misty's comment and Nellie, Laura, and the rest of their circus crew join in the fun. Jeremy looks at me and shakes his head as if to say *I told you so* about hanging with my torn-down crew. And I'm with him now. This is getting to be a bit much for a sistah. Why am I fighting so hard to put us back together when it seems like my friends are the very ones tearing us apart?

"What, are y'all chilling now? Please say it ain't so." I look at Mickey, who smiles slyly, like there's a secret I'm not in on. The bell for lunch rings and Mr. A dismisses the class. The rest of the students file out as Mr. Adewale watches the end of our drama unfold.

"Everyone's realizing just how crazy you really are, Jayd. Hurts, huh?" Misty says. Usually her words are empty threats, but for some reason those hit home. I can't think of anything to say in response. She's right. It does hurt and I can't do anything about it.

"Okay, that's enough. You can all leave now. Here's your note back," Mr. Adewale says, stepping in front of my desk to block the hater rays coming at me from every angle. Nigel's even quieter, and now I know there's definitely something wrong with him. He would never let anyone talk shit to me like that.

"Jayd, are you okay?" Mr. Adewale says when they exit the room.

"I'll be fine. Thank you for your concern," I say, rising out of my seat and leaving his room, too. Before Mickey started hating on me, Mr. A was hot on my and Emilio's trail. I feel like the whole world as I know it has turned upside down and I'm buried underneath it. This weekend I just want to crawl under a rock and hide out. And I think I'll start my retreat right now and wait for this confusing day to end.

Driving down Artesia Boulevard and heading toward my mom's neck of the woods, I recognize all of the small side streets and landmarks that let me know I'm going the right way. The bank on my left, the gas station on my right. There are several fast food restaurants on either side of the street, as well as other businesses that tell me I'm heading in the right direction. But if it weren't for these familiar landmarks, I wouldn't know which direction I was headed. That's how I feel at school with my friends.

I know I'm not in familiar territory if Mickey and Misty are hanging tight. I know I'm going in the wrong direction if I end up married to Rah and sharing my wedding with his baby mama. I know this is a warped existence if Nigel proposed to Mickey, when I know he's feeling quite the opposite way. If I trust my visions and know that the way I'm feeling is what's real, then how do I balance everything else out, and set my world straight again?

I turn on my left blinker to indicate I need to change lanes. As usual, the haters are out this sunny Friday afternoon, and no one wants to let me into the left lane. This turn onto Hawthorne Boulevard is always difficult. Finally, one brother lets me get in front of him and I wave thanks in my rearview mirror. I barely make it through the light, leaving the kind stranger behind. I wish friendships had the same traffic laws. There should be some sort of signal when we're all turning on each other so no one gets left in the dust.

"It's bigger than hip-hop," my cell sings, announcing a call from Mama. I put Dead Prez's song as her personal ringtone because she's the realest person I know. I'm sure she would've preferred Aretha Franklin or Anita Baker. But she won't hate on old school hip-hop because it has the same roots as the music she loves.

"Hola," I say, putting the cell on speaker. These cops around here would love to pull my black ass over and cite me for talking on the phone while driving.

"Hello to you, too," Mama says, sounding exhausted. She's been working day and night to fill her clients' orders, as well as dealing with all of my shit. "Are you planning on working at Netta's tomorrow?"

"Yes, ma'am," I say, glancing at the indicator on the dashboard that shows my gas tank is nearly empty. I wish I did have a choice between working at Netta's over the weekend and catching up on my rest, but unfortunately my funds are suffering.

"Good. I would like for you to look through your spirit notebook and brush up on your dream notes. Have you been keeping track of all of your dreams?"

"Uhmm, not really. I think they're permanently etched into my memory." Once you've been burned and attacked, as well as all of the other stuff that's happened in my dreams—whether walking or not—it's pretty hard to forget them.

"Don't be so sure, little lady. Make sure you write down everything you can recall in your notebook, you hear? I want to take a look at it tomorrow when you come to the shop." I have enough work to do, but I know Mama doesn't want to hear me complain. At least there's no traffic to deal with on this street, making my afternoon a little bit smoother.

"I thought you were taking Saturdays off?" I ask. Mama's been working too hard and resting too little lately. She needs to take her own well-being more seriously.

"I will take a day off when this love rush is over. You know these people out here are desperate to get their hands on anything they think can bring them more of everything they desire, whether it's good for them or not." Sounds like some of my friends have become Mama's clients.

"Okay, Mama. But please get some rest. I'm worried about you." I'm almost to Inglewood now, and can't wait to lie down on my mom's couch.

"Girl, don't worry about me. I've been doing this for a long time and don't plan on stopping anytime soon. By the way, how was your day, baby?"

"Oh, it was a day," I say, not really wanting to divulge to Mama all of the details of Misty's coup. She's taking over in almost every area of my life and I'm too tired to fight her effectively.

"Well, I know that. But I asked you how yours was. Uh oh, what did Misty do now?" Mama knows when I've had a bad day.

"She helped Mickey get Nigel to propose to her, when I know for a fact Nigel was not a willing participant in the engagement." I turn onto my mom's street, now only three blocks away from her building. Boys and girls alike are chilling outside, ready for the weekend. One guy in particular catches my eye as he puts a fresh coat of wax on his Cutlass Supreme. The red paint sparkles in the afternoon sun and his boys look on, completely entranced by his arm movements. I wonder if I gave him five dollars, would he wash my mom's car?

"Really?" Even though Mama answers nonchalantly, I know there's more behind it than innocent concern. "How's Misty looking these days?"

"Great," I say. I'm not going to front. She's got a new swagger in the past couple of months, that I quietly envy. When I look at my reflection these days, all I see is bags under my eyes and none of them come with a Gucci tag.

"I see." I know she does. Whatever she's thinking about is probably a clear picture in her mind. I always wanted to know how Mama's vision looks through her eyes, and my mom's, too. I got a brief glimpse of my mom's vision when I was her in one of my dreams. I wonder how it looks to see my thoughts from her point of view. But Mama's powers are the fiercest.

"Yeah, she's been on point lately." Mama's quiet on the other end of the phone as I park my mom's car in her spot and prepare to make my exit. I can feel Mama looking for something in my answers, but I'm not sure what it is she wants to hear. I felt her powers a little bit when we shared the vision of Maman getting beat by her husband, on Christmas Eve. But that was only an ounce of Mama's strength, and it was enough to knock me out then. Had I not been wearing my mom's gift to me, which ironically ended up being the same dress Maman received as a Christmas gift, I probably wouldn't have been pulled in like I was. Mama, on the other hand, needs no assistance jumping in and out of her visions.

I guess that's why she was—and still is—revered as a queen not to be messed with.

"Jayd, did I ever tell you the story of the day I married Oshune?"

"No, I don't think you did. You're not talking about your initiation, right?" I've heard that story so much I think I lived it.

"No. I'm talking about the day I was crowned. It was quite an event, but it almost didn't happen. I was under so much scrutiny from the law that I almost went to jail instead of the temple where my coronation took place. It is a marriage ceremony where you dedicate your life to serving the orisha and their devotees. Once a priestess slips on those rings there's no turning back."

"Rings?" I repeat, envisioning the gold bands on Mama's left hand. "Aren't those your wedding rings from Daddy?" I open the front door to my mom's house and shiver from the unwelcoming cold chill that always greets me. My mom probably hasn't been here all week.

"No, dear. The wedding set on my right hand is the one your grandfather gave me. The thin bands on my left hand represent my union with Oshune. That is how I got the title Ayaba. It literally means 'wife to the king' and Oshune is a female king."

"And Daddy didn't have a problem with you not wearing his ring on your left hand?" In my mind I can see the five thin circles held together by one thick gold link on the backside of the set. I've always envied how beautiful the rings look on her smooth hands.

"Whether he had a problem with it or not is irrelevant. He knew what he was getting into when he married me. It bothers him more now than it did then, I admit. But he jumped in with his eyes wide open. The point that I'm making is that all relationships are difficult, especially ones where you have to lead and serve at the same time. But our ancestors have mastered this already. Find out the common message in all of your dreams after you write them down. And be prepared to talk about them tomorrow. Now get some sleep and I'm going to get back to work."

"Good night, Mama, and I love you."

"I love you more, little Jayd. See you tomorrow. And take your pills," she adds before hanging up. I'll be so glad when I'm out of this mess and done taking those damned pills. In the meantime, I'll have to keep up with my dose until Misty's off my back. If they'll help me get my sight back on point, then I'll be one step closer to kicking Misty's ass once and for all.

"If you want the marriage to be over you have to take off the rings," Mama says as my mom and Aunt Vivica get ready to leave Mama's house. The baby me looks at my mother and smiles, knowing she's in safe hands with Mama.

"I intend on taking them off and pawning them, like my wedding china and everything else that belongs to me in that house. Come on, Vivica, let's go get my stuff."

"Lynn Marie, you need to leave well enough alone, girl. Don't go back to that house and whatever you do, don't pawn those rings. The only way to shed your past is to bury it." My mom didn't listen to her about burying my caul and she isn't hearing her now either. Damn, my mother has a hard head. That must be where my rock comes from. The next scene shifts to my mom outside of my dad's house.

"Give me Jayd's things. And my wedding gifts," my mom says to my father as she opens the door, stepping into the kitchen while my aunt Vivica waits outside by the car. I think they watched Thelma and Louise *one too many times.*

"Now's not a good time, Lynn Marie," my father says, pulling his robe closed to hide his silk drawers. My mom

looks around the kitchen and notices two wine glasses on the counter.

"You've got somebody in here, for real?" my mom yells at him.

"Lynn Marie, get out of my house," he says, trying to block her from coming in.

*"*Your *house? Don't you mean* our *house, or at least that's what you said over the phone last night. Who's the dumb bitch this time?" My mom charges out of the kitchen and through the dining room toward the living room. "You," my mom says. It's the same waitress from the Valentine's Day drama I dreamt about, and the broad is still wearing the necklace he gave them both. Damn, she's stupid.*

"Now that's enough, Lynn Marie. It's Thanksgiving, for Christ's sake. Don't you have somewhere to be?" My mom looks from my dad to his mistress, who is dressed in nothing but a robe matching my dad's, and smiles sinisterly.

"You know what? Since you're stupid enough to go back to this fool even after you found out what a jackass he is, you deserve to be his wife. I'm over it." My mom takes off her wedding rings and begins to hand them to the girl, who looks from my father to my mother in total shock.

"You told me she moved out already," the girl says, backing away from my mom's advance. Smart move. "I can't be around no voodoo witches." My mom—like all Williams women—hates to be called a witch. One of our great ancestors, Tituba, was one of many African captives living in this country who were accused of being a witch, because she understood how nature works. She was eventually hung during the Salem witch trials, after her master's children falsely accused her of practicing witchcraft. Needless to say, calling any priestess in our lineage a witch are fighting words.

"I'm not a witch." My mom's green eyes begin to slightly glow and, catching the fire's reflection, they look more fierce than usual.

"Please don't hurt me," the lady cries, backing away from my mother's gesture. My mom laughs at the trick's reaction to her power and looks back at my father, who doesn't know what to do. Unexpectedly, she tosses her wedding band and diamond engagement ring into the fireplace.

"Are you crazy?" my father screams, pushing my mom onto the couch and almost stepping on his date to get to the fireplace. "Do you know how much those rings are worth?"

"Go fish," my mom says, rising from the couch and storming out of the house without getting what she came for. She doubles back, goes into the kitchen, and retrieves from the stovetop her cast-iron skillets that Mama gave her as a wedding present. My daddy reaches for her arm and she raises the two skillets up like swords. He backs off and she and my aunt Vivica get in the car and roll out.

"Jayd," I hear someone calling in my dream. It's not my mom or Mama but it feels real, like when they're here with me. "Kill her!" When I come into my next vision, I'm running from an angry mob, with Misty leading the way. Stones begin hitting me in the head and all over the rest of my body. I trip and fall into a deep pit and the crowd gathers around it, burying me in a storm of stones.

"Wake up, Jayd. Now!" I hear my mom's voice yell.

"What the hell was that?" I ask aloud. I wake up alone in my mom's apartment. That felt too real to be a dream, but at least I'm dreaming regularly again, or so it seems. I look at the clock on the wall and notice the time. It's seven in the morning, which means I slept the entire night and stayed in place. I can't wait to get to the shop and tell Mama and Netta about this latest blast from the past.

~ 11 ~
Dreaming Eyes

"Me and those dreamin' eyes of mine."

—D'ANGELO

When I arrived at the shop this morning it was already packed with the Saturday regulars, including three of Ms. Netta's nosiest clients. I've had to wait until the end of the day to get some feedback on my dream last night. We're all tired, especially Netta. But she lives for hearing good stories and telling them, too.

"Your mama was always good at throwing some shit in a fire. That girl never listened to anyone outside of her own head," Netta says, refilling the shampoo and conditioner containers by the basin. Mama's busy restocking the client boxes with personalized products while I sweep the floor. It was a great workday. I made enough tips to take care of my gas for the week and that's always a plus.

"That's what happens when you don't control your power, Jayd. It will take over and drive you mad if you let it. Then you'll lose it completely."

"Anything else interesting you want to share?"

I don't know how to tell them about Mickey's latest accusation without them judging her, but that's not my problem.

"Mickey thinks I'm trying to steal her man."

"Which one?" Netta asks. And that's a very valid question when it comes to Mickey.

"Nigel." They both look at me in utter amazement. "I know it's ridiculous, right?"

"Girl, nothing about your little friends surprises me anymore." Mama looks bored of my drama but I still need her advice. And while Netta's touching up her hair from this week's earlier do, now that she's finished with her work for the shop, there's nowhere Mama can go.

"I'm not the one Mickey needs to worry about. His parents have recruited his ex-girlfriend Tasha to be his caretaker while he's at home. And now that he's back at school Mickey's jealousy is in rare form. But the best part is that apparently he proposed to her, ring and all. And the last time I talked to Nigel he didn't want anything to do with Mickey or her baby." I continue my work while Netta puts the finishing touches on Mama's hairstyle. Sitting in Netta's chair is all the therapy Mama needs.

"Has Mickey had any contact with Misty lately?" Mama looks like she's thinking hard about something and I know it's not what type of hairspray Netta's spritzing all over her crown, because she made it herself.

"Yeah. Apparently they're hanging tight like glue these days. I must be in a dream world if the two of them are becoming best friends." Mama yawns, indicating just how tired she really is. She should be, as hard as she's been grinding lately.

"Who's at our door this time of evening?" Netta asks, responding to the ringing bell. We each look toward the glass window in the front of the store and see Nigel staring back at us. Netta buzzes the front door open, allowing my friend in.

"Hey, Jayd, Mrs. James and Ms. Netta," Nigel says, walking into the shop and surprising us all. What's he doing on this side of town on the weekend?

"What are you doing here?" I ask, giving him a hug. Netta

pretends like she's still doing Mama's hair, but we all know she's finished.

"I need you to touch up a few of these braids before I go to this interview in the morning. I want to look my best," Nigel says, taking a seat in the empty station next to Netta's. There are three stylist stations in the shop and I hope one day I'll get to put my stamp on one of them.

"Interview for what?" I ask, getting fresh towels from the cabinet and draping them around Nigel's clothes. His braids last a long time, but a few are a bit frayed. I can fix these in no time and still get out of here before it gets too late for me to enjoy what's left of my Saturday night. Rah texted me earlier to see what I was up to, since his little brother, Kamal, and Rahima will be at his grandmother's house for the night. But I haven't had a moment to hit him back yet. I'll get to it as soon as I put these braids in Nigel's hair.

"It's with our pastor, about me and Mickey's engagement. We're both excited about it." Mama and Netta no longer hide the fact that they're actively listening to our conversation and tuned in for all of the details.

"Really? Because when I talked to you last week you weren't even sure if you wanted to claim her baby, let alone take on a marriage." Now that I can get back in his head maybe I can get the truth out of him.

"You were right to go off on me the other day, Jayd. I need to do the right thing, and that's marrying Mickey and making an honest woman out of her."

"All the Bibles in Compton couldn't make that girl honest," Netta says under her breath, breaking her and Mama's quiet observing. Mama shoots Netta a look that shuts her up—for now. I unbraid a few of his cornrows and begin the process of putting them back in place.

"I agree you need to do the right thing, but a few days ago

your feet were as cold as a penguin's toenails. What changed?" Nigel instinctively tilts his head to the right, already knowing I'm going to ask him to do that so I can get behind his ear. Nigel's silent for a moment, trying to come up with a good answer. Or he doesn't know the answer, which is my guess. And from the look on Mama's face she's thinking the same thing.

"I wish I'd never been shot," Nigel says solemnly. With my hands in his head, the night of the shooting comes back to the front of my thoughts. I continue manipulating the thick strands of his soft hair into precise braids, redefining the parts as I go.

Mama catches my eye in the mirror, sharing the painful memory with me. Nigel's completely unaware of the exchange going on in his own thoughts, but Mama's working through me. As I braid, Mama weaves the thoughts floating in my mind. We both see the bullet exit Mickey's man's gun and enter Tre's chest, then exit through his back before finally settling in Nigel's shoulder.

"Remove the cloud over his eyes, Jayd. If I can see it you can, too," Mama says aloud. I can't really tell if I'm dreaming or awake. And Netta combing Mama's hair is no help. I feel hypnotized by her steady hand movements and by the unique comb reserved just for Mama's hair.

"What's going on here?" Rah asks through the window, breaking up our session. "I've been knocking on the door for five minutes." Netta buzzes Rah in, waking us all up. And we were so close to removing the veil over Nigel's mind. Damn Rah and his bad timing.

"What's up, man?" Nigel says, but Rah doesn't look pleased to see his boy.

"What's up is you and Jayd kicking it behind my back. What's that all about?" Nigel looks up at Rah like he's lost his mind. Now he knows how I feel about Mickey's accusation.

"Rah, why are you tripping? You see we're handling business," I say, massaging some of my special almond-oil blend into Nigel's scalp before letting him up.

"I've been texting you all afternoon, Jayd. That's why I'm tripping."

"Well, you know where I am. No need to get pissed," I say. Nigel looks at his reflection, obviously pleased with the results. He pulls out a twenty and drops it on the table before rising from the chair. He looks completely unfazed by Rah's tone. I wish I could remain as cool as he is.

"Thanks, girl. I look good," Nigel says, giving me a hug and heading out the door. "I'll holla at you after our meeting, Rah. Good night, Miss Netta, Mrs. James."

"Good night, Nigel," they answer in unison. Netta buzzes the door for Nigel to leave and Rah's apparently right behind him.

"Rah, wait," I say, following them out. Nigel hops into this green Impala, turns the music up and pulls out.

"For what, Jayd? I was worried sick about you and you couldn't even bother to return a message." Rah paces back and forth while Mama and Netta look on. Why do we always have to go through some mess?

"I think your own guilt has gotten the best of you." The words fall from my lips and into Rah's lap. He can deny it all he wants, but I know Rah too well to be falling for his games. Whenever he gets jealous it's because he's doing wrong, not me. And after last week's disappearing act he's got no room to talk.

"I saw the way you two were looking at each other, Jayd. Don't tell me it was nothing." Rah unlocks the car door and gets inside, turning up his already loud music.

"Rah, I was just braiding his hair. And yes, I was looking into his eyes but it's not what you think." Rah starts the engine, puts the car in gear and begins backing up while I'm still talking.

"Whatever, Jayd. I'm out." Oh no, he didn't.

"Rah, what the hell is wrong with you?" I look back into the shop at Mama and Netta shaking their heads in disbelief. What just happened here? I thought my life was difficult before. Now I long for the days of my unusual dreams and dramatic friends, minus Misty's spell. This shit right here is too much for me.

"Jayd, go back to your mother's house and get some rest. You're going to need it," Mama says through the open screen door. She's right. I need to sleep this madness off and start over again tomorrow. Maybe what just went down between Nigel, Rah, and me will make more sense in my head tomorrow morning. Whether I'm ready or not, I have clients all day tomorrow and need to be in the right frame of mind to get my work done.

"Can you see her?" a voice asks in the distance. I can't see anything and I know my eyes are open. Maybe I'm wearing a blindfold or something, but why? And who else is here with me?

"Yes, I can see her," the female voice says to who I assume is another woman standing closer to me. I reach my hands out in front of me and grasp nothing but air. "Did it work?"

"I think so." I feel hands moving fast in front of my face. It feels like someone's in front of me, but I can't see a thing. "She's as blind as a bat during the day." Blind? Oh hell, no. I don't like this at all. We've done the blind thing once already. I can't go back there again. Not being able to watch television, text, or drive was a living nightmare. If I didn't value my sight before, I now know just how precious it is.

"Good. We've got her sight. Now it's time to finish her and her legacy off for good." What do they mean, they've got my sight? And who the hell is that talking? These women feel too

old to be Misty or Esmeralda, but they're definitely related somehow. I can just feel it.

"Ouch," I say, burning myself with the hot tool in my hand. Was I dreaming while standing here? This is getting to be a bad habit. And I thought sleepwalking was cruel.

"Jayd, what the hell did you do to my hair?" Shawntrese asks, shrieking at the clumps of hair in one of my hands and the running blow-dryer in the other. I must have dozed off while drying her fragile hair. Oh shit.

"Oh no, Shawntrese. I'm so sorry." After yesterday's mind trip with Nigel I've been feeling off. When Shawntrese came over this morning I wasn't ready to do her hair, but she insisted. I could just feel that something bad was going to happen and it did.

"Sorry my ass, Jayd. Look at me!" She snatches the loose strands out of my hand and puts them in my face. I've never seen her this pissed and I don't blame her.

"You can't work on stressed hair when you yourself are stressed. That's like a sick doctor trying to heal people: not the best combination, little lady."

"Okay mom, I've got it."

"Do you really, because I don't think you do. And wait until Mama finds out. She's going to have a field day with this one," she says, taunting me more like a big sister than a mom.

"Jayd, what the hell are you going to do about this?" Shawntrese demands. I wish I knew.

"There's some of Mama's hair-grow balm in the back of my medicine cabinet. Give it to Shawntrese and tell her to apply it three times a day. And make sure you put some on her scalp now so it can start working. Her new growth should be in by morning. I'm out." Now that's mother love.

"I've got just the thing for you, girl. I'll be right back," I say as I go and retrieve the balm. "And the next time I tell you I can't do your hair, please trust me."

"Next time? Girl, please. There won't be a next time," Shawntrese says, snatching the small jar out of my hand and walking toward the front door. Not her, too. I'm losing all of my friends and clientele at the same time. I think I'm going to be sick.

"Shawntrese, I'm sorry. Please let me make this up to you. I can start by rubbing this in your hair." I reach for the container but she pulls way from me like I've got a contagious disease.

"Jayd, ever since I found you outside with no shoes on when you were so-called babysitting, you've been acting strange. Get it together, girl." Shawntrese opens the front door and walks across the hall to her apartment, slamming the door behind her. She's right. I need to snap out of it, and soon.

I didn't sleep well at all last night. I tried calling Rah numerous times, but to no avail. I look around my mom's empty apartment and can still smell the burning hair lingering in the space. I wish I could sleep the rest of the afternoon away, but I have to get back to Mama's and prepare for school tomorrow. It's already been an exciting weekend and it has definitely taken a toll on a sistah. When I get to Compton I'm going to take a bath, swallow my prescribed horse pills, and pray for a restful night's sleep.

"All hail, His Royal Highness, Ogunlabi Adewale the First, and Her Majesty, Queen Jayd," the crowd says as they bow before our feet. Mr. Adewale is seated next to me on our thrones. We are outside in an open market type of environment and the sand is hot beneath our feet. We're dressed in matching traditional West African royal garb. Our purple-

and-white outfits are heavy and making me sweat but we still look damned good up here.

"Let the bembe proceed," one of the elders says in Yoruba officially starting the party for the orishas. I only know bits and pieces from our prayers, but for some reason I now understand the African language completely.

"Jayd, did you hear me?" Mr. Adewale asks, handing me a stack of papers. I can only assume he wants me to hand them out, since I didn't hear a word he just said. I've been in a daze all morning. I don't even remember driving to school, let alone getting through my first three classes. By the time I got back to Compton last night and talked to Mama about my impromptu vision while doing Shawntrese's hair, it was late. Mama made me take a cleansing bath and then straight to bed.

"I'm sorry," I say, taking the papers and rising from my desk.

"As you all know, the Multicultural Festival is coming up in March. I would like this class to participate in a healthy debate as part of the opening ceremonies. In order to do that, we have to practice our skills as well as pick a topic to debate on. There will be two teams of three. The top six debaters in the class will be divided and teamed up at the team captains' discretion. So, let's begin."

"Hey, Mr. Adewale. I have a good multicultural topic," KJ says, smiling at me as I continue passing out the papers. "Interracial dating: pros and cons." Everyone in the class snickers except for me, Jeremy, Emilio, and Mr. A.

"I want this class to be fun but controlled. We can learn about each other's similarities and differences more authentically by being freed up a little bit. But don't take advantage of the situation, and there will be no disrespect in this room, understood?" Mr. Adewale looks from KJ to me. I reclaim my seat and try to focus on the present moment. I've been so caught up in my involuntary daydreams that I barely know what day it is. "Alright, let's get back to the class."

After school I will talk to Mr. A about the vision I just had. Maybe he has a little more insight into the meaning. If my dream is accurate, he can see more with those hazel eyes than he's letting on.

After drifting through the rest of my day, I'm glad to hear the final bell ring. I walk over to Mr. A's classroom and find him seated inside studying, as usual. He's always reading something.

"Got a min?" I ask, knocking on the open door before stepping into his empty room. I look around the hallway to make sure we don't have any spying eyes. The last thing I need is someone eavesdropping on what we have to chat about.

"Sure. What's up with you today, Miss Jackson? You seem a bit distracted."

"I had a daydream about you and I need some insight." He knows all about my lineage already. It feels good not having to explain to someone the significance of my dreaming.

"I'm listening," he says, putting down his textbook and giving me his undivided attention. I tell him the entire dream about us being married, and he doesn't budge. I thought he'd give me more of a reaction than that.

"Have you ever heard of Oyotunji?" Mr. Adewale asks. It sounds familiar, but my mind is in such a state that I can't see clearly.

"No, can't say that I have."

"Well, it's an African village in South Carolina. My ancestors are Gullah folks and I grew up there until I was a teenager and moved to New Orleans with my mom."

"Why did she move?"

"Let's just say she wasn't happy as a fifth wife. But I miss the village to this day. It's the only place I know of where I can be completely comfortable as a priest. You should look it up." Yeah, with all of my free time on hand, maybe I will.

"Wow, I didn't know there was an African village in the United States."

"There's a lot you don't know. But that's why I'm here," he says, smiling brightly. If anyone can dig me out of my funk temporarily, it's this man.

"Is there a support group for people like us?" I ask, taking a Snickers bar out of my backpack to snack on. It's been a long day and I don't recall having lunch. I'm really bugging if I can't remember eating. Luckily my growling stomach has a memory all of its own.

"You mean people born with cauls, or all Africans in general?" He can be such a smart-ass when he wants to be. Too bad I find that irresistible about him.

"I mean caul babies."

"I wish. It's rare to find us at all, let alone a group of us. That's the best thing about the village. Everyone's spiritual lineage is not only respected but nourished, unlike out here in the wilderness. It's the politics you have to be careful of when living there."

"A group would be nice, especially when it comes to helping us decipher the true meaning of dreams," I say. Mr. A takes an apple out of his briefcase and begins snacking with me. It's our first lunch date. Too bad it's not under happier circumstances, but I'll take what I can get.

"Look, Jayd, just because we were married in your dream doesn't mean that's what you're really feeling. It could mean that we have to partner up in another way. Don't take your dreams so literally." Something about the way he's speaking sounds familiar.

"Yeah, I hope you're right. So tell me, what does your caul do for you?" Mr. Adewale looks deep into my eyes. From the feel of it, he doesn't have the gift of sight like we do, even if his eyes can get a sistah caught up in the rapture.

"If I told you that, I'd have to change schools," he says, smiling at my stern look. I'm going to focus on him with what little energy I have left. Ever since my mom taught me that trick I've used it well. Catching my drift, Mr. Adewale gets serious and tells me about his talents. "Like you, I have a lineage and it stems from my father's side. We are children of Ogun, the deity of iron, honor, and war."

"I know of him from our studies on the various orisha. But that still doesn't tell me about your powers." It's getting late and I need to get going. Since I don't have to be at Netta's today, Mama's going to wonder where I am if I don't get home soon. She's stricter than ever before now that I have my own wheels.

"Patience, little queen. I'm sure you know that you catch more bees with honey than vinegar." Mr. A switches his weight from the left foot to his right, and crosses his arms over his chest. His left shirtsleeve pulls up slightly and I notice the green-and-black beaded bracelet similar to the yellow-and-gold one Mama wears on her left wrist.

"I've heard that many times before," I say, telling the truth. I'm known for having very little patience.

"My father's people are known for their listening skills. Helps when we're hunting. And we can also tell when someone's being less than honest." He gives me that same look of recognition he gave when he first met me. He knew then that I was hiding something from him and I knew he knew more than he was saying at the time.

"Damn, that's a gangster-ass skill to have," I say. Mr. Adewale can't help but smile at my ghetto props. But for real, that's some baller shit. I wish I could tell when people were lying to me. If I had that skill, Misty and I would have never been friends in the first place. That alone would have warded off a lot of misfortune in my life.

"You'd better go on and head home before your grandmother comes looking for you." He's got that right. All I need is Mama worrying about me, especially with all that's going on our world.

"Oh, she doesn't drive." Mr. A seems amused by my words.

"We both know she doesn't need a car to look for you," Mr. A says, and he's right. It's a trip to talk to someone about my grandmother at school. A nice trip, but still it feels weird. "And try to get some solid sleep. The people in my lineage sleep light because we come from hunters. You need the opposite to honor your gifts. It's important, Queen Jayd." I would answer him back as King Ogunlabi but I don't know how he'd take it.

"Will do. And thank you for talking to me. I've been feeling slightly out of it lately, and I don't have anyone who understands what I'm going through."

"Well, I'm here anytime you need to talk. And it doesn't have to be just when you're not feeling well. But seriously, Jayd. Get your rest. You're going to need it to make it through your destiny." He's got that right. So far it's been one hell of a road, and I don't see it getting easier any time soon. "And whatever you do, keep a cool head. Your enemies will try and ruffle your tail feathers, but don't let them. You're a different kind of bird altogether. If you always remember that there's a crown on top of your head then you'll never lose a battle."

He could've fooled me. I feel like I've completely lost this war with Misty and I'm too tired to do anything about it. This madness has got me sleepwalking, losing my sight, and it's messing with my money. Losing my friends is the most challenging casualty of the whole encounter. I feel like I'm in a bad dream and any minute I'm going to wake up and everything will be okay. Trc will be alive, Nellie and Mickey will be bugging me about mundane shit and, most importantly, I'll be well rested and back on my A game. Maybe tonight will be the night I get some solid sleep and this hellish nightmare will be over, once and for all.

Once I made it home it took me awhile to settle down, with all the homework and spirit work I had to do. When I finally do drift off I fall into what feels like someone else's dream. I don't know how, but I know when I'm in my own thoughts and this is not feeling familiar at all. It feels similar to when I walked through my friends' dreams after they drank my mom's special party punch, but this time I'm not a quiet observer. It actually feels like the same thing is being done to me, but not for any kind of good.

"She's in," I hear a voice say. In where? And how the hell do I get out? "Hurry, say the chant before she wakes up." I hear a sudden drumbeat and begin to focus on that sound instead of the female voice, and in doing so Misty comes to the forefront of my vision.

"Give me your eyes for now and always. Let me have your sight, free of haze." Misty turns around and throws a look at me, her eyes now a blindingly bright blue.

"Don't look into their light! She's taking all of your powers, Jayd, not just your sight. When she dreams your dreams, she dreams of everything she wants to be through you. A dream snatcher is the worst kind of hater there is. You need to check her, and now, Jayd, before this goes any further," my mother yells. My head is pounding as I try to resist Misty's gaze, but the sound of the drumbeat in the background grows louder and with it I'm losing my strength to keep from looking at Misty.

* * *

"Jayd, get up. You're going to be late," Mama says groggily from her bed. After last night's weird dream I know I'm in for a hellish day. Yesterday I was so busy at Netta's I didn't have time to think. And with the regular short periods on Tuesdays, I didn't even notice the day go by. But today will not be so easy.

While I was at the shop yesterday, Mama and Netta warned me against Misty and Esmeralda's constant dream harassment. Luckily I've been taking my pills as prescribed, and whatever's in those huge things has helped me get stronger in my dream world. I still can't fall asleep when and where I want to, but I'm beginning to master the art of waking up.

When I make it to campus, the Valentine Day buzz is everywhere. There's always a rush week before any holiday, and with the dance next Friday the push is on to sell as many tickets as possible. There are also student cupids running around campus shooting people with plastic bows and arrows, indicating that they have a secret valentine. I wish one of them fools would shoot me. It'll be the last shot they ever take.

"Good morning, Jayd," Ms. Toni says with hella attitude. Why is she irritated, and so early?

"Good morning, Ms. Toni," I say, opening my locker. Something about the way she's looking at me tells me not to give her a hug right now.

"I saw you in Mr. Adewale's room Monday afternoon, Jayd. And it didn't look like a normal tutorial session to me," she says, leaning in close to me so our business isn't heard by the other students passing by. No wonder she's got her panties all in a bunch. She thinks I'm trying to get at Mr. A. She's not entirely wrong, but I'd never jeopardize his career—or mine, for that matter.

"Ms. Toni, it's not what you think. I've been having some problems and Mr. A . . ."

"Mr. Adewale, you mean," she says, cutting me off. Ms. Toni's breathing so heavily on me that I can smell the coffee and cigarettes she had for breakfast. She should really stop smoking. "You used to talk to me when you had issues. But now that Mr. Adewale is working here on a regular basis I hardly see you anymore. Tell me that's a coincidence, Miss Jackson."

"Not really. It's just that with everything going on . . ." But Ms. Toni's not having it this morning. I guess I should stop trying to explain and just let her talk, because she's not interested in a word I have to say.

"Jayd, I don't know what's gotten into you, but you need to wake up and snap out of it. This is not a game, little girl. You're playing with your life and his. So think carefully about how you are perceived when you're receiving this advice you think only he can give you."

Ms. Toni walks into the ASB room where her office is housed and closes the door, leaving me in the main hall, completely dumbfounded. I hate it when she's mad at me. What a way to start my school day. Wednesdays always feel longer after short Tuesdays. And with AP meetings at both the nutrition break and lunch, today will no doubt feel like an eternity.

English and Spanish were especially grueling this morning, with pop quizzes in both classes. I'm sure having Mr. Adewale as my teacher in two classes will eventually make me a better student, but right now I'm not feeling the love for his teaching style. And with Ms. Toni up my ass about associating with him, I'm not sure I should continue confiding in him, even if he is the only person at this school who gets me.

On my way to the English hall where my first AP meeting will be held, I notice Misty sitting in the quad with KJ and friends. Please tell me this trick isn't braiding hair. When the hell did she learn how to cornrow? Misty never had the patience or style to braid before. Noticing my amazement, Misty can't help but say something.

"What, you think you're the only black girl who can braid hair? You're so full of yourself, Jayd. Get over it already," Misty says, cocking KJ's head to the side just like I would. Most people would have the client hold their ear back instead. I don't even have a comeback I'm so shocked. Misty's snatching my life right before my eyes, and I feel powerless to do anything about it.

"Hey, Jayd," Jeremy says, falling into step with me as I continue my trek across the yard. I grabbed a churro to snack on during the meeting. Hopefully the sugar will keep me awake. "So you didn't answer me about Valentine's Day next Saturday." Jeremy's so sweet. But the last thing on my mind is celebrating another damned holiday when I'm still feeling ill from the last one.

"Next weekend is too far away." Jeremy smiles down at me and I can't help but smile back. Jeremy continues with his love day plans, completely ignoring my protest.

"I was thinking we could catch a movie. How about that new horror love story that's out? I think it's called *Voodoo Valentine* or something like that. The previews look scary as shit." This is the problem with dating a white boy who knows nothing about our history. I want to cuss him out on so many levels I don't know where to begin, so I won't.

"Jeremy, I can't deal with this right now. I have to get to my meeting," I say as we approach Ms. Malone's class. She's the best English teacher on the AP track, and I'm glad I have her this year. "But for the record, I hate horror films." I walk into the classroom, leaving Jeremy and his dumbass movie behind. If I can make it through the rest of the day without hurting someone it will be a miracle.

* * *

Misty braiding KJ's hair has been bothering me all day. I can't explain why, but I do feel like I'm the only black girl at this school who should braid, even if it's the furthest thing from the truth. Misty's invading my territory and I can't focus long enough to figure how to kick her ass once and for all.

"*A diva is a female version of a hustler,*" Beyoncé sings, announcing a call. It's Rah. I haven't heard from him since he stormed off at Netta's shop over the weekend. I haven't tried to call him because I've been too involved in my own shit to worry about him and his jealous tendencies. Besides, I'm not the one in the wrong this time around. He's been screwing up a lot lately, and I'm sick of it. Whether or not Misty has anything to do with his mistakes, I think he should still know better.

"Sorry how I acted with you and Nigel Saturday. My bad," he says as soon as I flip the phone open.

"Apology accepted." For now. I make my way to the crowded parking lot, ready to leave Redondo Beach behind for the afternoon. The sooner I get home the quicker I can get started on all of my homework, not to mention my spirit work. I have to record my dreams in my notebook, and with the various visions I've had I can't seem to keep up.

"So I was thinking we should stay in for Valentine's Day. You know, just chill. How does that sound?" I can tell by the tone of his voice that his version of chilling is making out all night. It's been awhile since we've had a night to ourselves, but I'm not going out like that, especially not after the way he's been acting lately.

"Oh, I see. You want to run around making project twins with me and your other woman. Well, no thank you to being one of your baby mamas," I say through the cell. My head is getting hot and that alone is blurring my vision. Luckily I'm safe in my mom's car, where none of the other students notice my escalating conversation.

"Why do you keep talking about having my baby, Jayd? What aren't you telling me?" Rah knows I'm not pregnant because my name's not Mary and my baby's name—no matter when I have it—will not be Jesus.

"Rah, I'm under a lot of pressure," I say, holding my head in my hands. My headache is coming back and I know it's because of this argument. "And why can't you go to the dance anyway? It's the day before the actual holiday." He pauses slightly before answering.

"Because Nigel and I are going to the dance at Westingle Friday night. It's business, baby."

"Business my ass, Rah. Y'all are going with Trish and Tasha, aren't you?"

"It's not what you think. Nigel needs to talk to the coaches up there and see if they'll let him back on the team, just in case your punk-ass school kicks him out."

"Tell me anything, Rah," I say, starting the engine. I knew Nigel wasn't ready to marry Mickey, no matter what Misty tried to do to him on Mickey's behalf. Whatever they did to my boy didn't stick after me, Mama, and Netta got in his head last weekend. Rah pauses and lets out a sigh, like I'm the one being difficult. He'd better check himself and quickly.

"I see you, boo. No matter what you're going through, Jayd, I got you. You know that, right?" Rah's insincere sincerity has worked my last nerve for the last time. Who does he think he's dealing with? In my family we take seeing someone very seriously. Rah's just trying to win my sympathy and it's not flying.

"Forget seeing. You need to recognize, Rah." I need to remind him of who he's got in me—forget what he's heard from any of the broads he's dealing with. What is it with guys and pulling stupid shit on us like we're too blind to see the blatant disrespect and disregard for our feelings? "I don't really give a damn what they teach you fools about communication, but I'm done with trying to rationalize the shit. I told you exactly what I wanted and needed and you chose to ignore my request time and time again. So I'm done asking. I'm out," I say, hanging up the phone and heading home. How did we get to this point in our relationship yet again?

"I hate it when people refer to voodoo and they don't know what the hell they're talking about," Mama says, banging pots and pans in the kitchen. Even though I haven't been home for a good two minutes, I can already tell she's in a mood. "These fools on the news compared a crooked-ass Wall Street's lack of financial prowess to a voodoo curse. What the hell?"

"Mama, don't let them work your nerves. You know how it is," I say, peeking into the steaming pots. Mama's making a pot roast with red potatoes and carrots. I can also smell her homemade rolls baking in the oven, or rather burning. "Mama, is that smoke?" I ask before opening the oven. The white cloud escapes the hot space, choking us both.

"Damn it," Mama says, exasperated. She pushes me to the side and takes out the pan holding two dozen blackened circles. "I asked for one thing, and your grandfather couldn't be bothered to get me that. Where's the real Santa when you need him?" All Mama wanted was a new stove for Christmas, and if I recall, she asked for one last year and the year before that, but to no avail.

I guess Daddy's deaf when it comes to hearing Mama's wishes, but I'm not. I'm going to get to work on getting her one for Mother's Day. If I braid enough heads and work enough hours at Netta's, I should be able to afford something if I ever get my mojo back. And maybe I can get my mom and Bryan to chip in. It would make it a larger family effort, but that never works out well.

"We have to be our own Santas," I say, hugging Mama's shoulders. She looks like she's at her wit's end, and my issues with Misty aren't helping any.

"You know, Maman used to say that to me all of the time when I was a baby." Mama turns around to look at me. "If you don't keep your word you have nothing, Jayd. Remember that."

"Yes, ma'am," I say. I feel Mama on that one, for sure. Even little things like being on time are important in my world. And big things, like buying Mama a new oven, should be in Daddy's world. Maybe he needs a little reminder.

"So tell me, what have you seen lately in your dreams?" Before Mama can continue, the same news story comes back on the small kitchen television and again catches Mama's attention, reigniting her fire.

"Mama, why do you watch this madness? It's just there to piss people off," I say, washing my hands in the sink before taking a big ball of dough to bake another dozen biscuits. I don't know if there will be enough for everyone, nor do I care. As long as I get my share of the soft treats I'm good.

"Because it's nice to know where the world is, even if we're not always participants in it." Mama joins me in my kneading while continuing to watch the program.

"The investor says that his family has been cursed with bad luck for generations and sees this recent financial disaster as further proof that the curse still exists," the news anchor says. Mama's jaw tightens and the dough in her manicured hands feels the brunt of her frustration.

"If they only knew how stupid they sound, especially when there are real curses out there." I know Mama's talking about the one over my head. She's still worried about me sleeping properly, but I'm more worried about Misty reigning as the most popular black girl on campus, a title that once belonged to me. Not that I care about the words so much, it's the crown that I'm concerned with. This trick has managed to twist up my world by writing and chanting a few words Esmeralda gave her, and I'm not feeling this shit at all.

"I feel you, Mama. But they always compare voodoo with unknown tragedy. Isn't that sort of correct, no matter how ignorant the intent?"

"No," Mama says, throwing the sticky dough on the cutting board. "There's no mystery to how we do our work, at least not for the faithful. It's cause and effect, plain and simple. If someone did put a curse on him and his family, who did it and why? If he were concerned with the right shit, he'd be able to fix it. But no, he'd rather blame our innocent ancestors, who could care less about him and his money. Dumbass," Mama says, making me smile. I love it when Mama gets all riled up. And honestly, this conversation, and being in the kitchen cooking dinner with Mama, and not making a potion, is just the sense of normalcy I need. Life is crazy right now, and I'm not feeling very powerful in it.

"Could you pass me the bowl of butter, please?" Mama passes me the bowl of melted butter to dip the biscuits in before placing them on the lined cookie sheet without missing a beat of her rant.

"It reminds me of when that politician in Georgia hired a priestess do some work for her, and then stopped payment on the check when the priestess didn't agree to kill her opponent, which wasn't in the initial agreement. That politician was stupid and unfaithful because first of all, she didn't want to admit to requesting the work, even though the priestess had proof. And she dared to piss off a priestess. Had she truly had faith in the work in the first place, she would have never angered the priestess because who knows what repercussions would've followed? Magic, Jayd. That's what some people subscribe to, and they get what they deserve in the end, always. Every time."

"That's what Mickey wanted, and she got it from Misty, I guess." Mama shifts her attention from the tiny television screen above the microwave and looks deep into my eyes. I want to cry, I'm so frustrated.

"Mama, I feel like I'm living inside of a dream world where Misty's me and I'm Misty." Mama's eyes begin to glow as she probes my mind. I relax and let Mama do her thing. I remember last night's dream about Misty stealing my sight as Mama looks through my eyes.

"What have I told you about sleeping when you don't want to?"

"To control it."

"And, to wake up. If you'd done that, Misty wouldn't have been able to get in your head in the first place. Be purposeful in your intent to dream. Focus on what you want to dream about and watch it manifest, not the other way around."

Mama's right. I need to get out of this funk, and the only way to do that is by kicking Misty's ass the old fashioned way, damn the positive thinking. Tonight I'm going to request going all the way back to when Misty and I first became friends. As the saying goes, if I'd known then what I know now, I would've never gotten close to the broad in the first place. And that's what I'm working on fixing—no magic needed.

~ 12 ~
Deck the Halls

"Words are very unnecessary/
They can only do harm."

—DEPECHE MODE

Here we go again. I can feel myself walking around the house in the dark, but there's nothing I can do to control it. I hear chanting outside, and my feet are moving toward the sounds even if the hair standing all over my body tells me to turn away. I can't. I still have no control over my dream world, and this time I know there's nothing good for me to see.

"There she is," I hear Esmeralda whisper. Why is she outside this late at night? "Don't let her get away this time. We need her eyes." And who is she talking to?

"Don't worry. I've got her," Misty says. They are calling me outside onto the front porch. I haven't exited through the front door alone since my painful run-in with Esmeralda months ago that caused my original headache. Even in my dream state I should know better than to leave the house where Esmeralda could take another shot at me. "I'm going to cast a dream net. Make sure you get the vision as she sees it."

"I see it coming," Misty says enthusiastically. I can't help but dream, and she's trying to steal it just like my mother warned me about in my last vision. What the hell?

"Good. I'll keep her grandmother occupied. Remember

what I told you," Esmeralda says. What does she mean she'll keep Mama occupied? No wonder Mama hasn't come looking for me. Esmeralda's got something on her, too. Damn it. I need to get stronger, and fast, before they take us both out.

Misty's waiting for me next door on Esmeralda's front porch. Her eyes have again changed from light brown to blue, just like Esmeralda's. I can't let them get away with this. She has a bow and arrow, like an evil cupid, and here comes her godmother with the net to catch my dream. I have to wake up—now.

"Jayd, wake your ass up, girl. Now," *Mama shouts from behind me. Whatever Esmeralda tried to put on Mama obviously didn't work because I'm coming to.* "Control your thoughts, Jayd and wake up."

Mama holds onto my shoulders and leads me back inside. I look at Mama's fearful gaze with tears in my eyes. This is the last day we're going through this shit.

I know Misty hates me, but damn. Does she have to hate on a sistah all of the time? Even Muhammad Ali got a break from his opponents at some point, and Britney Spears herself even got a slight reprieve from the media. But Misty just never seems to let up. Mama says it's because she's an infallible force of nature. I think they should have hurricanes named after the girl. Like water and wind, she can be deadly when she's got another force behind her like Esmeralda's wicked ass.

Mama says Misty's presence is needed in my life—much like Esmeralda's is needed in hers—to let me know what I should and shouldn't do, how I should and shouldn't act, and who I should aim to be. And believe me, Misty gives me plenty of inspiration to be a different kind of sistah. And this morning I'm going to tell her exactly how I feel.

I approach Misty in the main hall with the attitude of ten thousand angry women. Unfortunately we have a crowd this morning, but I'm not tripping. She's still going to get an earful from me, and I don't care who hears it.

"Misty, I need to holler at you real quick," I say as she passes my locker. She stops with her entourage behind her and smiles.

"Damn, Jayd. It sounds like Nellie was right. You do need some love in your life," Misty says, causing the audience to snicker. "Another lonely Valentine's Day coming up, boo?" Misty needs to lose that smirk on her face and I'm in just the mood to be of service to my former friend.

"I doubt it. She's used to stealing everyone else's man. I'm sure someone will keep her company," Mickey says, standing next to Nellie. Okay, I know I'm tripping if they're all on the same side against me. This is just too much to handle—almost too much.

"What the hell are you talking about? I didn't take anyone's man." Why am I defending myself? I know these tricks are under Misty's spell, but still. As long as Mickey, Nellie, and I have been each other's allies, their better judgment should take over at some point. They know that's not how I get down. Besides, I don't need to take anyone's seconds. That's Misty's job, not mine.

"So you're not after Nigel or Chance?" Nellie asks. Her jealousy is unbelievable. Even before Misty twisted Nellie's mind all up, she was on that shit with me and Chance. I've had just about all I can take from the three of them.

"Nigel was your side conquest, not mine, or did you conveniently forget that you were jocking him even while Mickey was busy becoming his baby mama?" Mickey looks from me to Nellie, confused about who she's hating on at the moment. What difference does it make now? In Misty's twisted reality, Mickey and Nigel are engaged. But I guess even under a spell Mickey's still on red alert when it comes to her main man.

I look into Mickey's eyes and almost recognize the down-ass homegirl who used to roll tight with Nellie. I remember the first time Nellie introduced us. We could've easily become enemies, especially being from different sides of Compton, where colors determine our loyalty. But instead we became friends, and I want that back. I focus intently on my girl, like I did Mr. A. I can see her struggling against her anger, and I almost have her won over. But Misty steps in front of Mickey, blocking our view. She then turns around and faces Mickey, her eyes shimmering as she does so. Did anyone else just see that shit?

"Misty, what the hell are you doing to her?" I ask. Everyone seems like they're in a daze and I'm the only one seeing this shit for what it really is. "Mickey, don't look at her. She's manipulating your thoughts."

"Jayd, please. We all know you're the real manipulator here. You think you're so much better than all of us, but you're not. And without your friends and your men, you have nothing." Nellie says. She is on a roll today. I look at Misty, who's gleaming, she's so proud of her unwilling protege. She may have turned everyone else in this school into a zombie, but I'm not going out like that.

"Don't be so sure about that, Misty. Nellie, this isn't over by a long shot," I say, ready to leave this ugly scene behind.

"She's right," Mickey says. "You made me think you had my back with Nigel when instead you went behind my back and had your hands all up in his head. What was that shit all about?"

"Mickey, I braid hair. That's what I do. You know this. And for the record, I don't need to steal anyone else's man if I want to get a date."

"You mean with the little Spanish boy?" Misty says. "Do

you think anyone buys the little act you and your immigrant boy toy put on in class? So what, y'all can dance good together. His name's not P. Diddy and you sure as hell ain't no J.Lo, so get over it. We know you want our men and we're not tolerating the shit no more."

"Misty, please. I've already had your man, or don't you remember jocking my leftovers at the beginning of the school year?" The crowd we've attracted can't help but laugh at that fact. Everybody remembers Misty getting her ass kicked by Trecee, KJ's ex side-trick, who promptly got kicked out of school after that fight.

"What about my man?" Mickey says. "Why else wouldn't you help me get Nigel back unless you truly wanted him for yourself? If you're so damned powerful, how is it that Misty could do what you couldn't? She fixed me and Nigel and now we're engaged."

"Mickey, do you hear yourself talking? You're not even making any sense." Misty fixed them all right. I'm waiting for that other shoe to drop, and with any luck, it'll fall right on Misty's fuzzy head.

"Because she's a hater," Nellie says, adding her two cents. I know this trick is tripping, talking shit about me when it's a well-known fact that she's been after Nigel since he got here, damned if her best friend was the one dating him. And Mickey can't say shit about this topic. This madness has got to stop now, and the only way to accomplish that goal is to overthrow the ringleader.

"Misty, do you really hate me this much?" I ask, gesturing around us. She and I alone know what we're really talking about here. I wish I could battle her in the spirit world right now, because I'd kick her ass if I could. After getting into trouble because of Mickey recruiting me to forge her mother's signature on her absent note, the last thing I need is another visit to the office. And without Ms. Toni to back me up, the administration would happily crucify my ass.

"No, it's not that I hate you," Misty says, stepping up to me like she knows I won't slap the spit out of her mouth. "I just can't stand you being here. Ever since you came to South Bay it's been nothing but drama in my life."

"I find that hard to believe, Misty. I have a feeling you've always had drama around you, no matter the target of your bull," I say, opening my locker door. The bell for first period just rang and I can't be late, now that Mr. Adewale is my teacher. I look around at my former friends and other haters, not believing I'm back in this situation. How can everyone turn on me at once? The vision of me being buried by stones comes back to my mind and the dreadful feeling along with it.

"Jayd, why don't you just give it up? You're not going to win this one. And there's nothing you or your crazy-ass grandmother can do about it." Oh no, Misty didn't just call Mama crazy. To hell with keeping a cool head. Now I'm going to have to whip her ass like I should've done a long time ago. I grab Misty by her weave, forcing her to look inside of my locker. I read about one way to break a spell, where you get the person to look at their reflection and yours simultaneously. The magnetic mirror on my locker door should do the trick.

"Jayd, let go of me. Have you lost your mind? Oh wait, that's right. You have," Misty says, causing Laura and her newest sidekick, Kai, to laugh at my expense for the last time. KJ and his crew walk up just in time to get in on the jokes too, even if KJ's more scared of Misty now than he's ever been of me, and for good reason.

"Not a chance, Misty. Not until you take those fake eyes out. Come on, Misty. I miss your pretty browns," I say, antagonizing her to the max. She snatches her arm away from my grip and I reclaim it instantly. She's not getting away from me so easily this time. I should've kicked her ass several times by now and today is her lucky day.

"They're not fake. I bought them fair and square. And that makes them as real as I want them to be," she says, making the crowd laugh. If they only knew how deep that statement was, they wouldn't think her shit was so funny. KJ, like everyone else, probably thinks she's actually wearing contacts, unaware of the permanent physical change she's gained from Esmeralda.

"I bet you did. You need to ask for a refund. Those eyes don't suit you well at all." I continue to hold on to Misty, who looks a little less confident as I talk about her newfound sight. She can't handle what Esmeralda's giving to her, and she knows it. But her hate for me drives her on and it's going to land her flat on her juicy ass if she doesn't back down.

"Do you want to get into more trouble, Jayd?" I've always wanted to kick her ass, but was worried about the repercussions. Now's my chance.

"This will be worth the trouble," I say, snatching her by her extensions to everyone's amazement. KJ backs up from the scene. He knows better than to get involved in a chick fight, as he would call it. And he also knows me, so he really should think twice about saving his little piece of tail, because we all know that's all Misty is to him.

"Damn it, Jayd," Misty says, grabbing my hand as I pull her around to face the mirror. The spirit books says I have to get her to look at her reflection and mine at the same time in order to break the initial hold she has on my luck. But turning me into a dream zombie has to be broken in my dream world, and to do this I must deal directly with Esmeralda, because this trick has no real power. It's all in Esmeralda's hands.

"What's the matter? You can't face yourself?" Misty refuses to look up at our reflection. I've got to get her to do it at the same time or the spell won't be broken. Misty's stronger than she looks, or I'm just getting weaker with every passing day that Misty's got my power. But as Mama and my mom keep reminding me, even on a weak day I'm still stronger than Misty.

"Misty, are you going to just let her grab on you like that?" Laura asks, stepping behind me as I try to force Misty's head up. There's nothing Laura can do, but I wish the trick would try. I've got Misty overpowered, and unless one of her fake friends steps up to the plate, her ass is mine.

"Well, don't just stand there. Help me," Misty says, still trying to get my hands off of her cheap extensions. She needs to ask Esmeralda to help her get some money so she can keep up her hairstyle. Misty doesn't even need hairpieces, but I guess it makes her feel better.

"They can't help you, but I can. You know you're way out of your league, Misty. Look at yourself." Misty tries to keep her head down, but she can't avoid my gaze forever, just like I couldn't avoid hers in my dream at first. Before I can get her to look in the mirror inside of my locker, Mrs. Bennett turns the corner, coming to Misty's rescue. Damn.

"Problem, ladies?" the evil teacher asks. Why is she even in the main hall this early? You'd think she'd be preparing for class like the rest of the teachers.

"No, we're good. I was just helping her out," I say, loosening my hold on Misty, but not letting go. We're far from done.

"Your eyes are quite . . . interesting," Mrs. Bennett says to Misty, her blue eyes shimmering more than usual.

"Thank you. I just got them," Misty says. She and Mrs. Bennett lock into each other's eyes like it's some sort of secret code. I know I'm tripping now.

"If you want to take this up with the principal, I'll be glad to escort you to the office," Mrs. Bennett says, not losing her lock on Misty's eyes. They don't even know each other like that, but there's a different kind of recognition going on here. I step in between them, since nobody else seems to notice what's going on.

"No, we're good. Like I said, I was just helping her with her hair, and it got caught in the locker door. I was trying to be friendly." If Laura and her crew had stuck behind Misty, she'd happily have sent me up the river for this altercation. But Misty's not going to say shit, because I know she doesn't want to see me once she gets home. Esmeralda or not, Misty doesn't want to suffer a beat-down once we're back in our hood.

"Miss Jackson, I can tell the difference between a friendly gesture and a not-so-friendly one. I do have eyes that work very well. I can see what's behind this façade. That said, I think you and I should take a trip to the office. Close your locker, Jayd. Miss Caldwell, you can go now." Damn, this chick's still going to make me go, even without Misty's complaint—and she's the supposed victim here. This is some hater shit for real.

"I know you've been through a lot lately," Mrs. Bennett says, holding on to my right arm tighter than necessary as we head to the main office. Is she even supposed to be touching me? What happen to the "personal space" clause in the school's manual? I read that thing cover to cover when I tried to find a way to keep Mickey from being forced off campus by the administration. "Maybe you need some counseling." Why do I feel like I'm going in for a lobotomy?

"I'm good, but thanks for your concern," I say as we enter the double doors connecting the main hall to the main office. None of the secretaries look up when they see us: they're too used to seeing me escorted by Mrs. Bennett. She leads me to the Special Circumstances counselor, who's only here on Fridays—lucky me. When we walk into her office she instantly recognizes me from my last clash, which also happened to be with Misty. Mrs. Bennett gives her the rundown of why we're here today, including the fact that I witnessed my friends get shot last month.

"Miss Jackson, it is understandable that you might have some anger management issues after all that you've witnessed. I think it would be effective if you took a break from your normal routine and enlisted in our week-long intensive counseling course."

"I don't think so, but thanks anyway," I say, adjusting the heavy backpack on my shoulders.

"This isn't a choice, Miss Jackson. Either you voluntarily enroll in the program or risk suspension for your behavior. It's your choice." If that were true I wouldn't be here in the first place. An entire week of this shit?

"Fine. What do I have to do?"

"Every day you need to report to the counselor's office. Come prepared to write about your feelings. If it's a successful week you'll be able to go back to your normal schedule. If not, we may keep you in counseling a little longer. We really want to help you through your issues, Miss Jackson. You seem to be a very angry young lady, yet so gifted." Why do white folks always think we're angry? Okay, this time she's right. I get hella pissed when someone tries to jack my life.

I know the counselor wants to help, but she's bugging if she thinks writing about my feelings is going to help shit. How do I write about the fact that Misty and Esmeralda are invading my sleep, stealing my gift of sight, and trying to turn me into a sleep zombie for their personal vendettas against me and my family? I don't think there's a notebook big enough to write about this drama.

"And I'll review the writings as well," Mrs. Bennett says. Why is she so interested in what I do?

"Oh, Mrs. Bennett, that won't be necessary. Besides, whatever we discuss in our sessions is completely private, Jayd." Mrs. Bennett looks at the psychologist like she's lost her mind. "We can meet when I come back next week and discuss all of your writings."

This is going to be a long week. I need to chill out and cool my head off, as my elders keep telling me. I can take the weekend to work on me, since I have no clients scheduled, especially after what happened to Shawntrese last Sunday. After school I'll go to the ocean and officially start my week of cleansing before I head to my mom's.

As I sit here on the beach watching the setting sun, it reminds me of how all things have their time, even friendships. Some stick around for life, and some for only a moment in time. And then there are some that are worth fighting for, even if it seems as if their end time has come. All of my real friendships are worth fighting for. Mickey, Nellie, Rah, and Nigel are my homies for life, I pray. We've had some bad times recently, but the good ones ultimately outweigh everything else.

I look in my backpack and find the brownies Mama gave me from the portion she made for one of her clients last night. I almost forgot about them. And after my last sleepwalking episode on Wednesday she told me to wear our special jade bracelets until I'm one hundred percent better.

"I wish this picture were still accurate," I say, looking down at the photo attached to my backpack of me and my melted crew, minus Jeremy. Jeremy and I don't have nearly the same drama that me and the rest of my friends carry. Why is that, I wonder? A tear falls from my eye to the plastic picture frame and slides down, hitting my jade bracelets. The orange hues from the waning sun hit the wet frame and sparkle brightly.

Suddenly, the picture seems to come to life, taking me back to that night. What was in those brownies?

"Jayd and Raheem, stand here," Nellie says in the photo. "Okay, now Mickey and Nigel, stand on the other side. Me and Chance will stay right here in the middle." Nellie's always got to be the boss bitch, even when there's a professional photographer on staff.

"Don't worry, girl, I've got you," Rah says to me, sliding his hands around my waist and pulling me in close to him. We had fun that night, even if he and Jeremy were more jealous than Bobby Brown of Whitney Houston at any awards show.

"Okay, everybody. Say money," Mickey says as the photographer snaps the shot, forever freezing in time a moment that's long gone.

I wish it were that easy to make a friendship permanent.

"You can, and I've got just the thing for you," my mom says, intervening in my personal "woe is me" moment. She has a way of answering my call before I can make it.

"I hope it's not another tea or punch, because I haven't had such good luck with either of those," I say aloud, kicking the sand beneath my feet. It's getting late and cold: two signs that it's time to go. One of the various couples walking along the beach look at me strangely and I don't blame them. How are they supposed to know that I come from a long line of voodoo priestesses and as a result, my mom can talk to me via psychic wavelengths? I forget I must look like a crazy girl when I respond to my mom out loud.

"Are you okay?" the white lady asks as her husband and collie dog run up to me, looking at me with pity in their eyes. They probably think my boyfriend just broke up with me, and right before Valentine's Day. In their minds, that's probably enough of a reason to go crazy. As if.

"Yes, I'm fine. Just praying about a bad day disappearing," I say. The couple smiles and walks on, with their pooch not far behind, satisfied that the unseen person I'm talking to is God. I wonder what it must be like to be that normal.

"Oh no, you don't, at least not for long," my mom says, picking up where we left off. *"You'll never be normal like that, powers or no powers."*

"How do you know that?" I ask.

"Because our ancestors are still former captives in this reality, period. That couple's world is very different from yours. It's our powers that can help us through it all."

"I'm not so sure about that one," I again audibly voice. My day was horrible, just like this entire new year has been so far. My powers haven't helped me through shit.

"That sounds like doubt, Jayd. Never disrespect your powers or the source they come from."

"What good are my powers if the people around me think I'm crazy? And to top it off, I can't even help my friends when they need me most. My powers aren't useful, they're torture," I say, bringing more tears down with every word. I don't care what anyone thinks about me now. I know I'm crazy, and I'm ready to admit it.

"Jayd, don't you dare call yourself crazy. That's worse than calling yourself a witch. This is all a part of the curse Misty and Esmeralda have on you. They weren't strong enough to make you fail, so now they're making you doubt yourself. And if they are successful with their hating, it'll definitely lead to your self-destruction. As long as you believe in yourself and the purpose of your lineage, you will succeed and get out of this mess. But if you doubt yourself for another minute you will be beaten."

"I don't want to play this game anymore," I say, ready to

leave both the beach and my destiny behind. The sun appears close to the water, giving the horizon a red glow. Soon it will disappear, taking this unholy day with it.

"You have no choice in the matter now, young one. You chose your destiny before you got here, and you have to walk it out, no matter how tired you are."

"But I feel . . ." I begin, but my mom's not having it today.

"Nobody gives a damn how you feel, Miss Jackson. Get your ass up, dust your shoulders off and keep it moving, little queen. I may have screwed up my destiny, but I'll be damned if my daughter does the same thing. You've got too many people depending on you, starting with your dumbass friends."

"Jayd, what are you doing here?" Jeremy asks, speaking of my friends. It's hard to hear him when he's wearing a tight, black body suit and dripping wet. Sometimes I forget how beautiful this boy really is. He's also the only one of my friends who is seemingly immune to Misty's visual hater virus.

"I needed a place to clear my head." Jeremy takes a seat next to me in the sand. Even with the cold sea breeze coming in from the ocean, this boy's presence still warms me up inside.

"That's why I come here on a daily basis. The ocean has a way of doing that," he says, smiling down at me. I feel like crying again, I'm so pissed at myself for getting in trouble—again. If I could undo my hotheaded actions I would. But it's too late for regret now.

"Yeah, it does. I wish I'd come this morning. Maybe the day would have turned out better." I don't want to tell him about Mrs. Bennett catching me snatching Misty up, but he'll eventually find out. There are no secrets on that campus, even if it is the second largest high school in Southern California.

"I got into a bit of an altercation earlier and now I have to spend the next week in involuntary anger management counseling." As the words escape my mouth tears again fall down my cheeks. He strokes them away before kissing me on the forehead.

"What happened?" I know Jeremy's sincere but I can't help but feel he's being paternalistic with his concern. And I'm in no mood for a daddy lecture from him right now.

"You wouldn't understand if I told you."

"Look, Jayd, you're right. I don't know what you're going through, and I never will if you don't tell me," Jeremy says, putting my right hand between both of his. "Let me in. Let me help you, and if I can't help, let me help you find whatever or whoever can." It's nice to have someone want to take care of me for a change. But the fact that my great-grandmother's lover was Jeremy's great-grandfather complicates things for us a bit. And it's not like I can tell him that small detail in our shared family history.

"You're so sweet," I say, wiping away the last of my tears.

"Come on. You can tell me all about it over dinner." Jeremy rises from his seat next to me and dusts the sand off of his damp body.

"Sounds good," I say. I'm too hungry and broke to turn down a free meal. I get up and follow him toward the showers, where he can change back into his school clothes. "I'll wait for you to pull around." I head to the street where my mom's car is parked, ready to leave the drama behind, but not before my mom finishes our initial conversation.

"I know it seems like this insanity will never be over, Jayd, but hang in there. It's always darkest before the light. And right now, you are in the eye of the storm."

"Yeah, a storm named Misty," I say, opening the car door and getting in. I throw my backpack on the passenger's seat and close the door.

"Good. You've identified the enemy. Now do something about it. You're not a victim, Jayd. Quit acting like one. I've got to get back to work now. Bye, baby," my mom says, finally checking out and leaving me to focus on following Jeremy. She's not giving me any love this evening. Maybe Mama will be more sympathetic when I check in with her once I make it to Inglewood tonight.

After slamming down the Italian dinner Jeremy treated me to this evening, all I can do is pass out on my mom's couch, but not before talking to Mama. She hasn't stopped going off about my mandatory week of head shrinking for the thirty minutes we've been talking on the phone, and I'm ready to fall out. Mama's more pissed at me for losing my cool than getting mandatory counseling, which she doesn't think is such a bad idea, given the circumstances.

"Take this week off from your social scene and focus on getting your mind right. Ever since your winter break you've been having a lot of issues. I told you to keep track of your dreams. Now I want you to systematically write down everything you'd want to change for the better if you could. Write them down as the dreams you wish to have. I'll see you Sunday, baby."

"Good night, Mama," I say before we finally end our call. I settle into the plush couch and think about Mama's advice. I wish I could go all the way back to the first week of school and whip Misty's ass properly. She's gained too much footing in the past couple of months. If I could have it my way, I'd undo all of the mess she's created this school year, starting with gaining my friends back. Without them, nothing seems real.

~ 13 ~
Home for the Holidaze

"My life's make-believe without you."

—SAM COOKE

It's been a week since I started my anger management counseling courses and I'm just as pissed off as I was when they first began. This school sucks. But at least I was shielded from all of the impending Valentine's Day bull. With it being the week of the dance, ASB is in overdrive and so is my nausea.

My teachers sent my classwork to the counseling office and I finished all of it in two days, leaving me plenty of time to focus on my spirit work and on strengthening myself. I admit, being separated from all of my school drama was an unexpected benefit. And with the dance being tonight, everyone's too focused on their dates to worry about me and my crazy-ass issues.

I wrote down some sorry bull for the school psychologist to read this morning. It was mostly about my childhood, or rather the one I saw on television last night. She ate up my fiction and let me out early for lunch, thank God. Now I can focus on the real. Mama has a plan to get Misty and Esmeralda off my back once and for all. Me, my mom, and Mama are coming together tonight after the dance to implement the plan. Making it through the rest of the day without killing one of these cupids walking around campus is going to be the real challenge.

"Jayd, can you put two braids in my hair? I want to wear it wavy for the fiesta tonight," Maggie says as soon as I exit the main hall, heading to the lunch area. The sun is blinding this afternoon and I almost run straight into my short friend.

"Sure," I say, following Maggie to a bench in the quad. She can also give me the rundown on what's been up on campus this week, not that I need the whole story. Mama again gave me the okay to braid hair, but I can't wash anyone's head until I'm completely healed.

"So what's been up with you, *Mami?* I heard you got detention for smacking Misty. Good for you," she says, taking a piece of gum out of her Dolce & Gabbana knock-off and smacking it loudly.

"Girl, nothing much. Just boys, girls, and drama. The usual," I say, not giving her any details. As Netta says, the hairdresser listens more and talks less.

"You need to find you a white boy," Maggie says as I part her soft hair. "Oh, you already did that. Well, that's why I say let the young blood take a shot at you, *Señorita* Jayd. You won't know if you like it until you try it, yeah?"

"He's a sophomore. He can't even drive." Emilio is fine, but the last thing I need is another dude to deal with.

"Now see, that's where you're wrong. He just turned sixteen and he can drive, he just doesn't have a license in this country. You'd think with a black president the laws would have changed a little too, no?" I force Maggie's head back and look at her like she's lost her mind amidst this racist montage called South Bay High. All hating is unfortunately contagious.

"You did not just say that shit."

"No, I didn't. It was a slipup. But seriously though, you'd think he could bend some rules."

"I like President Obama just the way he is." And that I do. I may not like my men younger than me but older is just fine.

"También." We both laugh at our mutual jocking of the first black president of the United States of America. Fine is fine, no matter the age or job description. I just want to be Michelle for one day, badass gear and all. Now that's a dream I'd be willing to walk through on a daily basis.

"Perfect," Maggie says, looking at her reflection in the tiny compact mirror from her purse. The warning bell for fifth period rings and students begin rushing to class. From what I can see, Misty and her crew are absent today. I haven't seen Jeremy, Chance, or Nellie around either.

"Glad I could help." Maggie pulls a ten dollar bill out of her purse and hands it to me. I smile at my girl. She appreciates my work and I appreciate getting paid for it.

"I'll see you tonight, Jayd, and think about what I said. Emilio's a cutey." Yes, he is, which means he's probably more trouble than he's worth.

My phone vibrates in my pocket. I pull it out to see another call from Rah. He's been jocking me all week and I'm not in the mood to deal with him. He's going to the dance at his school tonight, and me mine. As far as I'm concerned nothing more needs to be said. How is it that I always end up alone? I'm dealing with two dudes and neither of them are here when I need them. Why do I keep going through the same shit over and over again?

"Because it's in your blood. Haven't you seen enough of our collective drama by now to understand that?" my mom says, intervening in my otherwise quiet stroll to drama class.

"Thanks, Mom," I think back. I know she's right, but I refuse to believe it's permanent. *"I'm in class now, Mom. I'll see you tonight."*

"See you later, baby. And Jayd, don't worry. Life gets better after high school. Trust me." I sure do hope so, because

this school thang is enough to drive a sistah crazy, for real. I never did answer Jeremy back about going out tomorrow night. I'll think of how to reply to him later. Right now I'm going to immerse myself into being someone else for the hour. I'll get back to reality when I get home.

I hate getting dressed up over Mama's house, especially when I'm not prepared. Mama sprung this new plan on me this morning before I left for school, and now it's in full effect. The worst thing about trying to get cute here is having to do it around my trifling uncles, who have left the bathroom in a funky state of disarray this afternoon. I would've been better off getting ready at school.

I walk into the kitchen and look through the bare cupboards for something to snack on. Carrots are the only edible thing up in here. They will have to do until I can grab something at the dance. ASB always has good caterers for their events.

"Hey, baby. You ready for tonight?" Mama asks, coming in from the spirit room through the back door with her faithful companion close behind her. Lexi claims her cozy spot under the table while Mama leads the way to her room.

"I guess," I say, following her. My phone vibrates in my pocket. I hope it's not another call from Rah, and it's not. Instead it's Jeremy I'm avoiding this time. I open my phone and read Jeremy's words on the small screen.

Hey, Lady J. I realize I forgot to ask you out properly for tomorrow night. Will you be my Valentine? I hope so.

"What's that look all about?" Mama asks, sitting down on her bed. She looks like she needs a long nap.

"Jeremy wants to take me out to see some new love-thriller movie Saturday night. It's called *Voodoo Valentine* or something like that," I say, biting the carrot hard and making a loud snapping sound. I sit down on my bed, wishing I could take a nap myself. But I know that's out of the question. I need to get ready for tonight and I don't even know what I'm wearing yet. The only dress I have here is the red one from Christmas Eve that my mom gave me. I'm not sure I should wear that one after the vision Mama and I shared of Maman with the same dress.

"It's not the carrot's fault Hollywood can be ignorant, nor is it Jeremy's." I know Mama's right.

"But I expect more from him," I say.

"He's not a mind reader, Jayd. If you want him to know about you and your lineage, tell him. He might be more understanding than you give him credit for."

"Maybe, maybe not. Look, I've already lost all of my other friends over this mess. I can't afford to lose another one."

"You haven't lost anything if it's not really yours to begin with. And friends that leave so easily aren't really friends at all. I have work to do to prepare for your long night. I'll be in the back if you need me." Mama rises from her bed and kisses me on the cheek. She then places a small vial containing the tincture for Misty. "I'll see you when you get home, and don't take too long. Have fun and good luck."

"Thank you, Mama," I say as she leaves me to get ready. My phone vibrates again. Damn, I'm on fire today. This time I answer. I guess I can't avoid Rah forever.

"Jayd, what the hell is up with you? You won't talk to me or nothing and I didn't even do anything," he says into my cell. No hello or nothing, but I can't blame him. Just like he can't blame me for protecting myself.

"Not yet, but you will. It's just a matter of time before you hurt me again, and I can't afford it anymore. For real, Rah," I say while going through Mama's closet. The red dress is really the only thing that fits me. Mama's a good eight inches taller than I am, and her hips are bigger. Any dress I wear of hers would have to be hemmed.

"Jayd, girl, you are tripping," Rah says. I don't have time for this right now.

"Rah, I have to get ready for the dance. You have fun at your school dance and give Trish a big kiss for me. Bye," I say, not giving him a chance to respond. I still need to whip my hair up before I roll out in a couple of hours. I'm not staying at the dance for too long, but I want to represent properly while I'm there.

"Jayd, you should wear the dress. It was obviously meant for you and it brings you closer to your ancestors. Wear the dress and the jade bracelets and not just for the good luck they bring, but also because they look stunning on you, regardless of their history." I look at my reflection in the mirror, holding the embroidered scarlet fabric up to my skin. It is a beautiful outfit.

"Mom, the last time I wore this dress me and Mama had a vision together. That wasn't fun, and it's not what I'm looking for tonight," I say aloud while gathering my toiletries. I can only hope the small bathroom has aired out by now.

"True, but it also helped protect you from being completely sucked into the vision. You have to think of your visions as blessings, Jayd, not burdens. Otherwise no matter what you do, they're always going to come with a sense of dread for you. And eventually, they'll just stop coming altogether. Then who would you help? See you later." My mom's right. I need to fully embrace my lineage and love us for the powerful women that we are. I again catch my reflection as the five jade bracelets fall down my arm. I look like all of the women who came before me. And, like them, I'm running this shit, not our enemies.

* * *

When I arrive at the dimly lit gymnasium crowded with couples, I scan the area, intent on my goal. And of course Misty's nowhere to be found.

"Have y'all seen Misty?" Maggie looks at me with pure disdain at the mention of my frenemy's name. I feel the same way. But right now I need to find her so I can slip her this potion and get the hell out of here. Mama and my mom will be waiting for me at Mama's house, and I want to get this over as soon as possible.

"Oh, *mija,* you look gorgeous," she says, eyeing my outfit. I did clean up rather nicely if I do give myself props. "Her and KJ came in awhile ago. Why do you want to know?" Maggie asks.

"Because I've got something for her." I scope the large auditorium, looking through the close-knit couples dancing, scouting for my prey. Where the hell is she? Misty's hard to miss in the largest of crowds. I hope she's enjoying my vision because her time playing Jayd in her personal after-school special has just about run out.

"I thought you came with Rah. But if not, Emilio's here and he would love to be your escort for the evening." Maggie is forever playing matchup. It's not that I'm completely opposed to dating someone younger, but Emilio comes with an entire host of issues I'm not ready to entertain. Right now I have enough on my plate to sort out as it is.

"Rah's looking for me, and I don't want to be found," I say to Maggie, who looks amused by my dilemma. Knowing Rah, he'll make an appearance at some point tonight.

"Wow, Jayd. Do you ever just chill, *chica?*"

"Not nearly enough." When this is all over I'm going to soak in lavender for about a good week. Maggie's right. I need to relax in the worst way. I'm too young for all of this madness.

"There she is. How could you miss all of that?" Maggie asks, pointing toward the food table.

What Maggie doesn't know is that these days I can miss just about anything. Misty and KJ have gone all out for the Valentine dance, dressed in matching red outfits. His pimp suit makes him look exactly like the handsome ass that he is. I'm sure his ego is unbearable these days since the basketball season has gotten off to a great start, with KJ leading the way, as usual. So far the boys' basketball team is undefeated, with no worthy adversaries in the local competition. I bet KJ can't get enough compliments about his skills. And if I know Misty, she's filling his big head with all of the bull it can hold. Misty's skintight leather dress and matching boots are fierce, but a bit much for a girl our age. She looks like she should be working a corner somewhere, instead of attending a high school dance.

"I'll check you later, girl. I've got to handle something real quick." Before I can make it all the way across the gymnasium floor Nellie, Mickey, Nigel, and Chance walk in, temporarily distracting me from my goal. We should all be here together.

"Jayd, I've been looking for you all night. Did you just get here?" Rah asks, catching me off guard. Damn it. I don't have time to explain shit to him. Right now I've got to get to Misty before her powers grow any stronger.

"I did. And I'm about to leave." My jade bracelets fall down my arm, reminding me I'm on the clock.

"Wait a minute, girl. I got all dressed up and came here with flowers and shit, ready to dance with you all night, and you're leaving?"

"I'm sorry, Rah. But you said you weren't coming and I've got to get home. I've got business to tend to."

"Business with Jeremy?"

"No. With my ancestors," I say. Rah looks at me and then

across the room at Misty. Now he gets the picture, and I'm glad. The last thing I need is another fight on my conscience. I don't know exactly what Mama's got planned, but whatever it is, I know I'm going to need my mind to be as clear as possible to deal with it.

"Do you need some help?" I thought he'd never ask.

"I could use a distraction for KJ." Rah looks across the room and catches KJ and Misty groping each other like they're in a motel room all alone. I catch Mickey looking at them, envious of their public display of affection. She and Nigel have lost that lustful feeling. KJ continues holding on to Misty's backside like it's going to leave if he lets go of it. Whatever spell Misty has him under is making me and everyone else sick to our stomachs.

"I got you." Rah walks over to KJ and steps right into his face. "When's our rematch?" Perfect. Talking about KJ's humiliating loss to Rah will surely keep him preoccupied while I take care of my nemesis.

I walk over to the scene, noticing that the plastic cup in Misty's hand is still full of punch. Good. It'll be easy to get her to drink the potion if she hasn't taken a sip yet. After all of that groping on the dance floor I'm sure she'll be thirsty.

"I wish I had some single dollar bills on me," I say, catching Misty's attention. KJ and Rah are staring each other down.

"And I'd gladly take all of your money," Misty says, smiling at me like she's won some shit. Her blue eyes are shining bright tonight. Let's see what they look like after she wakes up tomorrow morning. When Misty turns around to check on her date, I quickly pour the potion into her drink. She then downs the drink before returning to the dance floor without KJ, who's now in a heated debate with Rah. I catch Rah's eye to signal I'm out. My job here is done. The sooner I get back to Mama's, the sooner this nightmare will be over.

* * *

I pull up to Mama's house and notice that my mom hasn't made it yet. My uncle Bryan looks like he's headed to his night gig at the public access radio station and needs a ride.

"What's up with you, little Jayd? You look nice," he says, sitting on the front porch. As I make my way up the driveway I realize how tired I am.

"Nothing much. I'm just sick of going through shit, you know what I mean?" I step up next to him, ready to go inside.

"Going through what, Jayd? You're not going through shit. As far as I can tell, it's all in your head and you control that, if nothing else. You ain't gotta go through shit you don't want to. Most of us don't have that luxury, niecey," Bryan says, playfully punching me in the leg. He hasn't called me that since I was a little girl. His new girlfriend is making him soft. I like it.

"When did you become so wise?" I ask, smacking him on the back of the head.

"Always been. You just didn't know, shawty," he says, getting up to meet his girlfriend at the curb. I guess he doesn't need a ride after all, not that I would be of much help tonight. I open the front door and head to the back, ready for my date with destiny.

"Hey, Mama," I say, entering her bedroom.

"Hey, baby. How did it go?" Mama asks, lighting nine white candles and giving the room a warm feel.

"Perfectly."

"Good. Now we just have to wait for your mother to get here." Since we have some time to kill I decide to ask Mama about her past in the African village. There's so much I don't know about my grandmother.

"Mr. Adewale used to live somewhere called Oyotunji. Ever heard of it?" I ask. I plop down on my bed, ready for the scoop.

"Yes. I lived there briefly before I met your grandfather. Strange place," she says, putting the matches down on the shrine.

"What happened?"

"A lot." Mama shakes her head from side to side at the apparently stressful memory. "But I learned a lot about people's character while I was there."

"Maybe I should move there for a little while. I might know how to deal with Misty better."

"Oh girl, Misty's little mess is nothing compared to the women there. I once had this lady invite me to stay in her home. Now mind you, her family and friends had stayed with me before and I always hosted them to the best of my abilities. But this heffa changed her mind after I had already extended my trip to stay with her, and she said it was because Legba told her to do so. Jayd, there's genuine purpose and then there's everything else. Character dictates how a devotee behaves with orisha, and some people use the orisha as a way to excuse things they want or don't want to do. If this were really the case with this lady, she would've asked Baba Legba before she offered me to stay in her home, not after. That's just plain rudeness and cowardice."

"But maybe she didn't have a bad feeling until after she invited you to stay." Mama looks at me sideways. I guess she already thought about that.

"Or maybe she wanted to appear hospitable while others were looking and then blame her actual intent on Legba, who'll take the blame, but not without repercussion. Me showing my ass in the end wasn't good either, but again it's all call and response, action and reaction, and she was an elder. She should've known better, just like Esmeralda. Knowing when and how to ask the question is part of the wisdom in divination, Jayd. Anything else is a mockery of the system's power."

"Is she telling the story of how one of her wives in Oyotunji didn't let her stay at the house after she already invited her?" my mom asks, walking in the door and surprising us both. She came straight from work and looks nice in her office attire, pantyhose and all. I miss watching my mom get ready for work. "Mama, you've got to let it go."

"Almost wife—and it was just plain rude, period." I haven't had a chance to talk to her in-depth about her life in the same village where Mr. Adewale grew up. It's weird to think of Mama having a life before she was married to Daddy. It's even stranger to think of her as being anyone's third wife. Mama's got diva written all over her. I don't know exactly what went down between her and the dude she almost married, but I know it's a juicy story and well worth the wait.

"Whatever. All I know is that it was ages ago. Don't you know holding on to the past can you make sick?" My mom makes herself comfortable on the edge of my twin bed, kicking her shoes off.

"Yes, I do," Mama says, glaring at her eldest child. "That's why we're here, isn't it?" They both look at me, and seem remorseful that I'm suffering. But I know with the two of them on my side I'll be okay. I just hope this works.

"So we're really going to do this? Go back and change what happened?"

"Yes, Jayd, we are. Are you ready? Misty should be next door at Esmeralda's by now, and we don't have any time to lose. The potion will wear off soon if we don't get moving." I shake my head, not sure what I'm agreeing to, or if I'm truly ready.

"Lynn Marie, hand me the book and then make the veve for our baba." My mom picks up the heavy antique binding with our lineage's history in it and passes it to her mother.

"I used to love drawing this cross," my mom says, taking the cornmeal off the dresser and pouring it on the floor next to the family shrine.

"For us, Legba's veve is an apotropaic symbol, Jayd, one that wards off evil and opens the road for clarity and focus so we can pick the right way to go. When you see this symbol in your dreams or in this reality, pay close attention." Mama can be cryptic sometimes. All of this information is too much on a sistah's mind if I'm supposed to be falling asleep.

"Oh Jayd, stop bitching," my mom says aloud. I hate when she reads my mind and then scolds me aloud for thinking what I think. What the hell kind of fate is this? "I can still hear you, little girl."

"What's the point of me having thoughts if my mind is under constant supervision?" I ask.

"Enough, girls. We have work to do." Mama begins pouring the libation to the ancestors, chanting a song I've never heard before. I slowly give in to the melodic drumbeat coming from Mama's hand movements. The pulsation of the heavy thumps course through my body like a cold chill, like when I dreamt of Misty taking my sight.

"At least now we know how and when Esmeralda and Misty took your powers. And we also know that Misty is the mule, not her mom, which is beneficial to us."

"How is it beneficial that I have to go to school with my mortal enemy, who also happens to live around the corner from me?"

"It's always in our benefit to have our enemies close and accessible, and Misty just so happens to be both."

"Not to mention stupid," my mom says, chewing on her gum fast, like it's going to jump out of her mouth if she slows down. "The girl's elevator's not going all the way to the top floor, if you know what I mean."

"Lynn Marie, that's enough," Mama says, slamming the spirit book closed. Her eldest daughter works Mama's nerves like no one else can. It's funny to see them together. Jay's mother is never around. The older my mother gets the more she favors Mama, and that's definitely a compliment. "You don't talk bad about other people's children. I know I taught you better than that."

"I do when they're trying to kill my baby. That girl is deaf, dumb, and stupid as far as I'm concerned, and Jayd needs to know it, just like that." Mama rolls her jade eyes at my mom, who promptly mirrors Mama's movements. "Jayd, you need to kick this girl's ass in both the spiritual realm and the physical. There are times to play nice and then there are times to fight dirty. This is a time to fight, Jayd."

"I already did that and it got me put on lockdown for a week."

"I think what your mother is trying to say is that there's a difference between choosing to let your powers go—like some stupid people do—and having them taken from you unwillingly," Mama says, causing my mother to sigh. I know she gets tired of Mama rubbing that fact of life in her face. I'm sure now my mom thinks it would've been easier to keep up with her lessons than hear this shit almost every time she and Mama talk.

"I thought you weren't supposed to call people's children stupid," my mom says, rising from her cozy position on the corner of my bed and pacing around the room. Mama always brings out the teenager in my mom.

"Other people's children. I can call my own children whatever the hell I want to, especially when I'm telling the truth." Mama smiles at my mom, who's now completely frustrated with our conversation. This is the longest she's stayed at Mama's house in a while without it being a family holiday, like this past Christmas. I'm sure she'd rather be celebrating Valentine's Day weekend with her boo, like everyone else in love.

"Okay you two, back to your corners." I always play referee between the two of them. Mama says it's part of my destiny and not to complain, because I chose to be in this moment before I was born. I wish I could choose to be out of it just as easily.

"Okay, ladies, we have work to do and it starts with Jayd falling asleep and you sticking with her, Lynn Marie. Here," Mama says, handing us each objects from the tiered shrine next to her bed. "Now that we have asked Legba to open the road we can get to work. We'll need all of our ancestors to help us out of this mess," Mama says, leading the way out of the house and to the back. The spirit room is where it all goes down.

When we get to the backyard, we hear loud chanting and drumming coming from next door. Lexi begins to howl at the sound of Esmeralda's voice. I guess they figured out Misty's been slipped a magic micky.

"We can do better than that," Mama says, continuing her steps to the backhouse where the spirit room is housed. We can smell the cigarette smoke coming from the adjacent garage where my uncles chill. How they stay in that dark-ass, musty space doing nothing all day with the door down is beyond me.

"Mama, I've never seen you so competitive before," my mom says, walking into the small house and looking around like it's the first time she's been back here. We each remove our shoes at the threshold. Mama closes the door behind her before placing the objects on the table. I instinctively go to the small shrine at the back of the room to place my objects down while my mom gets reacquainted with the energy in this space.

"No, Jayd. Set them here on the table. You too, little Lynn." Mama directs us both to wash our hands and get ready to get down. "Lynn Marie, hand me that bata drum behind you. Jayd, lie down on the floor in front of the shrine.

We don't have any time to waste. They're already there waiting for us."

"Where, Mama?" I ask, a little scared of where she's sending us.

"In the past. That's what we're going to use Misty's dreams for. The sooner we get there the sooner we can return. Lynn Marie, you need to open with a song to Legba so he can help you guide our child in the right direction. Once you're asleep I'll take care of the rest."

"Esu ma se mi o," my mother sings, beginning our opening chant. I'm glad she's praying for less confusion, because I don't know what the hell is going on.

"Remember, Jayd. Birth and death are the only two things that cannot be negotiated. Everything else in between is malleable. Focus on everything you wrote down that you want to change and get to it, girl. You have a lot of work to do." I begin to drift off with the sound of my mother's voice carrying me along.

Once inside my dream world, the first thing I notice is that it's very bright. The light's almost blinding, but I can make out several shapes ahead. I begin my trek to Misty's dream, which is where I'm going to change as much as I can before she wakes up. Mama's drumming is still audible, but the further I walk into my dream the softer the beats become.

As I drift off into my alternate reality, visions of women dancing with snakes creep into my thoughts. My dream vision is hazy, but I can make out Maman Marie's silhouette among the fire-lit circle of bodies. I stare at her fierce body movements as she matches the fast tempo of the drums, beat for beat. I can't tell if she's dancing to the drummer or the drummer's playing to her. Either way, they're in perfect sync.

The next image that comes into my mind is of Legba's veve, like the one at the shrine in Mama's room. But instead of just one, there are hundreds of them lined up in a row, like a trail.

"Follow the veves, Jayd. That's Legba leading you home." *I can see the illuminated symbols leading back out of Misty's dream, which is where the light is leading up ahead.*

I now see images that don't belong to me. They must be a part of Misty's dream. As the shapes become clearer I notice that one of them is Misty's grandmother, who passed away a couple of months ago. That's when Misty and her mama joined forces with Esmeralda and my nightmare began. If I could bring her back to life it wouldn't help much. According to Mama, and from my brief interaction with the woman, she was as evil as Esmeralda is, but without the powers.

"Jayd, focus," *my mom says.* "We don't have all night. Get in and out as quickly as possible." *Damn, why does she have to put so much pressure on a sistah? I hear her though. I don't want to be here any longer than necessary.*

I concentrate on the first violation of Misty's personal life, which came from Mickey. Seeing Misty's thoughts up ahead, I focus intently on going back to that day Mickey called her out in front of the lunch quad for catching gonorrhea, after she ratted out Mickey's pregnancy. I felt as helpless then as I do now that Misty's taken her revenge out on me.

"I'm in," I say to my mom. I can feel her mind relax a bit, knowing that I'm on the right path. Now I have to carefully undo everything that has been done over the past couple of months, ending with all of the drama we went through this past Christmas. The drumbeats are hard and heavy now as I begin unweaving the tangled web where Misty and Esmeralda are holding my sight captive.

"In your visions there was something distinctively powerful about each situation. Use that power now to help you get your sight back," *Mama says. I can hear her in my mind just as clearly as I can hear my mom. Like I said before, Mama's gangster with her powers.* "Stay focused on the drums and they will carry you home."

"Now fight her, Jayd. You're not alone." *My mom's words resonate deep inside of me and I'm ready to beat Misty at her own game. If she can steal my sight without my permission, I can damn sure go into her dreams and get it back without hers.*

"The potion is working." *I can see through Misty's eyes, and for now she can't do anything to stop me from taking my vision back. I see all that she sees, carefully undoing everything she and Esmeralda have done. It's like I'm unraveling an intricate woven mind web. I'm sailing through the pictures in Misty's mind, making them how they would have been had she not prayed for something different. This is the last time I sleep on my job.*

It feels like when I'm sleepwalking as one of my ancestors again, except this time I'm my friend-turned-enemy. If there was a mirror around I think I'd go completely insane seeing myself as Misty in her dream. That's a picture that would be forever etched into my mind. I guess this is how Lady Macbeth must've felt when she was sleepwalking after she murdered the king. My sleepwalking doesn't stem from guilt, but it is just as destructive as hers was. Fortunately in my case, what's done can, and most certainly will, be undone come hell or high water.

"Jayd, summon our ancestors and elders through your mojubas. It's time to finish what they've started." *Mama reminds me of my prayers. I call on my ancestors' names like I did at Tre's service, like I'm supposed to do on a daily basis. They all appear in my dream, ready to help me back home. I also see Tre in my vision. He smiles and I smile back at him. I hope he knows I'll keep his memory alive, even if he's not my kin.*

"Okay Jayd, it's time to go. Make sure you've put everything back in place the way you envisioned it," *Mama says. From what I can see, everything is as it was before Misty went on her hater rampage. I just hope it sticks in reality. I guess I'll find out when I wake up.*

I rub my sleep-encrusted eyes with my knuckles and yawn loudly like I've been asleep for days. I push myself upright in my bed and see Mama standing over me. Why is she looking at me like I was dead and now I'm coming back to life? I look around the small room and start to come to a little bit. I feel hazy, like I did after my breast reduction. I was under anesthesia for several hours and when I finally woke up I didn't even know what day it was, much like I feel right now.

"Jayd, are you hungry, baby? Here, have some breakfast," Mama says, placing a breakfast tray on the bed beside me.

"What time is it?" I ask, taking a banana off of the tray of food. I'm starving.

"A little after eleven."

"What? I'm going to miss the entire school day," I say, ready to jump out of bed and get dressed, damn the shower. With all of my recent absences I can't afford to miss another day.

"It's Saturday, Jayd, remember? Yesterday was the Valentine's Day dance. You came back here afterward." I look at Mama, completely dumbfounded by her words. I'm never here on the weekends. And I damn sure don't remember any dance or coming back to Compton after. Why would I do that?

"Mama, I'm drawing a complete blank," I say, stuffing one of the mini croissants into my mouth now that I've inhaled the banana. Mama's put a complete spread out of fresh fruit, croissants, and yogurt, with juice and tea to accompany it. Mama rarely makes breakfast, let alone serves it in bed to me or anyone else. What gives?

"I know, baby. But as the day progresses you'll get your memory back. And the more sleep you get the more rested you'll feel. Eat up. And don't forget to take your pills. You only have one more dose left." I notice the bottle of medicine on the tray with Dr. Whitmore's label on it.

"My dreams," I whisper, remembering part of my dream last night. "They're back to normal."

"Yes, baby, they are." Mama pats my head and smiles as I continue devouring my food. It feels weird being here on a Saturday, but if this is how it is I'll be here more often.

"No, little one. Mama's only doing this to help you gain your strength back. Once you're up and running again it's back to the regular grind for you," my mom says, setting me straight. Mama looks at me, knowing my mom's in my head.

"Tell your mother she left her scarf here. You can take it to her this afternoon when you go over there."

"I assume you heard that," I think back to my mom. My mouth's too full to speak.

"Yes, I did. Rest up, baby, and I'll see you in the morning. I didn't get to see my man last night since I was fooling around with you, so we're going to make up for it tonight, especially with it being Valentine's Day and all. Smooches and I love you, girl."

"Last night? What happened last night?" Mama stops putting her laundry up and sits at the foot of her bed directly across from mine. She stares at me so intently, forcing my eyes to lock with hers. Her eyes begin to glow and mine feel like they're glowing right along with them.

Through Mama's eyes, I see everything that happened last night, right down to me getting my sight back from Misty. I look under the blankets and notice I'm fully dressed from last night, but my bracelets are gone. Everything must be back to normal, or at least our version of it.

"You can walk out the front door again. No need to sneak around the back. Esmeralda won't try that shit again. She now knows just how strong your brown eyes really are." Mama looks at me with tears in her eyes. She was really afraid of losing another daughter in our legacy to Esmeralda's evil ass.

"I'll never allow myself to become that distracted again," I say, joining her on her bed and hugging her tightly. I didn't realize how much I'd miss my dreams until they were out of my control. I'm so grateful Mama and our ancestors were there to help me regain my sight.

"Yes you will, girl. But now you know how to get back on track. And more importantly, you know how to work your vision. That's the most important thing. Cherish your gift, Jayd, and you'll never lose it again."

"Yes, ma'am," I say, wiping away my tears.

"Now, get up and get moving. The day's almost gone and there's work to be done, especially since you have your sight back. Our clients are waiting, my dear." Every day Mama stays on her grind, and so do I. I feel like my old self, and that's a blessing indeed.

I didn't bother showering before changing my clothes, since I'm going straight to my mom's house. I packed my bag in record time and am ready to leave and enjoy the new day. Walking out of the house, I see Misty and her mother leaving as well. I wonder how she feels now that I've stripped her of the powers she tried to steal from me. Maybe she has amnesia just like I did this morning.

"Good morning," I say to them both. I don't want to be rude, even if they did try to kill my vision. They both look at me, scolding me with their weak eyes. Misty's have returned to their normal pretty brown and I'm glad for it. I smile in recognition: they do remember the fight they just lost.

I can't wait to get to Rah's house for the Valentine's Day session this evening. If all is well in the world, my crew should be tight like glue. There's nothing like being home for the holidays, and every other day of the year. And the best part about being home is chilling with my friends.

Epilogue

It's so nice to be back with my friends for a regular session. The entire crew is here and we are chilling hard, just like old times. Tonight we're at Nigel's crib because his parents are out for the evening. I was able to fix what I could, but some things—like Nigel's parents hating Mickey and me—haven't changed a bit.

"Personally, I'm glad that nigga's locked up again. Some people should never get out of prison," Rah says, throwing down the local newspaper after reading the article on Tre's murder. Rah's right about that, and I know he doesn't take prison lightly since his father is locked up for life. Rah's not about any black man being on lockdown for anything petty.

"I'm done tripping off that shit. I'm sorry your boy Tre got blasted, but none of us got hurt, and that's the most important thing," Nigel says, rubbing Mickey's belly like he used to. And to think, this moment almost didn't happen. It's happening now and that's all that matters.

"I have to take this call," Rah says, excusing himself from the rotation. Chance and Nellie are cozied up in the corner like they're really in love. I hope for his sake they are. Mickey takes the blunt from her man and passes it to me. I smile at my girl and she smiles back, knowing she's tripping for that move.

"I'll give it to Rah," I say, rising from my spot on the futon and walking toward the bedroom door.

"Who's that in the background?" I ask, hearing a female's voice through his cell. It's too far away for me to make out. Maybe his mom is home for a quick change between sets at the strip joint. He hangs up his phone and takes the lit blunt, looking at me pensively before answering.

"I wanted to tell you this before, but you were having your sleep issues and whatnot." When Rah stalls in his explanation I know whatever he's done is bad. Very bad.

"Who was that?" I repeat. He continues to avoid giving me a straight answer by telling a long-winded story that I'm not interested in hearing. I ignore most of his words, but the last thing I do hear is Sandy's name.

"Sandy's out of jail and in your house? Why?" I'm ready to throw the phone across the hallway. It's bad enough I just went through hell and back, now I have to deal with his evil baby-mama drama. Enough is enough.

"Because she needed somewhere to be released to. She's under house arrest and if she stayed with her grandparents the only way I'd ever see my baby girl is by driving to Pomona on the weekends, and I can't have that. She needs her daddy and her daddy needs her." I feel for Rah but this isn't going to work.

"Wasn't there another option? What happened to you going for full custody? Isn't this the opposite direction? You're the one who turned her in, remember?"

"Yes, I do, and that's why I've got to help make this right, Jayd. I don't want Rahima growing up with her mama in jail and shit." What he's not saying is that he doesn't want his daughter growing up like he and his brother are now, and I can understand that. But this is not the answer to my prayers, or Rahima's.

It sucks that going back and giving our recent past a makeover had to have consequences that I have to deal with so personally. The universe really has a sense of humor, allowing Sandy to move in with Rah so he could have Rahima twenty-four seven. Yeah, that was some real funny shit right there.

"This is some twisted mess, Rah. You know that, right?"

"One man's twisted is another man's normal, Jayd. I don't know what else to say, baby. You just have to trust me on this one." Rah's words hit too close to home for me. Him living with Sandy is crazier than anything I'm used to, and I don't know that I trust him enough to deal with his new dysfunctional family drama. But what else can I do?

A Reading Group Guide

Drama High, Volume 9: Super Edition

HOLIDAZE

L. Divine

ABOUT THIS GUIDE

The following questions are intended to enhance your group's reading of DRAMA HIGH: HOLIDAZE by L. Divine.

DISCUSSION QUESTIONS

1. Have you, or anyone you know, ever experienced sleep-walking? If so, was it scary?
2. Why do you think Jayd's gift of sight is through her dreams? What are the benefits of this type of gift? What are the disadvantages?
3. If you could choose a gift of sight to have from the Williams women's lineage, which one would you choose and why?
4. If you could change one event from your past or the past of someone close to you, what would it be and why?
5. When someone sleepwalks, where do you think his or her mind is? Why do you think some people sleepwalk sometimes?
6. If you were Nigel, how would you have reacted to being shot over Mickey? Do you think he should break up with her? Do you think she deserves being singled out by her friends as the one to take the blame?
7. Should Nigel get a paternity test? Until then, should he claim Mickey and her baby? Explain.
8. If one of your friends needed your help, would you do anything in your power to help him or her, even if it meant risking yourself? Why or why not?

9. Should Jayd continue dating Rah, even with all of his drama? Explain.
10. Do you think Jayd can trust Mr. Adewale? Do you know of a teacher like Mr. A?
11. Was Mickey justified in her reaction to Jayd's reluctance to help her out with Nigel, and his reaction to Mickey's role in his being shot? If so, what could Jayd have done differently to help her friends?
12. Do you think Misty deserves to have powers like Jayd's? If so, what do you think her powers should be?
13. If you were in Rah's place, would you have allowed Sandy to move in, or found another way to deal with the situation?
14. Do you think Jayd should entertain the idea of dating Emilio? What kinds of challenges would dating him present? Could it be a good experience for them both? Explain.
15. What are your daydreams usually about? Has anyone ever caught you daydreaming, and if so, how did it make you feel?
16. Have you ever dreamt of something and it came true? Do you think you could intentionally make this happen?

With our first super edition of Drama High we are introducing Jaydisms: simple solutions to everyday issues the way that Jayd would handle them. Here's the first of many to come! Enjoy~

Jaydism #1

When you want to relax like Jayd, adding a small amount of lavender essential oil to your bathwater or favorite lotion, soap, shampoo, conditioner, or just about anything else can make all the difference. You can even place a few drops of the oil in your laundry to scent your clothes, or sprinkle it on your linens for a restful slumber.

Stay tuned for the next book in
the DRAMA HIGH series,
CULTURE CLASH

Until then, satisfy your DRAMA HIGH craving
with the following excerpt from the next
exciting installment.

ENJOY!

Prologue

This weekend was the first one in a long time I spent hanging with my crew. After our hellish holidays it was nice being back to normal with my friends. Well, all except for Rah. He's completely lost his mind if he thinks allowing Sandy to be under house arrest at his house is the way to go. If it weren't for his daughter, I know he would've had no problem letting her trifling ass be prosecuted to the full extent of the law for stealing his grandfather's car.

I just got my conditioner set in my hair for the next thirty minutes. I feel like cooking a big breakfast this morning, but it'll be nothing like the spread Mama made for me yesterday. My memory's still coming back from our collective vision quest. I walk into the kitchen and check the fridge for some food. As usual, there's nothing in here to cook. Damn. I hope there's some grits in the cabinet. My mom loves hot cereal and so do I.

I check the cabinet and find what I'm looking for, but not before I'm interrupted by someone at the front door. Who's this knocking so early on a Sunday morning? Maybe it's Shawntrese, wanting to get her hair done before church. I look through the peephole and see Jeremy looking back at me. What's he doing here?

"We're making this pop-up thing a habit, aren't we?" I say through the door, unlocking the multiple bolts and letting him in. Jeremy has seen me look all kinds of ways. Now he gets to see me with my plastic shower cap on and I could care less. That's what he gets for coming by unannounced.

"Good morning to you too, Lady J. I had to come check on you since you're not returning calls," he says, walking inside and kissing me on the forehead. I haven't even checked my phone this morning. I passed out when I came home from Nigel's last night, and put my phone on silence to make sure I stayed that way.

"You want some grits?" I ask, sashaying back into the kitchen to finish cooking my breakfast. I open the freezer and find some protein to accompany my meal. Thank God for frozen food. Who knows how long these turkey sausages have been in here. In my opinion they look good enough to eat.

"What's a grit?" Jeremy asks, as serious as a heart attack. I turn around and look at him, shocked he's unfamiliar with one of our staple foods. I guess he's not familiar with chitlins and pig's feet either, although I haven't had either one of those since I was a child.

"How can you not know what grits are? Your mother's from the South." I gesture for Jeremy to sit at the dining room table while I get out the necessary tools needed to cook. I put water in both the pot and the skillet, ready to heat this small kitchen up.

"Yeah, but she doesn't cook everything southern. My dad's Jewish, remember? Some things we never got accustomed to, a grit being one of them."

"It's not 'a grit.' You don't eat just one," I say, smiling at my silly friend. "And it's like porridge made out of ground corn. Interested?" I begin pouring the white grains into the measuring cup, waiting for his response. From the look on his face I'd say the answer is no.

"I'll pass." His loss. I pour the cereal slowly into the boiling water and check on my sausages cooking in the skillet. This is going to be a slamming meal. "So, how was the dance?"

"It was okay. I didn't stay for long," I say, mixing the cereal until it's thick and smooth. I reach back into the refrigerator and pull out the butter. I take a knife out of the dish drain and put about a tablespoon of butter into the grits and then sprinkle in some salt. All I need now is brown sugar to make this meal perfect. I have about twenty minutes before I need to rinse the conditioner out of my hair. I hope Jeremy wasn't expecting my undivided attention this morning, because I'm all about me right now.

"And how was your Valentine's Day?" Jeremy asks while I pour the grits onto a plate and then place the sausages next to the cereal. I sit across from Jeremy at the table and dig in.

"It was cool. I chilled with the crew, nothing special. And on Friday night I was busy with my family, so I was glad too for the session last night." I offer Jeremy a sausage and he takes it. Something about Jeremy's eyes tells me that I'm missing something here.

"You were so busy you couldn't respond to my text about plans we had for the holiday?' His text? I forgot all about him asking me to be his valentine and about the stupid movie he wanted us to go see. But I can't tell him why I didn't remember until just now.

"You seem to pick and choose your holidays, Jeremy. I'm sorry I was caught up and I told you I didn't want to see a horror movie anyway, especially not one as demeaning as the one you chose." I continue eating without apology. If I told him that me, my mother, and my grandmother were busy fighting off Esmeralda and Misty in the spirit world because they were trying to steal my dreams, I don't think he'd believe me.

"How is a movie about voodoo dolls and shit demeaning to you, unless you're a voodoo witch?" I stop in mid-bite and look into Jeremy's blue eyes, now full of anger. He's about to piss me and the women in my lineage off, if we don't end this conversation right now.

"It's priestess, not witch." Did I just say that out loud? From the look in Jeremy's pretty blues I guess I did.

"What's the difference?" he asks, taking another sausage from my near-empty plate. I can feel the conditioner in my hair losing it's minty tingle, indicating it's about time for my rinse.

"What's the difference? I know you know better than that, Jeremy," I say, finishing the last few bites of my breakfast. "A witch stems from European Wicca beliefs. Voodoo is African and we are priests and priestesses, not sorcerers, witches, or any other name you might want to call us by." I know Jeremy loves a good debate, but he can save it for our fourth period class tomorrow afternoon. This is not a conversation I want to have with him right now.

"We? Us? Is there something you're not telling, Jayd?" Some things he'll never understand and I'm not in the mood to teach him.

"Yes, there is, and I'm going to continue not telling you as long as you have an attitude about it." I look at the wall clock and realize I've gone over by one minute on my conditioner. "I have to rinse my hair. I'll be right back," I say, wiping my face with a napkin before rising to head back into the bathroom where I've set up hair shop.

"Whatever, Jayd. Call me when you're ready to be straight with me, without the attitude." Jeremy gets up from the table and walks out of the apartment. What the hell just happened here? And why is he accusing me of having an attitude when he's the one acting like a three-year-old? Whatever the reason, it can wait until tomorrow, unlike my hair. I should've never answered the door. Maybe I can rinse away some of his negativity with my conditioner and start fresh tomorrow—no attitude included.

~ 1 ~
Black Girls

"Light skin, dark skin, my Asian persuasion/
I got them all that's why these girls out here hatin'"

—JANET JACKSON

For once, it's good to be back at school. Stepping out of my car I notice the air feels new this morning. I guess it's because all of the bad things Misty did, including trying to steal my dreams. All that was undone when I took back my sight and snatched her weaved head up while trying to undo her evil spell. It's nice to have received the benefits of the mandatory week of anger management counseling I had to endure without suffering the consequences. It's also nice that Nellie, Mickey, and I are speaking again. I need my girls to make it through these long days.

"What's up, bitch?" Nellie asks as I approach my girls in the main hall. Now that I'm driving myself instead of taking the bus, I've managed mornings better, so I don't arrive on campus so early. And Nellie's back to getting a ride with Mickey, as it should be.

"Who you calling a bitch?" I ask, looking around for someone else. I know she's not talking to me or Mickey, because those are definitely fighting words where we come from.

"You, bitch." If it weren't for the smile on Nellie's face, I would think she was serious.

"We don't do that," Mickey says, correcting our girl. She

rolls her eyes at me and smiles, knowing how bougie Nellie can be.

"But Tania and her girls say that to each other all the time." I wish we could have changed Nellie associating with the ASB clique permanently, but being crowned Homecoming princess changed Nellie. Then Misty lost her damned mind after Mickey busted her out for having the clap. So much had changed with my crew. "It's a term of endearment."

"Not for us it's not," I say, walking with my girls from Mickey's locker to mine. The warning bell for first period rings in the hall, putting the fear of detention in everyone present, especially me. With Mr. Adewale as my new first-period teacher, my days of excused tardies from my former Spanish teacher football coach are over. Mr A is serious about his shit and I'm serious about staying on his good side.

"What's so bad about calling your homegirl a bitch if it's said with the utmost love and respect?" Mickey and I look at our girl and shake our heads in disbelief. Nellie's clueless on certain subjects, and the black girl code of etiquette is one of them.

"Look at Tania and her girls and then look at us," I say gesturing to the bitch crew entering the hall from the main office. "Now you tell me what's the difference," I say, opening my backpack and switching out my books. I need to clean my locker, but I'm afraid of throwing anything away, especially after what happened last time: Misty went through my trash and found a note, then used it to try to incriminate me when Mickey and Nigel ditched class, which is what got us into trouble in the first place. I'm glad that's all behind us, but I'm not putting anything past Misty after what we just went through.

"They're rich and we're not. Well, y'all aren't, but you feel me," Nellie says, flipping her straight hair over her right shoulder.

"You ain't balling either, Miss Thang," Mickey says, checking Nellie. I'm so glad we're back to us, I don't know what to do. Dealing with them one-on-one was too much for a sistah to handle.

"We're black, Nellie, and they are not. We don't go around calling each other bitches, hoes, or any other derogatory term, because of the history attached to the words for us and our ancestors." I slam my locker door shut and begin speed walking toward my first period class, with my girls in tow. They can afford to stroll their class late, unlike me.

"Jayd, you really should let go of all that negativity. History's in the past. Leave it there." I stop in my tracks and stare at my girl. Mickey laughs at my reaction, but I know she feels part of what I'm saying. My ancestors are probably crying right now they're so mad, and so are Nellie's.

"Nellie, have you ever heard us refer to each other as bitches and then hug afterward?" I'm liable to smack a female instead of embrace her if she calls me out of my name.

"Hell to the no," Mickey says, taking a pack of Skittles out of her purse and eating them. Mickey looks at Nellie with a dare in her eyes and Nellie returns the stare. My girls are crazy. I'm just glad we're all on the same side again. As small as the black population is on this campus, we can't afford to be at odds with each other. It's bad enough the three of us don't get along with the South Central clique, where the other twenty-plus black students chill. Without each other, Nellie, Mickey, and I would truly be lost. I remember that feeling, even if my girls don't, and it was a lonely existence.

"Y'all are too sensitive. It's not that big of a deal," Nellie says as we exit the main hall. The morning air feels different with spring approaching. I love this time of the year and not just because my birthday's next month. Something about warm seasons makes school—and life in general—more pleasant.

"Good morning, ladies," Nigel says, greeting us all as we walk across the courtyard. He puts his arm across Mickey's shoulders and falls in step with us.

"Good morning," we say in unison. Even with the semester change, the three of them still share most of the same classes. At first I wasn't sure about having a general ed class, but it hasn't been that bad, with the exception of having to deal with Misty and KJ. Now that our crew is solid, I know it'll be live in third period for the remainder of the semester.

"What up, dog," Chance says, greeting Nigel before saying hi to us. He kisses Nellie on the lips and then big ups Mickey and me. "Good session this weekend, man."

"Yes, it was," Nigel says, reminding me of the last conversation that I had with Rah on Saturday. I haven't talked to him since I found out his baby mama is his new roommate. He's called and texted me a million times since then, and he can keep on blowing my cell up. Mama says if I don't have anything nice to say I shouldn't say anything at all. And whatever comes out of my mouth won't be good for Rah, so I'm going to avoid cussing him out for as long as I possibly can.

"Bye, bitches." Nellie says, running toward their first period ahead of Mickey and Nigel, with Chance right behind her. She thinks she's funny, but she's not. Calling each other a bitch is something Nellie needs to reserve for her white friends. We black girls are not feeling that shit in the least.

"That's your friend," Mickey says. Nigel laughs at his girl and I can't help but do the same.

"But you've known her longer," I add. We make it to my Spanish class where the door is wide open. Mr. Adewale doesn't count you as present unless you're sitting at your desk when the bell stops ringing. We have about a minute to go before the final bell rings, officially starting the school day.

Mr. A looks up from the stack of papers on his desk and at

me. His smile is reserved, but I feel more caution in his eyes than usual. Maybe Ms. Toni had the same conversation she had with me about him and me associating with each other on a friendly basis. I think she's overreacting, but what can I say? I know how these folk up here are, and with them being the only two teachers of color on the lily-white faculty, I can't say that I blame her. I just wish she had a little more faith in me.

"Don't remind me," Mickey says. As she takes her backpack off of her shoulders and passes it to Nigel to carry, I notice a new picture keychain hanging with our old shot from Homecoming.

"What's this?" I ask, taking a look at the photo. It's a picture of Mickey, Nigel, Chance, Nellie, Rah, and me from the Valentine's Day dance last Friday.

"What do you mean? You have the same one, remember?" she says, fingering the same set of photos hanging from my backpack. I'm glad there's a picture to prove we were all in attendance at the dance, because I don't remember any of it. And from the smiles on our faces it looks like we had a good time.

"My bad, girl. You know I'm sleep deprived." Luckily I'm not anymore, but I have to blame my memory loss on something, and that's part of the truth.

"We'll see you in third period, Jayd. We have a meeting with the principal at break," Nigel says as the final bell rings. I glance at Mr. A, who has his pencil and attendance sheet ready to mark the latecomers.

"Holla," Mickey says as she and her man casually stroll toward their first period. I missed Mickey being on the main campus. She talked with Nigel about the administration bullying her, and they've decided to stand up to the powers that be together. I'm glad she decided to stay and fight. We have to stick together in this wilderness we call South Bay High. Otherwise, they will pluck us out one by one, with us girls being the first on their exit list. I'm not leaving this campus until I have a diploma in my hand, and I hope Mickey feels the same way.

START YOUR OWN BOOK CLUB

Courtesy of the DRAMA HIGH series

ABOUT THIS GUIDE

The following is intended to help you get
the book club you've always wanted
up and running!
Enjoy!

Start Your Own Book Club

A Book Club is not only a great way to make friends, but it is also a fun and safe environment for you to express your views and opinions on everything from fashion to teen pregnancy. A Teen Book Club can also become a forum or venue to air grievances and plan remedies for problems.

The People

To start, all you need is yourself and at least one other person. There's no criteria for who this person or persons should be other than their having a desire to read and a commitment to discuss things during a certain time frame.

The Rules

Just as in Jayd's life, sometimes even Book Club discussions can be filled with much drama. People tend to disagree with each other, cut each other off when speaking, and take criticism personally. So, there should be some ground rules:

1. Do not attack people for their ideas or opinions.
2. When you disagree with a Book Club member on a point, disagree respectfully. This means that you do not denigrate other people or their ideas, i.e., no name-calling or saying, "That's stupid!" Instead, say, "I can respect your position; however, I feel differently."
3. Back up your opinions with concrete evidence, either from the book in question or life in general.
4. Allow everyone a turn to comment.
5. Do not cut a member off when the person is speaking. Respectfully wait your turn.
6. Critique only the idea. Do not criticize the person.

7. Every member must agree to and abide by the ground rules.

Feel free to add any other ground rules you think might be necessary.

The Meeting Place

Once you've decided on members, and agreed to the ground rules, you should decide on a place to meet. This could be the local library, the school library, your favorite restaurant, a bookstore, or a member's home. Remember, though, if you decide to hold your sessions at a member's home, the location should rotate to another member's home for the next session. It's also polite for guests to bring treats when attending a Book Club meeting at a member's home. If you choose to hold your meetings in a public place, always remember to ask the permission of the librarian or store manager. If you decide to hold your meetings in a local bookstore, ask the manager to post a flyer in the window announcing the Book Club to attract more members if you so desire.

Timing Is Everything

Teenagers of today are all much busier than teenagers of the past. You're probably thinking, "Between chorus rehearsals, the Drama Club, and oh yeah, my job, when will I ever have time to read another book that doesn't feature Romeo and Juliet!" Well, there's always time, if it's time well-planned and time planned ahead. You and your Book Club can decide to meet as often or as little as is appropriate for your bustling schedules. *Once a month* is a favorite option. *Sleepover Book Club* meetings—if you're open to excluding one gender—is also a favorite option. And in this day of high-tech, savvy teens, *Internet Discussion Groups* are also an appealing option. Just choose what's right for you!

Well, you've got the people, the ground rules, the place, and the time. All you need now is a book!

The Book

Choosing a book is the most fun. HOLIDAZE is of course an excellent choice, and since it's part of a series, you won't soon run out of books to read and discuss. Your Book Club can also have comparative discussions as you compare the first book, THE FIGHT, to the second, SECOND CHANCE, and so on.

But depending upon your reading appetite, you may want to veer outside of the Drama High series. That's okay. There are plenty of options, many of which you will be able to find under the Dafina Books for Young Readers Program in the coming months.

But don't be afraid to mix it up. Nonfiction is just as good as fiction and a fun way to learn about from where we came without just using a history textbook. Science fiction and fantasy can be fun, too!

And always, always research the author. You might find that the author has a Web site where you can post your Book Club's questions or comments. The author may even have an e-mail address available so you can correspond directly. Authors might also sit in on your Book Club meetings, either in person, or on the phone, and this can be a fun way to discuss the book as well!

The Discussion

Every good Book Club discussion starts with questions. HOLIDAZE, as does every book in the Drama High series, comes with a Reading Group Guide for your convenience, though of course, it's fine to make up your own. Here are some sample questions to get started:

1. What's this book all about anyway?
2. Who are the characters? Do we like them? Do they remind us of real people?
3. Was the story interesting? Were real issues that are of concern to you examined?
4. Were there details that didn't quite work for you or ring true?
5. Did the author create a believable environment—one that you could visualize?
6. Was the ending satisfying?
7. Would you read another book from this author?

Record Keeper

It's generally a good idea to have someone keep track of the books you read. Often libraries and schools will hold reading drives where you're rewarded for having read a certain number of books in a certain time period. Perhaps a pizza party awaits!

Get Your Teachers and Parents Involved

Teachers and parents love it when kids get together and read. So involve your teachers and parents. Your Book Club may read a particular book whereby it would help to have an adult's perspective as part of the discussion. Teachers may also be able to include what you're doing as a Book Club in the classroom curriculum. That way, books you love to read, such as the Drama High ones, can find a place in your classroom alongside the books you don't love to read so much.

Resources

To find some new favorite writers, check out the following resources. Happy reading!

Young Adult Library Services Association
http://www.ala.org/ala/yalsa/yalsa.htm

Carnegie Library of Pittsburgh
Hip-Hop!
Teen Rap Titles
http://www.carnegielibrary.org/teens/read/booklists/teenrap.html

TeensPoint.org
What Teens Are Reading
http://www.teenspoint.org/reading_matters/book_list.asp?sort=5&list=274

Teenreads.com
http://www.teenreads.com

Sacramento Public Library
Fantasy Reading for Kids
http://www.saclibrary.org/teens/fantasy.html

Book Divas
http://www.bookdivas.com

Meg Cabot Book Club
http://www.megcabotbookclub.com

HAVEN'T HAD ENOUGH?
CHECK OUT THESE GREAT SERIES
FROM DAFINA BOOKS!

DRAMA HIGH

by L. Divine

Follow the adventures of a young sistah who's learning life in the hood is nothing compared to life in high school.

THE FIGHT
ISBN: 0-7582-1633-5

SECOND CHANCE
ISBN: 0-7582-1635-1

JAYD'S LEGACY
ISBN: 0-7582-1637-8

FRENEMIES
ISBN: 0-7582-2532-6

LADY J
ISBN: 0-7582-2534-2

COURTIN' JAYD
ISBN: 0-7582-2536-9

HUSTLIN'
ISBN: 0-7582-3105-9

KEEP IT MOVIN'
ISBN: 0-7582-3107-5

BOY SHOPPING

by Nia Stephens

An exciting "you pick the ending" series that lets the reader pick Mr. Right.

BOY SHOPPING
ISBN: 0-7582-1929-6

LIKE THIS AND LIKE THAT
ISBN: 0-7582-1931-8

GET MORE
ISBN:0-7582-1933-4

DEL RIO BAY CLIQUE

by Paula Chase

A wickedly funny series that explores friendship, betrayal, and how far some people will go for popularity.

SO NOT THE DRAMA
ISBN: 0-7582-1859-1

DON'T GET IT TWISTED
ISBN: 0-7582-1861-3

WHO YOU WIT?
ISBN: 0-7582-2584-9

THAT'S WHAT'S UP!
ISBN: 0-7582-2582-2

FLIPPING THE SCRIPT
ISBN: 0-7582-2586-5

PERRY SKKY JR.

by Stephanie Perry Moore

An inspirational series that follows the adventures of a high school football star as he balances faith and the temptations of teen life.

PRIME CHOICE
ISBN: 0-7582-1863-X

PRESSING HARD
ISBN: 0-7582-1872-9

PROBLEM SOLVED
ISBN: 0-7582-1874-5

PRAYED UP
ISBN: 0-7582-2538-5

PROMISE KEPT
ISBN: 0-7582-2540-7